Hidden City

Also by Jim DeBrosse

The Serpentine Wall

Jim DeBrosse

Hidden City

St. Martin's Press   New York

Production Editor: David Stanford Burr
Design by Judith Stagnitto

Library of Congress Cataloging-in-Publication Data

DeBrosse, Jim.
    Hidden city / Jim DeBrosse.
        p.   cm.
    ISBN 0-312-06368-7
    I. Title.
    PS3554.E1768H5   1991
    813'.54—dc20   91-21824
                                                    CIP

First Edition: November 1991

10 9 8 7 6 5 4 3 2 1

To Béa

Where is the wisdom we have lost in knowledge?
Where is the knowledge we have lost in information?

—T. S. Eliot

Prologue

Clem Thompson kept one hand on the wheel, the other on a limp handkerchief for mopping his face and neck. It was almost sunset but still close to 100 degrees and no air conditioning in his Greyhound bus since the unit overloaded 80 miles back at a rest stop outside Lexington, Kentucky. The burnt-out grass along the roadside passed in a continuous, unfocused blur. All afternoon, the same; one long pale yellow river going north.

Clem looked in his mirror to see how the old Indian was holding up. He still looked cool as a cucumber. Maybe old people didn't sweat much. Maybe old Indians didn't sweat at all. Clem had never had an Indian on his bus before—at least not that he knew of. This one was carrying nothing more than a big gunnysack in his hand.

"Hey, chief!" Clem looked into the mirror. The old Indian was in the seat behind him. "You got family in Ohio?" The Indian had bought his ticket in Flagstaff, Arizona, a one-way ride to Cincinnati.

The Indian shook his head. He was a proud-looking old man with a gaunt tanned face, deep wrinkles, and a thin-lipped mouth. Any man less proud would have seemed ridiculous with long stringy hair and a red bandanna around his head.

1

Clem shifted into low for the long haul down Death Hill—a steep, winding stretch of I-75 that ended at the Ohio River. There was a sharp bend to the left, another to the right, and then the Kentucky hills parted and the Cincinnati skyline appeared all of a sudden like a cardboard pop-up.

"There you go, chief," Clem said, "Cincinnati, Ohio."

There wasn't much to see that day. The tight cluster of downtown buildings was fuzzed in a brown haze, the sun above them orange and pale. And the river was even sadder than usual—mud-rimmed and brown, still as a lake.

"You know, chief, you could have picked a better time to visit these parts. Worst drought in fifty years. Heat wave to boot. I ain't seen nothing like it, except maybe California about ten years ago. I was doing the San Diego to San Francisco run in them days."

Clem mopped his brow and neck, shifted back to cruise. There was a bridge ahead. A steel, humpbacked monster floating in the stew. "We should be at the station in about ten minutes, chief. You got somebody to meet you there?"

The old Indian reached for the gunnysack beside him and loosened the drawstring. He pulled out a folded piece of paper with grimy fingerprints around the edges. He held it out for Clem, who reached behind his ear and took it.

Clem flipped the paper open with one hand and stretched it flat over the steering wheel. He shifted glances between road and letter.

"Chief, I think you gotta problem. This letter's anonymous."

"Who is this 'Anonymous'?"

"What?" Then Clem shook his head. "Ain't nobody named anonymous. It means nobody signed this letter of yours."

"It does not matter."

"Okay, chief. I'm just looking out for you. We don't get many Indians on the run to Cincinnati—unless, that is, they're from Cleveland." Clem chuckled, but the Indian's proud face never changed.

Clem straightened in his seat and looked out over the dead stillness of the river. He had a bad feeling about the Indian. He didn't know exactly why. An old man like that belonged at home, with a fat old squaw to fuss over him, not gallivanting across country with no more belongings than what he could stuff into a gunnysack.

"I'll tell you what," Clem said. He took a pen from his shirt pocket, and holding the wheel with his left hand, set the letter on his lap and scribbled down a phone number.

"You have any trouble meeting your party tonight, you call me. I'll be at the Milner Hotel. Ask for Clem Thompson. You got that?"

He slipped the pen back into his shirt pocket, handed the letter back to the Indian.

The old man nodded and, carefully refolding the letter into a square, stuffed it into the sack.

"How do you say again . . . the name of this town?"

Clem told him, and the Indian repeated it, drawing out each syllable of the word so that it sounded almost like a chant: "Cin-cin-na-ti."

"You got it, chief. Straight ahead."

The bus entered the bridge with a loud thump and a deep rumble, and a flock of pigeons shot out from the girders and careened in an arc across the water.

1

The Odyssey 2000 beauty salon in the Duchess Hotel was a disco-inspired nightmare of wall mirrors and track lighting and gleaming chrome fixtures. As if through a time warp, the Bee Gees were being piped in, a muffled thumping that percolated through the deep-piled carpet. *Uhhh, uhhh, uhhh, uhhh . . . stayin' alive, stayin' alive* . . . Side by side in white vinyl chairs, three of the hotel's matrons were having their hair done, heads locked straight ahead, yattering above the music. The air smelled of harsh chemicals and strong perfume.

Rick Decker stepped up to the empty reception desk, grabbed a handful of Puffs from a dispenser there, and mopped his forehead. He was still sweating after the short walk from the parking lot. His underarms tingled from the shock of air conditioning.

Suddenly every eye in the place was on him.

"May I help you?" said the stylist closest to the desk. He was a pudgy young man, stuffed into a peach tunic that buttoned down one side. He smiled a big dimply smile as he brushed out a tint job. The woman winced a little with every tug of the brush, but there was no complaining. Beauty had its price.

Decker stuffed the wad of Puffs in his pants pocket and

4

pulled out a notebook. He forced a smile and identified himself as a reporter for the Cincinnati *Eagle*. "I'm working on a story about Cody Blair." The other hairdressers stopped working at the mention of the name. "I guess you know she's staying here in the hotel."

Dimples looked up without losing a beat on his victim's head. "You're telling me? We've had three reporters in here already this week." He gave Decker a quick once-over, from his scuffed Rockports to the tangle of reddish-brown hair that crashed to the right side of his head like a surf. The glance seemed to say, "Not bad, if it could be cleaned up."

Decker flipped open his notebook. Dimples watched, faintly amused.

"Tell me, does Ms. Blair ever drop in?" Why any teenager, much less a spoiled Hollywood brat, would step into this salvage shop for the dead was beyond Decker. But it was the only place he could think of to hide after the bell captain had spotted him in the lobby.

"As a matter of fact, one of our girls does her nails."

Decker squinted into the parlor's mirrored recesses, a kaleidoscope of glaring light. "Which one?"

Dimples smiled and shook his head: naughty, naughty. "I'm sorry, Mr. Decker. You'll have to talk to the manager."

Dimples pointed to an open, mirror-covered door at the back of the room. Decker didn't have to move. Like a mother goose protecting the nest, a round woman in a white smock bounced through the door and was on her way to inspect. Decker arranged his face into his best just-doin'-my-job smile.

"Yes?" It was a challenge, not an inquiry.

"I'm from the *Eagle*. I understand Cody Blair has her nails done here."

"Yes?" The woman could pack great meaning into a single syllable.

"I was hoping I could talk to the manicurist."

The manager slid a pair of half-glasses down her nose and

peered up. A quick, exaggerated smile played on her round face.

"Mr. . . . uh . . ."

"Decker. Rick Decker."

"Mr. Decker, one thing you should know about the Duchess is that we provide our guests with the utmost privacy. Miss Blair is here precisely because it's the one place in this city where she can be left in peace."

"Actually, I'm not here to disturb Ms. Blair. I just want to talk to her manicurist."

Again the smile. "I'm sorry, Mr. Decker. That's not possible."

"Could I at least get the manicurist's name?"

"I suggest you leave before I call the bell captain."

Decker slapped his notebook shut. "Thank you very much, but that won't be necessary."

Decker exited to the lobby as Dimples waved a tiny goodbye, wiggling the fingers of his hand as if to say, "Nice try."

Decker waved back, then blew a kiss to the manager. It was a perfectly chickenshit ending to a perfectly chickenshit day.

By 5:30 he was back at the *Eagle* building, glad to escape into its cool, cavernous lobby. The official temperature had reached 102 degrees earlier that afternoon, a record for August 23, and the worst day so far in a four-week-old rut of sweltering heat and drought. Decker felt coated from the haze and humidity outside—"slimed" was the term photographer Rebo Johnson had invented for it—and he stopped in the third floor men's room to rinse off his face and neck.

Afterward he took a quick drink from the hallway fountain, gulping the water to elude the taste. No such luck. It filled the mouth like chlorinated sludge, one more consequence of the drought. With the Ohio River at its lowest point in years, the algae count was out of control, and while the city treatment plants could kill the microscopic offenders, they couldn't eliminate the soil-like taste the little buggers left behind.

Only half refreshed, Decker stepped into the newsroom, a place he had hardly recognized since the paper had been bought out last winter by Delta Communications, Inc., one of the nation's largest newspaper chains. Gone was the open expanse of yellow linoleum and gray metal desks and beat-up chairs—what used to look like the bargain basement of an office furniture store. Delta had laid down carpet, brought in all new desks and chairs, and partitioned the room into a maze of cubicles, one reporter to a slot. *Rabbits in cages*, Decker thought. No more clustering around a reporter's desk to bullshit, tease, congratulate. The *Eagle* newsroom had been divided and, for the most part, conquered.

At least the air conditioning worked these days.

Like many afternoon dailies, the *Eagle* had been on the brink of folding when the new owners stepped in. Delta had refused to recognize the Guild, and the reporters knew there was nothing they could do about it. If they tried to strike, Delta would simply fold the paper and use it as a tax write-off. "Community service" wasn't part of the Delta lexicon.

Decker waited until he was safe behind his desk before he lit a cigarette. Smoking wasn't banned in the newsroom—not yet, anyway—but he was haunted by his own shame. After nearly three years without a cigarette, he was back at it again. Not one or two packs a day like before, but enough that it had become a sore point between him and Janet. "I couldn't call myself a doctor if I didn't nag you about it," she had told him. But she didn't nag, really. It was worse: She looked disappointed.

He still had the number of a hypnotist in Mount Adams taped to the shelf in front of his desk. Barry Stein, the assistant metro editor, swore by the guy. Stein had given up his pipe six months ago and now, of course, was a diehard crusader against the demon weed.

As if summoned by the scent of nicotine, Stein soon appeared at Decker's cubicle. His face was fixed in an impish half smile, a Jewish Mona Lisa. Stein seemed amused by everything at the *Eagle* these days. He could afford to be. He was leaving in a month, headed for a job as Tampa bureau chief with a respected Florida paper.

"Still hot on the trail of Cody Blair?"

"Jesus, Barry . . ." Decker shook his head and crushed his cigarette dead center in the tummy of a panda tray from the Cincinnati Zoo. He couldn't smoke around Stein anymore.

"That bad, huh?"

"Worse. I got kicked out of her hotel."

"Keep it up, Decker. You may win a Pulitzer yet."

"You can laugh, Barry. You wanna know how I spent the day in this heat? Driving to every goddamn fern bar and dance club in town, asking bartenders and waitresses if Cody Blair drops in at night. What's her favorite drink? What's her favorite food? How often does she go to the goddamn bathroom?

"And that's not all. Farlidge wants a breakout box to go with the main story—'Tips for Cody Watchers'—where I'm supposed to list the local spots where you're most likely to get a glimpse of the lovely Ms. Blair. This is what She-Ra calls 'reader friendly' news."

She-Ra was the current newsroom shorthand for Sally Beth Jordan, the *Eagle*'s managing editor and the overseer dispatched from Delta headquarters to whip the paper into shape.

Stein lost something on his smile. "So Blair's still not giving interviews?"

"Of course not. She just 'vants to be alone.' Her agent says she doesn't do interviews while on location. It disrupts her concentration. You betcha. Especially when she spends half the night at the Glass Onion shaking her bootie and getting smashed with the film crew."

"Just give it your best shot, Rick."

"Come on, Barry. What do you mean, my best shot? There's real stories out there I could be doing. The county infirmary has flunked three Medicare inspections in a row. They're about

8

to shut the place down, and I haven't written the first word about it. Farlidge has that candy-ass Menlo on the story, and all he's done is show up at press conferences. It's a joke."

Instinctively Decker reached for a cigarette from his inside sports coat pocket, then thought better of it. "Maybe it's a good thing Turk's not around. He'd probably go berserk with all these corporate types breathing down his neck." Decker cut it short before he turned maudlin. More and more these days he looked back on Turk Nystrom's death as the end of a newspaper era.

Turk's death and Delta's rise. They seemed to go hand in hand. At last count, Delta had two hundred papers in its fold, and its profit margins were the envy of the industry. The Delta formula was simple. Slash staffs and salaries to a minimum, then package the product with plenty of snazzy color photos and catchy graphics. The stories didn't matter, really, as long as they were short and bright and full of easy-to-digest, easy-to-use "facts." Fast news for a nation of fast-news junkies—the Delta creed.

Stein had quit smiling altogether, and Decker felt satisfied that he had finally pricked his guilt about leaving. After all, it was Stein who had lured Decker to the *Eagle* in the first place. To make a difference. And for three or four years they had made a difference, digging up more dirt than all the other media in town combined.

Stein took a seat on Decker's desktop. Although his newspapering philosophy hadn't changed, Stein, too, was looking more corporate these days. He was wearing white shirts and power ties. His hair—once a corona of black frizz—was tame now, cut close to his round head and going gray at the temples. Stein had traded in his wire rims for designer glasses, the big ovoid kind favored by Wall Street lawyers and Washington lobbyists. Somehow they seemed to diminish the thoughtfulness of his heavy-lidded eyes.

"You still won't consider coming with me?" Stein said.

Now it was Decker's turn to feel guilty. Stein at least was refusing to play by the new rules.

"You know the story, Barry. Janet's got another year of residency. After that, she takes over Daddy's practice. I'm stuck here for life." Decker surprised himself with his own bitterness. Was he really that angry with Janet? He decided to hell with Stein, and lit another cigarette.

"Have you thought about going over to the *Times*?"

Decker laughed. "The Cincinnati *Times*? Come on, Barry, what's the difference? They're both cartoon papers now."

"So you're going to stick around here and smoke yourself to death, is that it?"

"Barry, you're starting to sound like a lung association ad." He crushed out the cigarette anyway. "Janet wants me to quit and free-lance for a while."

"What's wrong with that? Some of us would love the chance."

"Be honest. You're as addicted to this business as I am."

Stein gave him a fatherly pat on the shoulder and hopped off the desk like somebody twenty years younger. "What are you now, Rick? Thirty? Thirty-one?"

"Hell, I don't know . . . thirty-two."

"You have to be at least forty before you can declare yourself a burn-out. So quit your bitching. Make the best of it."

"You sound like my mother, Barry—only she's dead. What's your excuse?"

Stein smiled and left, and the second he was gone Decker lit another cigarette. He swallowed his pride and got down to the task at hand. He zipped through his Cody Blair notes, hammered in a lead, and was searching for a zingy quote from a bartender at the Glass Onion when the phone rang.

"Hello, sweetie. Get me rewrite."

It was Janet—her voice registering not only in his ear, but in a kind of low-voltage current it sent through his viscera. So why, then, were things going so badly between them?

"You at work?" he asked. She rarely called him from the

hospital, except to say he shouldn't wait up for her. He hoped that wasn't the case—not a second night in a row.

"I'm on ER rotation tonight, which is why I called." Her voice turned serious and quiet, almost secretive. "We've had an extremely bizarre case show up here from the coroner's office. I thought you might like the scoop."

"Bizarre? Meaning how? 'Crack-addicted nun dies of overdose'?"

"Rick, seriously . . ."

"I *am* serious. All the news that fits—in six inches or less. That's our motto now."

"Listen. This could have enormous public health consequences. I can't really tell you over the phone. Do you think you could meet me here?"

Decker looked at his watch. It was almost six. Screw Cody Blair. He had all night to finish the piece if he wanted—as long as it was sitting in Farlidge's computer basket by morning.

"I can be there in about ten minutes. You can't give me a hint?"

"Just hurry."

2

Late afternoon clouds were teasing again—always threatening, that summer, but never delivering. Toward nightfall there would be a suffused flash of lightning, a distant rumble of thunder, but no rain—only the smell and promise of it. Some nights there might be a sprinkling here and there, but by morning the clouds had moved on, leaving behind a gritty, silver-brown haze that seemed to grow thicker each day.

Decker didn't bother with the Dart's air conditioning. On short drives, it only blew hot air around. He tossed his blazer on the front seat, dumped the dashboard shade into the back, and rolled down all four windows. When he pulled out of the *Eagle* lot, the back of his shirt was stuck to the vinyl seat.

It took him longer than expected to get through the rush-hour traffic downtown, but then he made good time along Reading Road and up Burnet Avenue to Cincinnati General. He was there in fifteen minutes, five later than promised, and asked for Dr. Shoemaker at the emergency room reception window. He stepped to the side and tidied up, unrolling his shirtsleeves and slipping back into his blazer.

Janet didn't spot him at first as she came through the double electric doors, and he watched her a moment the way a stranger might. Janet didn't draw stares. She wasn't leggy or chic, but had the kind of whispery beauty—healthy skin and hair, comfortable proportions—that invited closeness.

Now that she was Dr. Shoemaker, she had cut and permed her pale blond hair and started a makeup routine to give her a more professional look. But there was still a girlishness in the quick movement of her legs, the forward thrust of her shoulders, as though she might break into a skip or a run at any moment. Her white lab coat was buttoned over a dark suit, and her hands were stuffed in her pockets. Lately she had become self-conscious about her weight, dieting when Decker thought she didn't need to. Rib cages and backbones weren't his thing.

Janet looked around the waiting room, and in her tensed, unsmiling expression he could see she was fighting exhaustion. She had come home past one the night before, rousing Decker from a Carson-induced slumber in his wing chair, then left the next morning before he was out of bed.

In the last few months they seemed to be spending less time together. Or maybe it was the quality of that time. Their bed was becoming their only meeting ground, and lately both of them had been too tired or too preoccupied to do more than sleep. Worse, the last few times they'd tried, Decker had been unable to perform. Janet told him not to worry, which, of course, only made him worry more. He was on his way to becoming an all-around burn-out.

Janet greeted him with a smile and a quick hug, just long enough for him to feel her softness under the uniform.

"Does Higgins know I'm here?" Decker asked. Rollie Higgins was the hospital's publicity director. Lately he and Decker had patched things up, had even gone sailing together on Higgins' nifty 27-foot Catalina. Still, just between friends, Higgins vowed to have Decker arrested the next time he entered the hospital unannounced.

"No," Janet said, "and if you're quick enough, he'll never know."

He followed her through the double automatic doors, past

13

the ER nurses' station—doctors and nurses scratching away at paperwork—and down the hallway to a bank of gray elevators. She pressed the down button, turned and smiled at him, but she seemed distracted, as though carefully weighing what she was about to say.

He gave her an opening. "The morgue?"

She nodded, took a deep breath. "It was a DOA the coroner's office dumped here this morning. They weren't sure what to do with him, so they sent him to infectious diseases. I was one of the lucky people assigned to help Dr. Luken with the case."

"The case? Aren't we talking about a dead man?"

Janet nodded as the elevator jolted open. It was empty. "It's what killed him that has everyone in an uproar."

Decker followed Janet in, and she punched the old-fashioned press-in button for the basement.

"Let's cut the buildup," Decker said. "What killed this guy?"

"Plague," Janet said. The elevator doors closed with a reverberating thud.

"Plague? What kind of plague?"

"Bubonic plague."

"Wait a minute. You mean, as in the Black Death?" He grinned incredulously. "The Dark Ages? Rats? Self-flagellation?" Janet nodded and put a finger to her lips. Decker strained to lower his voice. "Let me see if I've got this straight now: Here in Cincinnati, on this very day, we have plague?"

"Uh-huh."

Decker rounded his lips. "O-o-o-kay. I see. Uh-huh."

"Just follow me."

The elevator doors popped open, and they stepped out to the basement hallway and turned right, a tangle of insulated pipe low above their heads. Halfway down the hall a security officer was sitting in a folding chair, his feet propped on a desk. He wore a paper surgical mask over his mouth and nose.

14

Janet sighed in frustration. "Lenny, I thought I told you. There's no need for that."

Lenny pulled down the mask. He was a fortyish black man with a gold front tooth. "It don't hurt to be too careful now, does it? I hear this plague stuff can go right up your nose and down your lungs. That's what they said over at the coroner's."

"Len-ny . . ." Janet wailed. "Oh, forget it. Can you let us in? I'd like another look at the body."

"You bet. But you got to sign in. You know how much hell I catch when people don't sign in."

Janet took a pen from her lab coat and scribbled her name in the time-honored scrawl of every physician—a cross between Arab script and a cardiogram.

"You signing your friend in, too?"

Janet smiled. "Can you pretend he's not here, Lenny?"

Lenny held up his palms. "You know how this place is about paperwork."

"I'll sign," Decker said. He scratched down his name, although Higgins might never invite him on his boat again.

"Is the post room clean, Lenny?" Janet asked.

She glanced at Decker, and Lenny laughed. "Oh, I see what you're sayin'. Yes, ma'am. The anatomy people were in there cuttin' up this afternoon, but Willie done clean everything up, from top to bottom. So you just take your friend right on in, and he won't have to worry about a thing."

Decker wasn't so sure. He'd seen plenty of morgues, but he'd also had some unpleasant surprises. Like the time he walked into the middle of an autopsy, just as the pathologist and his assistant were elbow deep in an open corpse and scooping out the entrails.

Lenny pulled a chain cord just above his desk, and the heavy double doors drew back with a loud clunk and an ominous grinding whir. Just as Lenny had said, the room was clean, a windowless expanse of glazed white brick and stainless steel.

Sitting empty in the middle of the room were two autopsy tables—long, shallow sinks, really, tilted at one end for drainage. In a corner the drain pipe from a wall freezer gurgled and swallowed. The place reeked of disinfectant and the faint fatty odor of a butcher shop.

Janet pulled a chain cord near a second set of doors on the left, marked "Cold Storage." They stepped through a cloud of chilled mist into a smaller room. Overhead fans churned the icy air. Along the walls on either side of the room were sets of pipe-metal bunks, each stacked four high and lined with pull-out trays. About a dozen bodies, maybe fewer, were scattered on trays throughout the bunks. Each was sheathed in a white rubber bag, like plasticene mummies. There was a silent tension in the room, as though one of the bodies might come to life at any moment and rip through the sheeting.

"Here," Janet said, reaching into a cardboard box just inside the door. She handed Decker a blue surgical mask.

"But I thought . . ."

"We'll be viewing the body. There's a slight chance of airborne organisms."

Decker snatched the mask and started tying.

Janet found plastic gloves in another box and snapped one on each hand. "You won't need these as long as you don't touch the body."

"Don't worry."

"He's over here."

Janet pointed to the second bunk on the right and asked Decker to bring a stretcher cart from a corner of the room. She positioned the cart length-wise at the foot of the bunk, then cranked it to the level of the body tray. It took both of them to slide the tray out of the bunk. When it was free, Decker lost his grip on the handles and the tray fell with a metallic crash onto the cart. The body pitched and rolled like a canoe in a wake and nearly fell off the cart until Janet slapped her arms over the bag.

Decker's breath whistled through his nose.

"You okay?" Janet asked.

"Yeah, yeah. I'm fine. The weight surprised me."

16

"They always weigh more than you think."

She slowly unzipped the bag, starting at the head and ending below the groin. The cold plastic crackled as she separated the two halves. Instantly a raw stench filled the air—sweet, acrid, like rotten potatoes. Decker retreated a step. He pinched the metal nosepiece in his mask to make sure it was in place, then leaned in for a closer look.

"Jesus . . ."

The face belonged on a cathedral door. Mouth twisted in agony, eyes pleading toward the heavens. The body was a bloated, ashen lump covered with purple-black bruises. An incision ran from windpipe to groin like a body zipper, widely stitched with thick black sutures.

Decker spoke hoarsely. "Christ, somebody must have worked him over with a baseball bat."

Janet shook her head. "It only looks that way."

She switched into her clinical teaching mode—something she managed to do without sounding condescending. It was her only flaw as a doctor. Decker pulled a notebook and pen from his coat pocket.

"As far as we can determine, he died from septicemic plague—in other words, a plague infection of the bloodstream. The plague bacillus releases several different toxins, which I won't go into here, but one of its nastier effects is to coagulate the blood.

"The bruises you see, then, are actually necrotic, or dead, tissue. The coagulopathy cuts off the blood flow to organs and tissues all over the body. You could almost say this man was choked to death from the inside out."

"The Black Death," Decker said softly.

"Exactly. Plague in its most virulent form. It can kill in as little as twenty-four hours after infection. We don't have a lab confirmation yet, but Dr. Luken is convinced. Now let me quiz *you* on something—what do you notice about this man's features?"

"Oh, come on, Janet." He didn't care to look.

"It's important," she said.

He held his hand over his mouth and nose and stepped closer. The face was a grayish, puffed-up mess, hardly human. But as Decker looked more closely, he noted the broad cheekbones, the hatchet nose, the wide mouth. Not a mouth, really; a runny, black-purple gash. In the final shuddering instant before death, the old man had evidently refused to cry out, biting down and clean through the swollen meat of lower lip. The tendons on both sides of his neck stood out like guide wires.

Decker shivered a little as he looked into the old man's eyes. Somehow they had retained a clarity and a defiance: dark flash of iris turned upward into the open lids. They seemed to blaze with a secret vision. Other-wordly. Ancient. Proud.

Decker knew almost instinctively: "He's an Indian."

Janet nodded. "Native American is the current term. We think maybe a Navaho or a Hopi. That would fit the demographics for the disease. But so far it's all we have to go on. They found no identification on the body. Nothing but his clothes."

Decker could see how the day had worn on Janet. Her face was drained of color, her eyes hollow and tired. She stared at the dead man's face as if it were some infuriating puzzle to be solved.

"Why don't you go home, Janet? Can't you take some time off?"

She glared at him. "Would you?"

Decker shook his head. "All right then, tell me about the demographics." He had his notebook ready.

"I spoke to some people at the CDC this afternoon. According to them, plague is practically unknown in this country, with the exception of one region—the Indian reservations of the Southwest. Of the ten cases reported in the country last year, all but one was found among Native Americans residing in New Mexico and Arizona."

"Why Indians?"

18

"I asked the same question, but it's obvious when you think about it. Apparently, there are whole populations of wild rabbits and prairie dogs out West that are rampant with plague. Fleas are usually the transmission vector. The Indians hunt the animals, skin them for meat and furs, and that's when the fleas go searching for a fresh meal."

"Wait a minute. I thought it was rats in the Middle Ages."

Janet took a deep breath. "That's what has everyone in a panic. They found our friend here in an alley behind the downtown men's shelter last night, less than fifty feet from a trash pile crawling with rats. The Health Department trapped a bunch this morning. They're under observation now."

Decker stopped his note-taking. "I'm confused. Do they think the rats gave plague to the Indian, or the other way around?"

"Either way is bad. Once the organism infects the rat population, it can grow virtually unchecked—unless, of course, you exterminate the rats. But it's more likely this man arrived in town already infected, probably from the Southwest. What worries us is that we found a number of rat bites on the body. I didn't tell you this, but that's another way to spread plague—by ingesting infected tissue."

Decker rolled his eyes. "Great image. All right, so how long was he dead when they found him?"

"The coroner says no more than four hours."

"Any idea how old he is?"

"They think about seventy-five, based on a dental exam. Discounting the infection, of course, he was extremely healthy for his age." Janet propped open the left eyelid with her gloved thumb. "You can see there's no clouding of the lens from cataracts. No arthritis in his major joints, either. And very little arteriosclerosis. The coroner says he had the heart of a forty-year-old."

Decker looked at the Indian's eyes again—hot black coals beaming upward from an ashen face. The eyes, it seemed, were still alive, straining to speak a language no one could hear.

19

Decker closed his notebook. He hadn't much for a story, just a lot of technical details and unanswered questions.

"What in God's name was he doing here?"

Janet looked down on the contorted face and shook her head. She lifted the back of his head, gently, trying to relax the straining tendons in his neck. It was no use: Death refused to loosen its grip.

"If we can get a story in the paper—and I think the sooner the better—someone may recognize this man," Janet said. "You can't imagine how helpful it would be to have a personal history. Not to mention some idea of how many people he might have exposed."

"Why not hold a press conference?"

"I wish we could. The problem is, Dr. Luken can't do a thing without approval from the health commissioner, and he won't announce until they get a confirmation from the CDC."

"When?"

"The lab work will take at least twenty-four hours, maybe forty-eight. The CDC didn't start their tests until this afternoon."

"Great. So meanwhile we could have an army of plague-infested rats roaming downtown."

Janet looked up at Decker, and for the first time he saw something like panic in her eyes. Her voice was low and a little frightened.

"It's like a bad horror movie, Rick. If plague were to gain a foothold among the men at the shelter, it could spread like wildfire. Especially if it becomes pneumonic."

"You'll have to explain."

"That's when the infection reaches the lungs. At that point, it becomes extremely contagious, because the victims cough and wheeze and spread the organism through the air."

"Like a cold?"

"Yes, like a cold, only much more deadly. You'll read cases in medieval literature where apparently healthy people went to bed at night and died of pneumonic plague in their sleep."

20

"Dandy . . ."

"All right, then, imagine what would happen if even one person with pneumonic plague spent the night at the shelter. To begin with, most of those men have compromised immune systems, because of drinking, old age, poor diets, whatever. Then when you consider how many of them are crammed into one room . . ."

"Epidemic city. I think I'm getting the picture now."

Janet's blue eyes took on a steely glare. "I just hope the health commissioner does."

3

Decker tossed his pack of cigarettes into the far recesses of his desk drawer, where he'd have to hunt for them, then settled back in his chair. The front wall of his cubicle was glass from desk level on up. He could see Farlidge coming down the hallway, straight from Sally Beth's office, in one of his charcoal suits and a fat yellow paisley tie. Farlidge pointed down the hallway toward his office, and Decker gathered up his notes and followed. Stein was already there, his body slumped down in one of the pseudo-art-deco chairs.

Farlidge had to squeeze around his desk to reach his leather executive chair. He was tall and paunchy, with delicate skin and straight brown hair that swept just over his right ear and stopped before it could get out of control. He wore a boxy little mustache, and it was that more than anything else that reminded Decker of *"der Fuhrer"* whenever he looked at him. His office was small—barely room enough for a desk, three chairs, and a potted Corn King—but Farlidge insisted always on meeting there, something he no doubt had learned in one of his management seminars.

Farlidge was only thirty, two years younger than Decker, eleven years younger than Stein. He was one of the fair-haired

Golden Boys on Delta's corporate fast track. He had worked four or five years as a reporter on one of the chain's smaller Florida papers, where he had won a number of in-house writing awards from Delta. From there the chain sent him through a three-month training program at its New Orleans headquarters and—*voilà!*—he emerged a metro editor in Cincinnati, bumping Barry Stein down to assistant. That was six months ago, and now Barry was about to set himself free.

"It's just as I thought, I'm afraid," Farlidge began, sounding helpless and apologetic, the way he always did when carrying out orders. "Sally Beth won't use an unnamed source."

Decker threw up his hands and jumped from his chair.

"Rick, sit down," Stein said calmly. "Let's hear this out."

"I've heard it too damn many times."

Stein caught Decker's arm and gave him one of his quit-acting-like-a-child stares. Decker sat.

"Ron," Stein said, "you know this isn't just any anonymous source. It's a physician, and one close to the case. If we use her name, she loses her job."

Farlidge leaned forward, looking more earnest than an altar boy. "But you know the policy, Barry. And, frankly, I think it's a good one. The public doesn't trust unnamed sources. Now if Rick could find somebody at the Health Department—"

Decker interrupted, gripping his chair arms to stay calm. "Ron, I've tried every person in the department, from the health commissioner to the goddamn night janitor. Nobody's willing to go on the record. Instead, they'll wait twenty-four hours, or however long it takes to do their freaking lab tests, and then throw a press conference for every newspaper and TV station within five hundred miles. And you can bet they'll hold it in the late afternoon—long after our deadline—so the TV mannequins can do it live."

Farlidge sat back, smiled coolly. "We take that chance. But as Sally Beth would say, our days of playing god are over. We don't create the news. We report it."

Stein spoke out before Decker could. "Is it playing god, Ron, to want to be first?"

"No, Barry, but what if it turns out to be wrong—"

Decker jumped in. "I've got two independent confirmations."

Farlidge grinned. "Both off-the-record."

"Come on, Ron," Decker said. "What really worries Sally Beth is how the Downtown Council will react. 'Plague in the Blue Chip City.' Nobody wants to read that shit, do they?"

"When plague is officially declared, we'll run with it, believe me."

"All right, Ron," Stein said, holding up a hand to quiet Decker. "We'll get it on the record. But you and Sally Beth think about this. You don't keep good reporters around by handcuffing them."

"Then quit," Janet told him at dinner. "We can get by on one salary for a while. We'll cut corners." She waved her hand around the table, as if candlelight dinners were one place they could start.

True, they could get by. They paid little in the way of rent—$350 a month for the wood-frame bungalow they'd found on the Ohio riverbank in Ludlow, Kentucky.

"Fine," Decker said. "I'll quit. I can fish all day and wait for you to come home."

The argument was tired ground; Janet's reaction was to get up from the table and start clearing dishes.

"I'll do that," Decker said, and took the plates from her hand. Whoever prepared dinner was spared the cleanup; that was their deal; and Janet had fixed one of her specialties—a stir fry of shrimp and Chinese vegetables, done to perfection with fresh ginger and tart raspberry vinegar.

Janet sat again, her voice insistent. "Rick, I can't just drop out of school and leave everything behind. Especially not now."

24

"I know," he said, more resigned than patient. He stacked the Fiesta Ware bowls and plates—part of the inheritance from Janet's mother—and went out to the kitchen.

Janet's mother had died last summer, and now her father was alone, eating haphazard meals and living in semisqualor above his office in Cheviot. He refused to hire a cleaning lady, although he grudgingly permitted Janet to make a sweep of the place on weekends. Otherwise, he appeared to be the same old "Doc" Shoemaker. Kindly, generous, quick with a joke. The last of the old-time family physicians. No one could *not* like old Doc Shoemaker, which made Decker all the more ashamed of being jealous of him. Janet's father was the one man Decker would never measure up to.

He sat again at the table, intent on smoothing things over. He poured more wine for both of them. "A great meal," he said. He turned to an imaginary waitress and dead-panned, "Would you send my compliments to the chef, please?"

Janet smiled and softened. She was in her domestic mode, far from the madding hospital crowd—a braless, jeans-clad college girl again, foot tucked under thigh. She was wearing one of his frayed Oxford cloth shirts, loose and half-unbuttoned. When she leaned forward to take his hand, there was a wink of unfettered breast. Casual. Just between friends.

"You know, Rick, we'll get through this, don't you?"

He nodded, a believer. After all, he had never expected it to last this long. Not him. Before Janet, he had made a point of disappearing before the other person had had the chance. The way his father had disappeared when Decker was thirteen.

When Decker started to clear the table, Janet left to take a quick spin on her bike around the neighborhood. On some days she biked the whole eight miles to work and back. She was tough. Not even a collision with a Pepsi delivery truck the summer before, and a broken leg that had her hobbling on crutches for months, had tempered her zeal for the sport.

Decker put the leftovers in assorted Tupperware containers and added them to the stock Janet would take with her to eat at work, no matter how stale, tasteless, or moldy. Janet refused to throw away food—a dictate of her global consciousness and, as even she admitted, of the middle-class guilt that came with being a doctor's daughter.

Decker quickly finished the dishes and set them in the drainer, then went outside to the porch for a cigarette and a look at what was left of the river.

Their house was the last on Butler Street. It sat on a small flat hill overlooking the Ohio, its front yard buttressed by a moss-covered limestone wall. The wall dropped five or six feet to an asphalt lane, and beyond that, a second hill tumbled to a small wood along the riverbank.

It had been Decker's idea to live on the river in Kentucky, away from their jobs, away from the city. A place where they could both relax, forget their cares, and watch the river go by. Only now, as in the past few weeks, the drought-stricken Ohio looked more like a stagnant pond than a river. The water was jaundiced brown by day, a sluggish, tarry black by night. Nothing moved on it now, not even the commercial barges and towboats, for fear of running aground. On either side, the naked banks were mud-cracked and eroded. Here and there big trees had fallen and overturned, their dry roots nerves exposed to air.

Decker leaned against the porch railing and lit his cigarette. He coughed. The day's lingering heat made even the first drag seem harsh and raspy. Well, maybe now he could quit again.

He took a deep breath. His lungs drew in the closeness of the night. Heat lightning flickered across the horizon. Silent. Angry. Impotent. He looked to the farther shore. The street lamps along the viaduct were haloed in fog, each light a tiny suspended orb. Upstream, he could see the nimbus of downtown lights, a pink corona against a background of brooding gray.

He tried his cigarette again—it was smoother this time—and looked downstream. The tug *Jo Ann McGinnis* was anchored fifty yards from port, tethered by steel cables to a small

26

pier. A light burned in the pilothouse; shadows played against the windows. Decker imagined how it was inside: the rank odors, the endless rounds of coffee and poker, the bored, restless crew waiting for the river to rise and work to begin again.

For Decker, that was the worst part of it. The waiting. Worse than the corn dying in the fields. Worse, even, than the taste of the drinking water. Everything, everybody, every life seemed on hold. Waiting for the rain to come.

Decker flicked his cigarette butt into the street, watched it spark on the asphalt.

He thought again about the Indian in the morgue. Teeth cut clean through his lower lip. Dead in some strange godforsaken town.

In a while, Janet came spinning down the street on her bike, sleek and shiny in her biker pants and helmet. She stopped in front of the house, snapped off her helmet, and lifted the bike easily onto her shoulder and walked it up the porch steps. She was red in the face, and her hair was matted in a wet ring around her head. She gave Decker a quick peck on the cheek on her way into the house. "What a night! I feel grungy as a bear."

Decker went back inside and finished drying and putting the dishes away. Then he poured what was left of the wine into two clean glasses and took them upstairs to the bathroom.

"Room service."

Janet was soaking in the tub, her head wrapped in a towel, reading an article in one of her medical journals. There were only so many minutes in the day.

"How thoughtee," she said, perching the journal on her uplifted knees and hoisting a glass. She took a sip and handed it back to Decker. "I need to finish this one thing," she said. She lay back against the sloping end of the tub, her shoulders shiny wet and pink.

Decker sat on the edge near her feet and sipped his wine. There was no need to look; he could feel the warm glow of her nakedness. She was more a force than an object to him now. All of a piece. The pale blond hair. The inner-lit skin; warm, scented like orange. And the strong-soft, yielding thickness of her body.

Janet possessed a healthy sexuality that had somehow survived her Catholic education intact. She was intense, almost reverent in her lovemaking, quietly attending to her own needs but always returning in time for his. She smiled during sex, something that had distracted him at first, like making love to a beaming madonna. Her love for him was so obvious and radiant he felt exalted and at the same time like an impostor. He could hardly bear to look into her eyes.

"Okay," she announced, smiling and tossing the journal to the bath mat. They clinked glasses again and drank, and now, oddly, when he had access to her, his thoughts drifted back to work.

"You know, I've been wondering about our Indian friend again."

Janet hugged her knees.

"It seems weird," he said, "I mean, that he wouldn't be carrying any identification."

"But a lot of transients wouldn't. Aren't most of them trying to escape from something—themselves?"

"True, if he'd been an alcoholic. But he wasn't."

"Well, it wasn't easy to tell from the condition of the body. But, yes, there was no liver enlargement."

"Wouldn't you agree, then, our Indian friend was mugged?"

"Mugged, or maybe looted."

"Exactly. And if he was, his ID was probably dumped somewhere near the body."

"But I'm sure the police must have looked."

"The police? Come on. They find a rotting body in an alley behind the men's shelter. It's dark. The body stinks to high heaven. They assume it's a wino. Case closed."

28

Janet handed her glass back, empty. "So I know where you'll be tomorrow morning," she said.

"I wish I could go now."

She made a face that said, "You jerk," and rose naked and dripping from the tub and reached for her towel. For a brief moment as she stood, he was staring straight into the smooth swell of her tummy, the clean, volute strength of her hips. He almost gasped with sudden lust and a kind of awe.

He put the two glasses down, and before she could step out of the tub, he was kissing her face and then her lips, and she was smiling and kissing back. Her mouth had a slight metallic taste—tangy, not unpleasant—the way it always tasted when she'd been reading or concentrating on something. It was the taste of her mind, he told her once.

She stopped and kissed him on the nose. "Can you give me five minutes?"

"Can you make it four?"

She laughed, but there was a touch of nervousness in it—a response, he knew, to his eagerness. She had told him not to try to prove anything. It only made matters worse. Easy for her to say.

He headed downstairs with the wine glasses, rinsed them, checked the lock on the back door for the second time that night, and snapped off the kitchen light.

In the bedroom he kicked off his shoes and stretched out on the bed, hands behind his head. The overhead fan circled lazily, a necessary adjunct to the inefficient air conditioner. He could hear Janet making soft splashing noises in the tub and then—*pop!*—the rasp and gurgle of water spiraling down the drain. She was humming something classical. Maybe Vivaldi.

He rolled over and his eyes fixed on the portable TV above the dresser. The clock next to it said 10:59. Somehow he knew he shouldn't—that if he turned on the set, the night would be ruined—but he couldn't resist a peek at the eleven o'clock news. He got up, pushed the "on" button, flipped to Channel 9. He stood there and watched.

There was an ad for a discount furniture store, the owner reclining in a Naugahyde easy chair, pitching his wares in a phony hillbilly accent. The Channel 9 news intro followed, and when the anchorman dispensed with the usual folksy smile, Decker knew there was some real news. "Good evening. For our top story tonight, we take you live to the Hamilton County coroner's office, where Channel 9 reporter Sam Delaney has shocking news on the death here of an unidentified man. Channel 9 has learned the cause may be bubonic plague—"

Decker hit the "off" switch with a force that set the dresser rocking on its legs. When he turned, Janet was standing in the doorway, her wet hair combed back and her skin glowing and her body wrapped in a loose terry-cloth robe. She wasn't smiling.

Decker jammed his feet into his shoes, plunked down on the mattress, and started tying the laces. His hands were shaking.

"I guess you heard that." He was hoarse with anger.

Janet untied her bathrobe. Her jaw was set. "Why should it matter?"

He didn't hear. " 'Channel 9 has learned.' Don't you love it? Don't you just love it! Christ . . ."

He got up and started out of the room. "I'm sorry, Janet, but I need a long walk or I'll go crazy."

From the door he saw her standing with her back to him, hands draped at her side, looking vulnerable and hurt. He almost went back and put his arms around her, but his gut told him it was too late.

4

Decker woke late the next morning and reached for the "off" button on the clock radio, even though it wasn't playing. It was 7:35. He wondered if he'd slept through the alarm or if Janet had forgotten to reset it before she left. He hurried through his shower and shave, dressed, and headed for downtown, skipping his morning coffee up the street at Pete's Diner, where he liked to rest his elbows on the cool marble countertop and read the competition.

Dawn had brought no relief from the heat and drought, although the sky was still gray and the air heavy with the threat of rain. The thickness of it played havoc with Decker's throat, still raw from so many cigarettes the night before. He tried not to think too much about last night. Not until he was caffeinated. Besides, today was a new day. "The first day of the rest of your life." Well, dammit, it was.

It was almost eight when he started across the Clay Wade Bailey Bridge. He rolled down the window, stuck his face into the fetid rush of air. Downtown loomed ahead, its tight cluster of buildings shrouded in haze. Ghost city. Unreal.

Over the bridge, he turned right onto Third, then left onto Elm and drove past the block of closed shops in the stillborn

Convention Square complex. The windows were filled now with flimsy promotional displays for the ballet and the symphony, put there by the Downtown Business Council. Anything to hide the emptiness.

The men's shelter was on the northern fringe of downtown, in the old Doppelman's brewery at Elm and Central Parkway. The brewery was a macabre spectacle of dark brick and sandstone, a 1920s kitsch version of a Bavarian castle, five stories high and a block long. There were fake turrets at every corner, notched stone cornices along the roofline, and, for use as a truck entrance on Elm Street, a double set of spiked wooden doors.

As a boy, Decker could remember walking by the brewery with his mother and looking through the wrought-iron grates over the basement windows and seeing the eerie glow from the long line of kettle fires. He was certain the devil lived there. It still gave him that feeling.

"Mad Gustav" Doppelman built the place in 1921, a copy of a sixteenth-century baronial palace he had once visited on the outskirts of Munich. Back then, too, Central Parkway was a canal that ran along the front of the brewery like a moat. But fifty years later, when Doppelman's became one more victim of Spuds MacKenzie and the Lite Age of beer, the city fathers could hardly wait to tear the place down. It was tacky, they said. A gargantuan eyesore. A nightmare for the city's modern corporate image.

Years of legal wrangling ensued, with the Doppelman family and a group of hard-core preservationists trying, and failing, to place the brewery on the National Register of Historic Places. Finally, just two years ago, the city won its battle in the state supreme court and was about to move in with wrecking crews. But then a group of activists, led by Eric Strider, broke into the brewery early one morning and declared the space a "people's sanctuary" for the poor and homeless.

Some people in town suspected that one, or all, of the three Doppelman boys—like father, like sons—had put Strider up to the invasion. Others, including Decker, thought Strider had simply seen the political opportunity and seized it, as was his way. Whatever the impulse, the occupation rallied enough public support that the City Council backed off.

But the shelter continued to draw political fire. Business leaders blamed it for downtown's precipitous decline. Two major department stores had pulled out in the last two years. Why? Not because the city was under siege by a ring of suburban malls, but because the shelter was funneling bums and wackos into the downtown shopping district and scaring away decent middle-class consumers who, quite naturally, were afraid of anyone not like themselves.

And now, Decker thought, an old Indian dies of plague in the shadow of the brewery, as though it were hexed by some ancient Bavarian curse. It was just the medieval touch Mad Gustav would have loved.

Decker parked on Elm just north of Eighth. The brewery was in the next block, its dark towers rising against a leaden sky. Doppelman's was the cornerstone in a decaying section of downtown known as the Crown, where open parking lots were spreading like asphalt cancer. Here and there was a gleaming new office center or a sand-blasted yuppie restaurant. But mostly there were cut-rate clothing stores, wino bars, fleabag hotels. Places that evoked the nostalgic seediness of a Hopper painting, when downtowns were more brick than glass, more grit than glitz.

Decker's long walk the night before had taken its toll. He felt the stab of shin splints as he made his way up Elm past a row of abandoned town houses. The windows breathed a musty, acrid smell, a mix of stale urine, rotted plaster, like dying old men.

To Decker's surprise, the sidewalks around the shelter were empty. No panhandlers. No wasted-looking men sleeping under their coats.

He soon discovered another surprise: The alley behind the shelter was roped off. There was a sign stapled to the caution tape. HEALTH AND SAFETY HAZARD. NO ENTRY. PER ORDER OF THE CINCINNATI HEALTH DEPARTMENT.

Decker bellied up to the tape. The alley was cool and dark, barely wide enough for two men to walk side by side. The brick pavement was dry and scattered with bits of broken glass and trash. He looked for rats, for clothing, for any sign that a body had been found there the day before, but there was only a couple of greasy-looking pigeons pecking away at a Styrofoam burger box.

He slipped under the tape, and instantly, as though he'd tripped a booby trap, a voice boomed behind him: "Hey, you! Come back here!"

A policeman was coming at him in a hurry across Elm Street, leather creaking, metal paraphernalia jangling. The sound of angry cop on the hoof.

"Buddy, can't you read?"

He was tall, rock-solid, too young for the standard-issue paunch. He was wearing knee-high rubber boots.

Decker smiled. Sometimes, not often, it helped with cops. He identified himself as an *Eagle* reporter and put out his hand. The cop only glanced at it. He was young, all right, with something to prove.

"I've got orders to keep everybody away from this building, and that goes double for reporters."

"You mean they shut the place down?"

"Cleared everybody out at five this morning."

Decker got out his notebook. "How many?"

"You'll have to contact the duty officer for a statement."

"I won't quote you. This is just for background."

The cop took off his cap, scratched the ring it left in his thick, sandy hair. He was a bit afraid, but also eager to talk. Anything to make a morning of guard duty go faster.

"Is that a promise?"

He *was* young. "Scout's honor."

"Well, it was close to two hundred men is what I hear. They took some over to Cincinnati General for tests, then bused the

34

rest out to Longview." Longview was the state mental hospital in Bond Hill, now named the Lewis Center, but only the shrinks called it that.

"All because of the body they found?"

The cop nodded and pointed. "Right down this alley, as a matter of fact. The health commissioner ain't taking any chances. He wants this whole block cleared until they finish testing the rats down here."

Decker shot a glance at the cop's boots.

"Yeah, well . . . I'm not taking any chances, either. Some fuckin' rat crawl up my leg—no way!"

Decker smiled. He'd tucked his trousers into a pair of hiking boots for the same reason.

"If it's all right with you, officer, I'd still like to look around. All I ask is one minute down that alley."

"Lookin' for what?"

"Maybe a wallet or a personal effect. Anything that might help identify the Indian."

The cop snorted. "Indian . . . Shit."

"You don't believe it?"

"Hell, that's some horseshit the coroner put out. I've seen enough of these men that hang out down here. He was probably some old hippie who liked to wear Indian love beads or something. Probably been doing IV drugs for the last twenty years. I'll bet that's how he got this plague thing."

Decker stared off down the alley, his eye picking up the glint from something flat and square. Broken glass? A wallet folder?

"I'd still like to look."

The cop shook his head. "Orders is orders."

Just as Decker had feared, Stein was charged up and rearing to go that morning. Decker barely had time to sit down with his first coffee and cigarette when Stein came into his cubicle. He was clutching the A section of the Cincinnati *Times*. A

35

front-page box just below the masthead carried the headline: Body Found Near Shelter May Be Plague Victim.

"I guess you saw this?"

"Yeah." Decker lit a cigarette, tilted his head back, and exhaled a long stream of smoke. Stein edged off a little. "They probably caught Channel 9 last night and got the coroner out of bed to confirm. They didn't advance it much. At least our follow-up will look that much better." Decker hated writing follow-ups. It was like cheating from someone else's exam— only you had to come up with better answers.

Stein pulled up the straight-back chair Decker kept in his cubicle, just for Stein, to accommodate his back problems. "You know, you look pretty beat. Are you sure you're up to this?"

Decker roused himself, grinned. "Sure. I only look like I had four hours sleep."

His walk the night before had taken him west through Ludlow and a mile or more to the Brent Spencer Bridge. A dense warm wind had been steady at his back all the way there, then full in his face on the return. He had thought for sure it would rain. When he got home an hour or so later, he found Janet in bed, curled with her back to him and her body carefully arranged on one side of the mattress. Decker knew what that meant. He could understand why, too.

Even so, he woke once in the middle of the night and found they were clinging to each other, as though their subconscious minds had overruled any fight their conscious minds had started. She was gone by the time he got up, although he vaguely remembered being stirred in his half-sleep by the close-in scent of makeup and toothpaste, and the ticklish warmth of a kiss on his cheek. Unless, of course, it had been a dream.

"It's going to be one hell of a busy morning" were the next words that registered with Decker. Stein was still in high gear. "Murdock called a press conference for ten. He's already closed the shelter."

"I know," Decker said. "I was just down there. The police have everything roped off."

"Then you know about the other press conference this morning."

"No, but let me guess—Eric Strider."

"He's calling his at eleven thirty. In the Legal Aid offices."

Strider was a former Bengals linebacker who had dedicated his life to social activism after a knee injury ended his mediocre football career in the mid-seventies. Every year or so Strider and his followers would "liberate" an abandoned building in the name of the homeless—a tactic guaranteed to get him media attention.

Decker glanced at his watch. It was almost nine. The Strider bash at eleven thirty would crowd the noon deadline for home edition. Decker might be able to stretch it to twelve fifteen, but with the possibility that Mullins, the copy desk chief, would suffer a stroke. "Maybe I should call Strider now," he said.

Stein shook his head. "I tried about ten minutes ago. He wants a grandstand audience before he'll sing."

"Dammit, if Strider thinks . . ."

"Calm down. I've talked with Farlidge about this. Here's the plan. You'll go to the commissioner's press conference at ten, then come back here to write your story. Someone else will cover Strider and phone you the notes."

"Who?"

"Angie Lapola."

"*Who?*"

"Angela Lapola." The name sounded like La-PO-luh.

"Wait a minute. You mean the one that looks like Annie Hall on acid?" Stein didn't smile. "Barry, she's a copy clerk, for Christ's sake."

Stein shrugged. "Farlidge says she's the only person we can spare. We've got three reporters on vacation, and two more covering the Pete Rose thing. Then there's the drought coverage: a cloud seeding this morning out in Butler County, and, get this, somebody's trying an Indian rain dance later today in

Loveland. And on top of all that, Sally Beth insists somebody sneak onto the set of the Cody Blair film for the first day of filming. It's going to be one stressed-out day."

"What about the Guild, Barry? Don't we have rules that say clerks can't cover stories?"

Stein broke into a cynical little smile. "What Guild?"

"But, Barry—a frigging copy clerk!?"

"So help her along. She's not as ditzy as she looks. She's been stringing for the neighborhood section."

Decker blew smoke, rolled his eyes.

"All right, her stuff is a little timid. But from what I've seen, it's professional. Farlidge says she's been begging to move into metro. She wants a chance to prove herself."

Decker crushed out the last of his cigarette. "You're right, Barry. One stressed-out day."

At 9:30 Decker was at his desk making a last-minute check of his carrying bag—a clean notebook, two pens (one blue, one red, for highlighting his shorthand), and a spare set of fresh batteries for his tape recorder—when the phone rang.

"Hi, Rick. Angie Lapola. You ready to go?" She was breathless with excitement. "I'm down in the lobby. My car's right outside the door."

"Wait a minute. Ready for what?"

"Didn't Barry tell you? The press conference at the Health Department."

"I thought you were covering Eric Strider at eleven thirty."

"I am. But Barry thinks it would be good background if I went to both. Don't you think?" Decker didn't answer. "I don't mind driving, really I don't. *Hector*'s right outside."

"Hector?"

"Oh, geez, I'm sorry. My car. It's a long story. Anyway, come on down. I'll meet you in the lobby. Okay? *Ciao.*" Click.

Decker stared at his phone. *"Ciao?"*

He didn't have any trouble finding Angie in the lobby. She was wearing an oversized man's sports coat—a silky green to set off her red hair—over a white T-shirt and a tight black miniskirt with patterned white stockings. The ensemble was completed, top and bottom, with a black felt hat and black slippers. On 99.9 percent of working women the outfit would have looked ridiculous. On Angie, who was young and petite and wired, it wasn't clothing; it was an outgrowth of her persona.

She approached Decker with a big, wide-open smile and a quick handshake. Her hand felt tiny in his. It seemed to vibrate.

"Isn't this exciting?" she said. Her green eyes propelled energy, never took it in. "I mean, it's a totally awesome story, don't you think? Plague and rats and politics and stuff. Hey," she said, "doesn't that have a neat ring to it? *Plague and rats and politics—oh, my!*"

Decker took a deep breath as Angie practically skipped ahead. She pushed through the revolving doors in such a rush that Decker was pulled through by the momentum.

Outside the sky was clearing and the sun was beginning to bake the streets again, the heat rising in waves from the asphalt. By late afternoon the false clouds would gather, the dry thunder would rumble, and the whole frustrating cycle would start anew.

"*Hector*'s over here." She pointed to a rusting Pinto parked three spaces up Broadway. A bumper sticker at the bottom of the rear window said, CAUTION—THIS CAR EXPLODES ON IM-PACT. There were other stickers: one for 97X, a New Wave rock station. Another for Greenpeace. A fourth said: ILLITER-ATE? WRITE TO THIS ADDRESS FOR HELP."

Before he could yank the door shut, Angie had slipped on her Raybans and was speeding off into traffic, the Pinto's unmuffled engine sounding like an explosion in a trash can. Decker hunted for his seatbelt.

"You know, I went bananas when Barry called me about working this story. For months I've been covering these boring, boring, BOR-*RING* suburban council meetings, and I thought, *My God, if I have to write one more story about sewer improvements or garbage collection rates or putting in a new traffic light somewhere, I'm going to scream.*" And she did—loud enough to be heard over the engine.

Decker gripped his door handle as Angie wove through traffic. On Reading, she swerved into the left lane to pass a Metro bus, cutting off a Type A in a Saab. The driver hit his horn, flashed his brights. Angie smiled into her rearview mirror and calmly flipped him off. Decker continued his search for a seatbelt.

"You know, Barry reminds me so much of my dad. He's like this big soft teddy bear you'd like to reach out and hug. Only you can't do that in the newsroom. Everybody would think you'd gone over the top or something. Sometimes, though, I think things would be a lot less uptight around that place if people would just let go and hug each other. Don't you think?"

Decker had his right hand behind his back, digging between the cushions for a seatbelt. Angie glanced at him quizzically.

"Yeah, I know what you mean," he said. "Actually, I've always wanted to give Farlidge a big hug."

Angie threw her head back and laughed. It was a high-pitched giggle, as loud as it was spontaneous.

"He's a major yup, isn't he? Somebody told me he's got like this really radical wine collection in his basement. Worth thousands of dollars."

"And a pasta maker," Decker added. "He brags about his homemade rigatoni."

"Mmmm. Sounds like my kind of guy," she said. "I'm really into starches."

Decker wasn't sure if she was kidding or not.

"Sorry about the seatbelts," Angie said, turning serious for a moment. "The previous owner ripped them all out. Said they violated his constitutional right to die young." She laughed out loud again.

Decker sat back, calculating the distance to the windshield. "It doesn't matter," he said.

"Hey, why don't you put in a tape?" She reached behind Decker's seat and pulled out a plastic trash basket. It was filled with tapes. "Take your pick."

Decker started sorting. They were mostly New Wave groups, with names derived from some cryptic language of the new generation. Firehose. Concrete Blonde. Oingo Boingo. Fine Young Cannibals. Decker decided on the last one, intrigued by the literary quality of the name. Angie popped in the tape, set the volume at a dull roar, and Decker was surprised: There was an acoustical guitar, lyrics he could actually understand.

"Not bad," he said.

"How old are you, Rick?" The question was direct, startling, like everything she did.

"Thirty-two."

She pointed to the trash basket. "There's some Beatles in there, near the bottom."

Decker laughed to hide his indignation. "Are you saying I'm too old for anything but the Beatles?"

"Oopsie. Did I, like, ruffle major feathers? Sorry. Anyway, thirty-two's not old. Men aren't interesting until they're thirty."

"Really? And at what point do women become interesting?"

Angie turned and batted her eyelids. "Women don't have to be interesting."

She downshifted for the long climb up Burnet Avenue to Pill Hill, so named because that's where most of the city's hospitals and medical offices where concentrated. The engine made a loud, sputtering noise, like a kid vibrating his lips into a vacuum cleaner hose.

"You know," she said, slowing her speech closer to the Midwest norm, "you're the reason I'm in journalism." They

41

were stopped for the light at Burnet and Oak. She turned and stared at him with wide-eyed earnestness, nodding. For the first time, he noticed she was wearing two different earrings. A white loop in one ear, a black triangle in the other. Was it a code?

He was off-balance again. "Me?"

"The Krieger stories," she said, as though it were perfectly obvious. "I was a sophomore at UC at the time. My parents wanted me to major in graphic design. You know how that goes. They're both art professors. My father's a sculptor. My mother's in commercial design. Anyway, when I saw how you and that other reporter, what's-his-name . . ."

"Turk Nystrom." Decker wanted to scold her for not knowing. Turk had been killed in a car crash during the investigation.

"Yeah, well, how you two guys turned this whole town on its ear. And then Krieger and that fire chief, what's his name?"

"Orsini."

"Yeah, both of them committed suicide, and then the FBI found this whole giant conspiracy. God, I thought, this is where the action is. This is what I want to do with my life. Not lock myself in some grungy art studio like my parents."

Decker squinted into the silvery heat up Burnet Avenue. The photons seemed to shimmer in the trapped air. "Actually, Krieger didn't commit suicide. His daughter shot him."

"She did? Unreal. Positively dee-lish."

Decker was glad when they arrived at the Health Department building at Burnet and King, but not so glad to see all the signs of a media feeding frenzy. The parking lot was filled with cars, the surrounding side streets jammed. There were a half dozen circus wagons from the TV stations, including one from CNN, all of them sprouting microwave dishes. Decker looked at his watch. Fifteen minutes to show time.

Angie circled the building, and finding nowhere to park, suddenly stopped the car in the middle of Highland Street. She closed her eyes and placed her fingertips lightly on the rim of the steering wheel. "All right, Rick, let's visualize a parking space."

"You're not serious?"

"Of course, I'm serious." She kept her eyes shut.

In a second or two she started the Pinto moving again and turned right onto Piedmont. A half block up, a station wagon was pulling away from the curb.

Angie grinned at Decker and patted his hand. "You've got to open yourself to what's out there, Rick."

5

The press conference was in the main auditorium on the second floor of the Health Department building. A sign taped next to the elevator door said so, but Angie didn't wait there. She went straight to the stairway.

"What's the rush?"

Angie held the door. "We want good seats, don't we?"

He stared at her. "It's not a rock concert."

But she skipped ahead, and Decker found himself following up the stairs after the echoing scuff of her slippers.

"Wow," Angie said, "it's a happening!"

Inside the auditorium TV crews were jockeying for the best shot of the conference table, its surface a tangled nest of mike cords and tape recorders. Already the first three rows of chairs were filled with reporters, about two dozen in all, including a couple Decker didn't recognize. They were young, East Coast-looking types, dressed in funky gray shirts and skinny black ties. Decker figured they were bureau reporters from *The New York Times* and the *Wall Street Journal*. Plague was one thing on a Navaho reservation, quite another when it was found in the heart of an inland city.

Angie deferred for once as Decker led them to seats in the back row. He liked quick exits, especially near deadline.

Angie sat next to him and started unloading supplies from a large canvas Greenpeace bag—a UC spiral notebook, a lavender felt-tip pen, an econo-pack of sugarless gum. She offered a stick to Decker, who declined. She flipped open her notebook, crossed her legs. The miniskirt took a long hike up her thighs. Decker couldn't help noticing they were nice thighs—shapelier, softer-looking than he would have guessed from the rest of her, which seemed to be all angles and bone, sinew and wiriness. She caught him looking from the corner of his eye, and smiled without embarrassment. He quickly turned away, setting his carrying case on the floor.

He was dying for a cigarette, just a puff or two, but smoking in the Health Department auditorium was akin to swearing in a cathedral. He looked at his watch. Not enough time to sneak outdoors.

Angie was gawking around the room, her mouth working on a stick of gum, her white shin pumping up and down over her knee like the rocker arm on a piston. Decker tried not to notice, but there it was, in the corner of his vision, up and down, up and down. One more thing to get on his nerves.

"God, just feel the energy in here," she said. "What a trip!"

"You betcha."

He said it sarcastically, but it was true. Ten years in the news business, and press conferences still made him antsy. They were every reporter's nightmare. Most of the time you went in cold—no background, no contacts, only a vague idea of what was going down. And then you found yourself surrounded by other reporters, like buzzards, fighting over the same bits of predigested news.

Actually, it didn't matter if it was news or not. The hyped formality of a press conference made everything seem like news—another study from another blue-ribbon panel on education, another drug bust by another sheriff seeking reelection, or another "breakthrough" in the treatment of cancer or heart disease, just in time for some agency's annual fundraising drive. If nothing else, the announcement became news because other papers might have something your paper didn't. Turk had had a name for it: cover-your-ass journalism.

A minute or two before ten, the health commissioner—Dr. Reginald X. Murdock—walked briskly out of his suite of offices at the front of the auditorium. He was trailed by a male aide carrying a collapsible stand and several large charts. The aide was followed in turn by Mayor Carl Bussmeyer, loping and grinning as always, and behind him, a fourth man in a white lab coat, whom Decker assumed was from the Centers for Disease Control.

Murdock took the middle seat, flanked by the mayor on his right and the CDC man on his left, while the aide set up the chart stand. As usual, Murdock was impeccably dressed—a double-breasted navy blazer, cut perfectly, over a crisp white shirt and a crimson tie. Murdock was black, a fact that seemed incidental once you got to know him. He was a Cincinnati kid who had climbed out of the slums of Over-the-Rhine, attended UC on a baseball scholarship, and found his way to Harvard, where he earned a dual M.D.–Ph.D. in public health administration. He was bright, arrogant, defensive, and his political views—like his starched shirts—were whiter than white.

As usual, too, Murdock had brought a prepared speech—why didn't he just fax the damn things?—which he read in his booming voice while the cameras flashed and the tape rolled. Angie, Decker noticed, was jotting down every word in precise Gregg shorthand.

"Where'd you learn that?" he whispered.

"Girls never tell."

Murdock began with a rundown of what everyone in the room already knew. The discovery of the body at the drop-in shelter two days before. Confirmed: a victim of septicemic plague. A male, possibly a Native American, estimated to be about seventy-five years old. Identity unknown. The Federal Bureau of Investigation had been contacted to help make the identification.

Then came the news.

"Tests on several rats trapped in a basement storage area of the shelter were found to be carriers of the disease, although final lab determinations are still in process," Murdock said. "Therefore, in the interest of public health and safety, I have made the decision to close the shelter and quarantine a one-block area surrounding the site until the rodent problem can be eliminated."

Murdock looked up from his prepared text, and the room exploded with questions. He put up his hand for silence.

"I would like to add a note of caution before this affair turns into a media carnival." He glared from behind a pair of rimless glasses, the lenses flashing in the TV floodlights. "While plague does constitute a serious public health threat, especially to certain high-risk segments of the population, the disease itself is treatable and is almost always curable with antibiotics. The important thing is that doctors in the community recognize the signs and symptoms of the disease at its earliest onset, and begin administering medication immediately. Plague has been known to kill those infected in less than forty-eight hours."

The hubbub started again. A medical reporter from a local TV station wanted to know the difference between septicemic and bubonic plague.

Murdock yielded the floor to the man in the white lab coat, Dr. Bradford Wolters, head of a visiting CDC investigative team on infectious diseases. He was a small, precise man with sandy blond hair and a neatly trimmed mustache. He seemed even more arrogant than Murdock, if that was possible, his sharp nose bobbing in air à la William Buckley.

"Normally with plague you'll find bubos—that is, swollen lymph nodes—underneath the victim's arms and in the groin area . . ."

"Would you spell that, please?" It was Otis Greenup, editor and staff of the Ludlow, Kentucky, *Enterprise*. Otis, who was at least seventy, lived for these moments.

Wolters was flustered. "Spell what?"

"Booboos, or whatever the hell it was you said."

The room erupted in laughter. Wolters waited for everybody to stop, then rattled off like a spelling bee contestant: "B-U-B-O-S. Now, may I continue?"

"Yes, sir, you may."

Wolters stuck his nose in the air again. "Bubo is the derivation, of course, for 'bubonic plague.' The swellings can grow very large—the size of an egg, or perhaps even an apple, if you believe the medieval literature. But in this case we—and I mean both Dr. Murdock's office and our own team—have found no evidence of lymph node swelling on the victim."

"So what gives?" someone up front blurted out.

Wolters answered again. "We're convinced this is septicemic plague, which is even more rare than the bubonic form. It's the same disease, really, caused by the same infecting organism. The only difference is that in septicemic plague, the bacteria enters directly into a blood vessel rather than through a superficial bite or break in the skin. It also kills much more quickly than the bubonic form."

Decker jumped on the next question. "Have you determined how the bacteria entered the victim's bloodstream?"

Angie elbowed Decker and smiled, as if to say, "Good question." Decker frowned at her.

"I'd like to answer that if I may, Dr. Wolters," Murdock said. Wolters folded his arms and deferred. "It could have happened several ways. An infected flea might have bitten directly into a vein, or the bacteria might have entered through a deep wound. A possible scenario was that the victim was skinning a rabbit or some other infected animal and cut himself."

A voice called out from the back of the room. It was Carol Dunaway, one of the better reporters at the Cincinnati *Times*.

"Dr. Murdock, the technical details aside, most of us here are wondering why an Indian would be skinning rabbits in the middle of downtown." This sent a ripple of cynical laughter through the auditorium.

48

Murdock threw up his hands. "I'll be honest with you, Carol. I wish we knew the answer to that. It may be the victim was infected elsewhere, then traveled to Cincinnati and died at the shelter. In the worst possible case—and one we think is less likely—he may have been bitten by an infected flea or rodent after, rather than prior to, his arrival here."

"But didn't you just say there were infected rats at the shelter?" someone asked.

"Yes, but chances are the rats were infected by the victim. We found a number of rodent bites on the body." Decker could feel the collective wince in the room.

An earnest young blonde from a local TV station asked the expected panic-in-the-streets question: Is it safe to go downtown?

Murdock said yes, by all means, although he recommended "avoiding possible vectors of the disease." In translation, that meant not walking through alleys where rats might be feeding.

Angie turned to Decker and whispered: "Damn. No more lunches from the dumpster."

Decker almost laughed, then gritted his teeth. "Take notes."

"Well, exc-u-u-se me."

"Dr. Murdock, can you tell us when the shelter will re-open?" This came from a local TV anchorman, a notorious womanizer who was pitched in the station's ads as "more than a newsman—he takes the time to get involved."

Murdock cleared his throat. The room quieted. Another bomb was about to be dropped.

"Before I answer that, I'd like to show you something." Murdock got up from his chair and turned to the display stand behind the table. His aide, a nervous kid with a deep tan and slicked-back hair, came running from the back of the room with the chart. It was an enlarged street map of downtown, with an overlay of green lines. The caption said: Storm Sewers in Downtown Cincinnati. The aide handed Murdock his pointer and disappeared again into the back of the room.

49

Murdock stabbed at a pink circle near Central Parkway and Elm. "Several factors have combined to make the shelter an ideal breeding ground for rodents, as well as an extremely difficult site for eradicating them."

Murdock droned on and on, but the upshot was clear. In the midst of the summer drought, rats in the sewer system were migrating toward the shelter, or more specifically, to the basement below it, where water was pooled from the old pipes that once supplied the brewery.

"Unfortunately, the leakage cannot be stopped without turning off the water supply to the whole building," Murdock said.

Murdock nodded and his aide came running from the back of the room. He slipped the second chart onto the easel—an enlarged blueprint of Doppelman's brewery.

"As many of you may already know, when the brewery was built in 1921, what we now know as Central Parkway was then part of the Miami-Erie Canal. Rather than excavating the site and risking flooding from the canal, the brewery was built over the first floor and basement of a preexisting structure. The result is that there are several subbasements below the brewery—a virtual labyrinth of underground rooms. Over the years this substrata has become a honeycomb of passageways and nesting areas for the downtown rat population. All this was discovered, I might add, after some rather harrowing explorations by our rodent control supervisor, Wayne Plaxton."

Murdock pointed to a balding man in a short-sleeve shirt and a loud striped tie. Somebody yelled, "Attaboy, Wayne!" and the room broke into laughter. Murdock's booming voice took command again. "The point is, there can be no effective control of the downtown rat population until the substrata below the brewery is excavated. Therefore, I am recommending to the Department of Buildings and Inspections that the current site for the shelter be condemned and that it—and several adjacent structures—be razed."

Suddenly Angie jumped from her seat, arm straining in the

air, vying for attention like a grade-school kid. Decker wanted to crawl under his chair.

"Dr. Murdock, sir. Sir, I noticed you said earlier that the victim had died *at* the shelter. Wasn't the body found in an alley behind the shelter?"

Decker raised his eyebrows. A good question. The kind a rookie with a fresh ear would ask. Angie was still standing at attention when Murdock launched into his answer. Decker pulled her down.

"I was going to address this matter at a later point, but since you asked, I might as well clear the air now. True, the first report of the body came from a passerby, who has asked us not to disclose his identity. This person spotted the victim in an alley adjacent to the shelter on Elm Street, early on the morning of August twenty-first. However, in talking to residents at the shelter, we learned something else. Several have told us that the body was first discovered in a basement storage area of the shelter on the night of August twentieth and physically removed by staff persons to the alley. . . ."

Pandemonium. Several reporters exited to the lobby phones.

"Please! Ladies and gentlemen, allow me to finish. As I was saying, the body was removed from the premises by staff persons at the shelter. No one at the shelter reported what they had found either to police or to our department. I have already contacted the county prosecutor on this matter to see whether charges of gross criminal negligence can be filled against those responsible . . ."

As the questioning continued, Angie smiled at Decker a little uncertainly.

"Did I do good?"

"Good? You did great, Ace."

Her whole face lit up.

* * *

At 11:46 A.M. Decker hit the "Count" button on his terminal, then lit another cigarette while he waited for the computer to squeeze his story into an exact column width and measure its length.

"Come on, come on . . ." The closer to deadline, the slower the computers. He had thirty minutes at most to wrap up his story, and Angie still hadn't phoned her notes from the Eric Strider press conference.

Finally the computer bleeped and the column measurement popped up in the right-hand corner of the screen—25 inches.

"Aaargh!" It was way too long, even without the comments from Strider. He'd have to excise whole paragraphs.

He typed, "Ron, how much room for 'plague'?" on the message line at the top of his screen, then zapped it over to Farlidge's terminal.

More waiting. He smoked his cigarette, flicked the ashes into his panda tray. The tummy was piled high now with dead butts.

Bleep! Farlidge's reply: "Keep 'plague' to twelve inches."

Decker stared at the screen. He couldn't believe it. He stood up from his chair and shouted over the partition to the city desk, where Farlidge was sitting with his back turned.

"Ron, are you serious? Twelve inches? This story is national news!"

Farlidge left his desk and started toward Decker's cubicle with a patient smile on his face that said, "Well, here we go again." He leaned against Decker's partition and said, "All right, how much do you need? Fifteen?"

Decker propped his feet on his desk, folded his arms. He was so angry he could feel the sweat breaking out on his scalp. "Ron, this is the first case of plague in this city's recorded history. Maybe the first in the entire Midwest. And on top of it, there's enough political maneuvering behind the scenes for a three-part investigative series. And you're telling me to write half a single newspaper column?"

"I'll be honest with you," Farlidge said, trying to be conciliatory. "Sally Beth assigned it a low priority. She doesn't think we should blow this thing out of proportion."

"Out of proportion? In other words, she's afraid to piss off the Downtown Business Council."

Farlidge came close to losing his cool. "No, I'm not saying that at all. Listen to me. She thinks this is a freak thing, not a major health threat. You heard what Murdock said. It's only a threat to high-risk groups . . ."

"Like old bums and derelicts and all the other scum this paper doesn't give a shit about?"

"You put it more bluntly than I would."

"Not much."

Decker put his feet back on the floor and rolled his chair over to his terminal. "All right, fifteen inches. But keep my name off of it. It's not my story anymore."

"Have it your way, Decker, but let's get moving."

Decker hated cutting almost as much as writing follow-ups. It was like losing weight via amputation. Still, he managed to trim seven inches from the story in about fifteen minutes, mostly by paraphrasing quotes and eliminating the more technical stuff from Wolters. He was still cutting and fiddling when Angie called at 12:10—ten minutes past deadline.

"You've got five minutes, Angie. That's it. Forget about spellings. Just read it off." He hit the split-screen key, moved his story to the left half of the screen, and opened the right half for Angie's notes, which he could then copy to the other side. He was poised over the keyboard like a concert pianist.

Angie was still riffling through her notes. "All right," she said. "Jammin'."

"Jammin'?"

"As in 'We be jammin'.' "

"Five minutes, Angie."

"Okay. First of all, Strider said he knows nothing about a body being moved from the shelter and dumped outside. He had no further comment on that question until he talked with his staff. Quote: 'I don't know who the health commissioner talked to about this, but he never talked to me.' "

"Good stuff. What about Murdock's recommendation for razing the shelter?"

"Strider said he wasn't surprised."

"What did he mean he wasn't surprised?"

"He said the city—and this is a quote—'has been trying to shut us down, one way or another, since the day we opened. But the people . . .' "

Decker stopped typing. "Forget the sixties bullshit. What else did he say? Did anybody see the Indian at the shelter?"

"Wait a minute." Angie riffled through her notes again.

Decker strummed his fingers on the edge of the keyboard, looked at his watch. "T minus four minutes and counting."

"All right. Here we go. He said the shelter's nightly log had no record of anyone fitting the victim's description. He said they keep track of everybody who comes in, even if they have to assign that person a name."

"Assign them a what?"

"A name. You know, guys who come in so loaded or freaked out they don't know their own name."

"Gotcha. Anything else? We've got to wrap this puppy."

"Well, the reason I called so late is that I cornered Strider after the conference."

"And?"

"I asked him point-blank if he thought Murdock might have a personal or political vendetta against him."

"Good—and?"

"Well, this is sort of off-the-record . . ."

"Angie, you don't let people talk off-the-record. Not on a story like this. Didn't they teach you anything in journalism school?"

"I didn't go to journalism school."

"Forget it. What did he say?"

"He said we should talk to this guy in the economic development office. He gave me a name and a number—"

"We don't have time. What else did Strider say?"

"He said he knows for a fact that there's a huge development project being planned for the block where the shelter's located. He said Murdock is one of the investors."

Strider, Decker knew, had his own stake in the area. He was the founder of ROT—Reclaiming Our Tenements—a nonprofit group that bought up slum properties with the idea of renovating them for the poor. But while the group now owned hundreds of such properties, less than a dozen had been fixed up. Strider blamed the city for refusing to give him money.

"And you're the only one who got this?" Decker asked.

"I caught Strider coming out of the john. His hands were still wet."

Decker looked at his watch—12:16. "It's too late for the home edition. We'd have to contact Murdock. I'll talk to Farlidge and see what we can do for the final."

"Jammin'."

"Good work, Angie."

"You mean 'Ace'?"

"All right, *Ace*."

6

Decker was too wound up to eat, even though Angie had brought him a turkey sandwich on whole wheat from Arnold's and placed it in front of him on his desk. He peeled back the top slice of bread. The meat was buried under a mound of alfalfa sprouts. It looked like a chunk of sod.

"Where's the mayo?"

"Silly. You don't need mayo. It's full of cholesterol."

She sounded like Janet, only Janet would have meant it. He thought about calling her, but there was too much going on.

He covered the sandwich and punched the phone number again for Sam Burke, assistant director of the economic development office. Sam was the contact Eric Strider said would confirm the plans for the shelter site. The number had been busy for the last ten minutes, and Decker feared someone else was already on to the story.

"Still busy?"

He slammed the receiver. "Yes, dammit. I'm about to give up on this guy." He lit another cigarette and tried to think if he had any other contacts at the development office. The only person who came to mind was a former director who had left the post two years ago.

"I can run down to City Hall," Angie said eagerly.

She was sitting in his straight-back chair, legs crossed, scraping around the bottom of a yogurt carton. Her leg was pumping up and down again, a loose slipper dangling from the end of her foot.

Decker looked at his watch: 1:20. "Forget it. By the time you walked over there and got into his office, we'd have to file for the final anyway."

As a joke, Angie had left her floppy hat on top of Decker's terminal, the brim sticking out over the screen like a visor. With the hat out of the picture, Decker got his first real look at her features. Her red hair was the wispy, orangy kind, feathered around her face and cut short around her ears, which were small and delicate but stuck out a little. Her face was thin, with a somewhat pointy chin, and her green eyes were wide and almond-shaped. In short, she looked pixieish.

When the yogurt container was scraped clean, she wedged her tongue against the spoon and closed her eyes. She was thinking.

"Wait a minute," she said. "Why don't we call Murdock and ask him straight out if it's true he has a financial interest in tearing down the shelter."

"Based on what? A rumor generated by Eric Strider?"

"We don't have to tell Murdock that."

"So young, and already so twisted . . ."

Angie grinned. "So what?"

Decker tried Burke's number again, and to his surprise, got through.

"Is it ringing?!"

Decker held up his hand for quiet.

"Development. Burke here."

Decker identified himself and got to the point. It was closing in on 1:30.

"Mr. Burke, I understand there's a project in the works for the old Doppelman's brewery."

Burke swallowed and then said, "You mean Crown Pointe?"

"Of course." Decker was smiling now. "Can you give me the details?" He winked at Angie.

"Well, it's all very preliminary at this point." Burke seemed a little puzzled by Decker's curiosity, although not outright suspicious. "We haven't been shown the plans yet, but there's been a lot of maneuvering in the background."

"Isn't it supposed to be some kind of big residential complex or something?"

"*Big* is an understatement. It's going to be massive—a mix of residential, retail, and entertainment. Or at least that's the rumor. There's a coalition of developers getting ready to make a big pitch to City Council. They want that block."

"Who does it belong to now?"

"Good question. The damn thing has been in and out of court so many times I'm not sure who owns it. Maybe Eric Strider owns it by now. One thing is certain. If the building is officially condemned, which is what Dr. Murdock wants, it reverts to the city."

"So what developers are we talking about?"

"I haven't seen the complete list, but I know Skip Flannery is one." Flannery, a flamboyant type who raced Indy-class cars and fancied himself another Ted Turner, owned the largest commercial development firm in town. "But it's going to take more than Skip to get this baby off the ground."

"Really?"

"They'll need forty to fifty stories to support a block that size. You're talking about a four-hundred-to-five-hundred-million-dollar investment."

Decker whistled into the phone.

"It could be more if they decide to go upscale—you know, trendy shops and theaters and such."

"You mean like the Back Bay development in Boston?"

"Exactly. Godiva chocolates and Dove bars at the movie concession stand. That sort of thing."

Angie pointed at her Day-Glo Swatch. Decker nodded.

"Listen, Sam, you don't happen to know if Dr. Murdock is one of the investors, do you?"

"You mean the health commissioner?"

"Yes."

"Oh, now I see what you're getting at," Burke said, a sly-dog tone coming into his voice. "As far as I know, the answer is no. But you can check it out for yourself."

Angie was leaning forward, a quizzical look on her face. Decker put his hand over the phone.

"He says no. As far as he can tell."

"No?"

"Yes."

Angie looked disappointed.

Decker spoke again to Burke. "Excuse me. You said we could check on that. How?"

"Under Ohio law, the partners have to register with the state. The record would be down at the clerk of courts office. It's an outfit by the name of Crown Pointe, Inc. That's Pointe with an *e* at the end."

"Figures," Decker said.

"I'll tell you one thing, though—if you promise not to say where you got it."

"Fine, Sam. I'm just looking for background right now."

"Murdock does own a number of properties in Over-the-Rhine."

Over-the-Rhine was a diamond in the rough, a decaying slum of nineteenth-century row houses, located north of Central Parkway, where the shelter was. The name had made sense once, a century ago, when the parkway was a canal and the neighborhood was teeming with German immigrants. Now it was empty storefronts, half-vacant buildings, and poor blacks leaning out of windows.

"I'm not sure what you're getting at," Decker said.

"You're not?" Burke laughed a little. "Take it from me—property values in Over-the-Rhine will soar if this project goes through. You'll have downtown's finest shopping within walking distance of the city's largest stock of old town houses. It's rehab heaven. The yuppies will be crashing their Bimmers to get there first."

Great quote. Decker wanted it. "Are you sure you want this off-the-record, Mr. Burke?"

"Are you kidding? We've got enough troubles in this department. We don't need a feud with Murdock."

After Decker hung up, he turned to Angie and took a deep breath. He felt the old news rush in his veins.

"It looks like Strider was right—in a way."

"In a way?"

"I'll explain later. I've gotta reach Murdock."

He punched the number for the commissioner's office and got his secretary.

"I'm sorry. Dr. Murdock is on the phone at the moment. May I take a message, or would you like to hold?"

"I'll hold, thank you. But let him know I'm on deadline. This is important."

Decker had talked to Murdock only once or twice before—the first time after his appointment as commissioner two years ago. He hoped Murdock would recognize his name.

Angie's leg was jumping again.

"Would you like a Valium?" Decker said.

"Me? You're the one creating an air pollution crisis."

Decker crushed out his cigarette and ran his tongue along the front of his teeth. They were coated with tar. Janet was right; he had to stop. The tobacco or the nonsmokers, one or the other, were going to kill him. He lifted his sandwich in both hands and took a small bite. The turkey was good, but the alfalfa sprouts were as dry and tasteless as straw. He checked his coffee cup. Empty. There was nothing to do but chew and chew.

Suddenly Murdock was on the line. Decker gulped his food, cleared his throat, hoarsely identified himself.

"Yes, can I help you?" Murdock sounded busy and impatient, but there was no time to soften him up.

"Dr. Murdock, one question. Is it true you own several properties in Over-the-Rhine?"

"Excuse me. But whom am I talking to?"

Decker made it clear this time. "Rick Decker. At the Cincinnati *Eagle*."

"And what was the question again?"

"Do you own properties in Over-the-Rhine?"

"If you're talking about my parents' house, yes, I do own that. Plus a number of other residences on the same block. Why is this so important, Mr. Decker?"

"Are you familiar with the Crown Pointe development project?"

"I've heard talk about it. What's your point here, Mr. Decker? I've got six calls waiting."

"Isn't it true the project would raise property values in Over-the-Rhine?"

"Why are you asking me? Why not call a real estate appraiser?" The voice was openly petulant now. Decker suspected that Murdock indeed knew what he was driving at.

"Wouldn't you have a personal financial stake, sir, in seeing that the drop-in shelter was condemned?"

There was a long pause on the other end. Decker didn't know whether it was fear or anger—maybe both—roiling in the silence. He had his pen and notebook poised.

"I won't dignify that question with a response, Mr. Decker." If Murdock had anything to fear, it didn't show in his voice. It was steady and filled with contempt. "I am the health commissioner of this city, and it is my sworn duty to protect the health and safety of its citizens. And that means all its citizens, Mr. Decker. Not just those who pay taxes or contribute to election campaigns, or those who buy your newspaper. Now, if you'll excuse me, I have other calls to attend to."

"Dr. Murdock, are you . . ."

The line was dead.

Angie finished the question: ". . . one of the investors in Crown Pointe?"

"Damn it. I should have asked that question first."

Angie cocked her head to one side. The leg was pumping again, a steady rhythm like a metronome. "Now what?"

Decker grimaced. "Now we talk to editors."

For the second time in two days, Decker found himself crammed into Farlidge's art-deco cell along with Barry and, this time, Angie as well. There was only enough room for two chairs in front of Farlidge's oversized desk, so Decker stood behind Angie's, leaning against the open doorway.

"I think it's clear we have to move slowly and carefully on this story," Farlidge said.

"You keep saying that, Ron," Decker said, "but it doesn't take long to check property records. The same goes for finding out if Murdock has an interest in the development. Angie and I could have it nailed down in time for tomorrow's first edition."

Angie turned her head and smiled at Decker for having included her. She had yet to say a word during the meeting.

Stein spoke up in his calm, reasoned voice. "Ron, it seems to me this is a straightforward conflict-of-interest piece about a public official. I don't see why we're agonizing over it."

Farlidge was leaning forward now, doodling with a pen along the margins of a fresh home edition of the *Eagle*. "Maybe so, Barry, but it's still politically sensitive. I'd like to run it by Sally Beth."

Decker spoke again. "You mean because Murdock is black."

Farlidge looked up from his doodling. "Yes, because Murdock is black. And because we've gotten our tit caught in the ringer on this type of thing before." Farlidge suddenly remembered Angie was in the room, his face coloring. "Excuse the metaphor, please."

Angie perked up. "Gee, I just hope nobody gets their balls caught."

That brought an uncharacteristic guffaw from Stein, which Farlidge chose to ignore.

"I assume you're referring to the Darrell Jackson fiasco," Decker said. Jackson was the highest-paid player on the Reds—a talented young outfielder billed as the next Willie Mays. The summer before, in the midst of Jackson's batting slump, the *Eagle* ran a front-page story speculating on the star's drug use, relying mostly on unnamed sources and a flurry of Major League rumors. The story had been generated by a "hot tip" from one of Sally Beth's society friends.

"You bet I'm talking about the Jackson story. We don't need another misunderstanding like that." The "misunderstanding" had called down the wrath of the local chapter of the NAACP, not to mention a threatening letter from Jackson's lawyer. It was one of the big reasons the *Eagle* had tightened its policy on unnamed sources.

Stein injected his note of calm again. "But this is hardly the same situation, Ron. We're talking about a matter of public record."

"Even so, I'd like to run it by Sally Beth before we action this."

" 'Action' it?" Decker said. He could hardly believe his ears—Farlidge was even talking like a corporate bullshitter now.

"In the meantime," Farlidge said, eyeing Decker, "I'm wondering what's happened to our Cody Blair coverage. Have we forgotten that she's still in town shooting a movie?"

"No, 'we' haven't," Decker said. He had come prepared. He pulled his notebook from his back pocket and started flipping through the pages.

"Let's see now. It seems Miss Blair is very fond of the local night life. She was spotted at the Flying Pig last Friday night— dancing and drinking until two A.M. And then the Drastic Plastic and Tobacco Road in Covington on Saturday . . . until three. In all cases, she was accompanied by at least four members of the production crew and a rather surly-looking body-guard."

Farlidge's eyes lit up. This was good. This was the stuff of page one. With a breakout box, of course, under the headline "Tips for Cody Watchers."

"She's evidently quite the party girl," Decker said. "The bartender at the Flying Pig said she was chugging half-bottles of Moët like soda pop Friday night. And the DJ said she hounded him all night to play music by the Dead Kennedys."

"The Dead Kennedys?"

Angie spoke up. "It's a punk group. She's dating the lead singer."

"Ohhhhhhhh." Farlidge liked that, and made a note to Decker: "Get that in. What about restaurants? Where does she like to eat?"

"She hits Chez Jean's about three times a week. Loves the beef cordon bleu, I'm told, although she only dares eat about a tenth of it. I'm also told she has a fondness for mellow red wines, particularly the restaurant's Cabernet Sauvignon Special Reserve. a hundred twenty dollars a bottle."

Farlidge folded his arms and slipped into his supportive manager mode. "Primo stuff, Decker. I'm sure Sally Beth will want it for One-A."

"Sure, Ron. Oh, and one other thing." Decker was trying hard not to chuckle. "Cody Blair is seventeen."

Farlidge nodded, as if it were only a trivial point. But when Angie giggled, the meaning sank in.

"Seventeen? You mean she's been seen drinking in all these places?"

"Like a fish, Ron. An underage fish, to be precise. Chez Jean could lose its liquor license."

This gave Farlidge pause for reflection. Chez Jean was the oldest and most respected restaurant in town. Practically an institution. Delta's top executives made a point of eating there whenever they visited town.

"I better run this by Sally Beth."

"Good," Decker said. "I'll wait before I 'action' anything."

Four fifteen P.M. If he was quick about it, Decker had just enough time to run over to the county courthouse and check the files in the clerk's office before the GOP hacks knocked off fifteen minutes early for the day. He was about to exit his cubicle when his phone rang. He considered ignoring it, but he was helpless. A phone rings, a reporter answers.

"Yes."

"Rick, do you have a minute to talk?" It was Janet, sounding determined about something.

"What's up?"

"I've been thinking a lot today. About us. About last night."

Suddenly, unexpectedly, Decker felt his eyes well up. It was as if he were eighteen again and had just asked out someone he had a crush on and realized he was about to be turned down.

"I see. You've been thinking, and . . ."

"I've been thinking about a lot of things, Rick, and what I've decided . . . I mean, what seems best right now is that I spend some time with my father. He really needs me, Rick, and to be honest, I'm not sure you do."

"What are you getting at, Janet?"

Her voice was firm now. "I won't be home tonight."

He'd seen it coming, but it didn't lessen the blow. He tried to keep his voice under control. "How do you know I don't need you, Janet?"

"I'm surprised you need to ask that. Really, Rick, this isn't something to discuss over the phone. Let's take a break from each other for a few days, then talk things out."

He tried to preserve some measure of pride. "Are you sure this is what you want?" But he recognized how phony he sounded the moment he let the words out.

"Yes, I am. For now."

"Okay. I'll call."

When he hung up, he felt suddenly tired, his weight sagging down into the chair. He had ten minutes to get over to the courthouse.

7

When he really had it down—
the kick, the stroke, the breathing—the water seemed to disappear and he became part of it, moving with the medium, not through it, the way light bends and tunnels through curved space.

But after forty and even fifty laps, he still had the sensation of fighting the water. Every few minutes or so, he adjusted some part of his technique—tightening his flutter kick, changing the angle of his hand entry, expanding his chest, raising his buttocks—but nothing worked. It was as if he'd lost his faith in the buoyancy of water.

He gave up short of his usual mile, found his towel and thongs and padded into the sauna. He sat alone on one of the toasty wooden benches, inhaling the sting of hot moist air, waiting for the panicked beating of his heart to subside.

Decker had gone straight to the YMCA from the courthouse, where he had arrived at 4:40 P.M. and found—just as he had feared—the clerk's office closed.

A minute or two in the sauna had the desired effect. His muscles warmed, loosened, his breathing turned slow and deep. He closed his eyes, remembering. A warm, breezy night in Miami. Like college kids, they sneaked up to the hotel's rooftop Jacuzzi, 2 A.M., slipped out of their clothes, slipped down into the bubbling liquid warmth. A cool wind, star-sent, rushed into their faces. "Moon over Miami," he whispered, laughing, and then they were kissing, grabbing at each other's slick flesh, slipping deeper into the water, with Janet on his lap and the steamy liquid lapping just below their chins, threatening, it seemed, to drown them both at the moment of climax.

He wondered if it could happen to them now. Ever happen again. That kind of spontaneity.

The door of the sauna burst open, startling him out of his reverie, and an old woman with dimpled thighs jiggled in. Decker stood up, holding his towel discreetly in front of his inflated trunks, and stepped out.

He went home around 7:30, had a beer on the porch, and watched the heat lightning pulsing in the clouds above Mount Echo. Then he went up to the empty bed, buried his face in Janet's pillow, and fell hard asleep.

He arrived at work an hour late the next day, and found himself playing catch-up the rest of the morning. Farlidge, per orders from Sally Beth, had zapped him first thing, assigning him a story about a farmer in Butler County who had raised a black-and-orange-striped sow. The farmer was offering the pig as a mascot to the Bengals football team, and Decker was forced to call the team's general manager for a comment. The story was going page one.

Then at 10:15, just when he'd finished with the porker piece and thought he could relax a minute with a cup of coffee and a cigarette, Bart Petkamp, the *Eagle*'s police reporter, called with a good inside tip: Murdock had decided not to press charges against Strider for allegedly dumping the Indian's body behind the shelter. "The cops think it's because he can't make it stick," Petkamp said. "None of the witnesses want to testify against Strider."

Decker called Murdock, got the expected no-comment from

his secretary, and banged out a brief by 10:45. Fired up again over the plague story, he walked over to the courthouse to check on the list of Crown Pointe partners. An hour later he was back at the *Eagle*.

He went straight to Vendville, where he bought two cans of diet soda and pressed one can against each side of his forehead. The five blocks to the courthouse and back had been withering. The temperature outside was already 95, with the humidity about the same, and still no hint of rain. He stood at the pop machine and finished the first soda in three long gulps, belched, and took the second can back to his desk. He was sweating in big spots through the front of his blue shirt.

Decker had with him a copy of the list of twelve partners in Crown Pointe Development, Inc. Murdock's name was not among them. In fact, Decker recognized only two of the names, neither of which surprised him. One was Skip Flannery, of course, and his development firm, The Flannery Group. The other was Theodore H. Andersen, retired CEO of the city's largest corporation and one of its most powerful behind-the-scenes movers and shakers. The *Eagle* wrote ad infinitum about City Council and its petty disputes, but it was people like Andersen who got the job done, quietly, without fanfare. Two years before, "Tireless Teddy," as he was dubbed by his business buddies, had headed up a blue-ribbon panel to study ways the city could revitalize downtown. He was listed as Crown Pointe's president and legal counsel.

While Decker was in the clerk's office, Angie had gone to the property records section to locate and confirm Murdock's Over-the-Rhine properties. Decker was disappointed that Angie hadn't returned yet, and not only because he was eager to find out what she had learned. He would have been hardpressed to admit it, even to himself, but he enjoyed working with her.

True, she could be exasperating—a wired, overeager pain-in-the-butt. But at the same time, she made his job seem new and fresh again. There were plodders and seekers in this business, and the seekers were becoming fewer all the time. Angie was a seeker. You could see it in the intensity of her eyes when she was on the phone or writing at the computer. Excited, concentrated, a little nervous, like a diver poised over water. Decker could remember when he was like that, when it seemed as if even the most routine story might take an unexpected turn and plunge toward a startling truth.

He returned to his desk, where he found a note from Farlidge to hold off on the Cody Blair story "until further notice." He smiled. With any luck, he wouldn't have to write "Tips for Cody Watchers" after all. He sat down, finished off the last of his soda, and started making calls to the offices of all twelve Crown Pointe partners, beginning with Flannery and Andersen. Neither, of course, was available at the time, but Decker left messages with their secretaries. He did the same with the ten out-of-state partners, including Dominic Jacubrizzi, president and CEO of a giant outfit in New Jersey that went by the idyllic name of Meadowlands Construction. Decker doubted any of the twelve would call back, especially Dominic.

He was about to light a cigarette when Janet stabbed into his thoughts again. Maybe he should send flowers. White mums, her favorite. Too corny? But maybe that was the problem. Maybe what he thought was corny was a natural display of affection to anyone normal. Maybe he needed to be a little cornier, a little more open and vulnerable. But, hell, if she didn't know him any better than that . . .

The phone rang. Decker was surprised to hear Tireless Teddy himself on the other end. He thanked Andersen for calling back—it never hurt to flatter a giant ego—and asked to be filled in on the Crown Pointe project.

Andersen chuckled a little. "Sorry, Rick, but no comment at this time."

"Isn't it true you're planning the largest real estate venture in downtown's history?"

"No comment at this time."

"I understand the site you're looking at is the men's shelter on Central Parkway. Any comment on that?"

"Nope." Andersen had a deep, folksy voice, the kind that seemed always on the verge of laughter, as if life were one big inside joke.

"Can you at least tell me when you'll announce?"

"Soon," he said, chuckling outright again.

Decker's patience had run out. "That's dandy."

He was about to say good-bye when Andersen turned chummy and confidential. "Rick, I wish I could tell you more. I honestly do. You know I've always been upfront with you boys in the press. But in this case there's just too much at stake for me to go shooting my mouth off before we have all our ducks in a row. I don't want to blow this deal the way our boys down in City Hall always do. I hope you can understand that."

"I'll have to," Decker said. "Just remember me when you're ready to talk."

Andersen chuckled again. "It's a deal."

Decker hung up, wondering why Andersen had bothered to call back at all—unless, of course, he really was a nice guy. It was more likely, though, he was trying to find out how much Decker already knew.

He had just finished zapping the gist of the phone call to Stein's computer when Becky Caudill, the receptionist, appeared at his cubicle.

"Rick, are you busy?"

He turned from his terminal and shook his head no. Becky was standing just inside his partition with an expression of pained concern on her thin young face. It could mean only one thing—an unannounced visitor.

Becky was the *Eagle*'s one-woman security system. Between phone calls with boyfriends and the never-ending task of typing wedding announcements into the computer system, it was her job to keep the crazies from stumbling into the newsroom and collaring reporters with their life's stories. She ran inter-

71

ference better than any Pinkerton twice her size. All it took was one withering stare from her hard gray eyes.

"Rick, there's some guy at the desk who says he knows you. A Floyd Deekins?"

Decker thought for a moment. "Deekins? Are you sure?"

"That's why I wanted to check with you. He's kind of rough-looking." Becky lifted her chin and tossed back her waist-length blond hair. She was quite proud of it.

"Rough-looking?"

"Well, not like a Hell's Angel or anything. He's just dirty and smells bad. I mean *real* bad. He's a little guy with a long ratty beard."

"A little guy with a long beard . . ." Then it hit him. "Oh, Jesus, it's Floyd. The homeless man I wrote about last year. Remember?"

"You mean the guy who lived in that tent on the river?"

"Yeah, that's him. Floyd Deekins. I'd forgotten his last name. Harmless as a fly. Go ahead and send him in." Why not? It would take his mind off things, and he was waiting on Angie to return anyway.

"Okay. But I'm warning you, this guy smells like he crawled out of a dumpster or something."

"He probably did."

Decker smiled to himself. He hadn't thought about Floyd in a long time. But the profile he wrote about the man—a sidebar to a larger story about Cincinnati's homeless—was one he was especially proud of.

Just then, Stein popped up at his desk. "Andersen say anything?"

"Not much. But he was his usual buddy-buddy self."

"Just one of the guys, huh?"

Decker looked through his glass partition down the hall. "I was expecting Floyd Deekins. Remember him?"

"Yeah, the homeless guy. Is he off the juice?"

"I don't know, but he wants to see me."

Stein smiled. "Need some change?"

"Get outta here."

Floyd was a wino; there was no denying that. And he had told Decker so many different stories about why he had left his wife and kids back in Spartanburg, South Carolina, that Decker didn't know what was true and what was alcoholic psychosis. But Floyd was a gentle, talkative little man, and amazingly resourceful.

Decker had spent most of a windy autumn day with Floyd, following him on his morning can collection rounds through the back streets of downtown and over the river to Covington and Newport, eating lunch with him at an Over-the-Rhine soup kitchen, watching him give blood at a plasma center, then later that evening helping him build a fire at his makeshift campsite underneath the Suspension Bridge.

After the miles of concrete and noisy traffic, Decker recalled the wondrous peace and solace of that evening—he and Floyd huddled around a fire, the wind in the treetops, the river lapping in small waves against the bank, and everywhere the sharp, loamy smell of leaves dying and returning to earth. It was hard to imagine that, barely two blocks from their wooded campsite, lay the heart of downtown.

In a minute or two Becky returned, this time with her arms folded in exasperation.

"Well, he's gone," she said.

Decker wasn't surprised. Floyd had a way of slipping in and out of people's lives, like a friendly ghost. "Did he leave a message?"

"No, he just said he wanted to talk to you about the plague story."

"What about it?"

"He said he had a tip or something. I thought he was just some old crackpot. I didn't mean . . ."

"Forget it. I'll go catch him."

Decker grabbed his notebook. If anyone knew the scuttlebutt on the streets right now, it would be Floyd. Decker bypassed the elevators and ran down all six flights of stairs to the lobby, through the revolving door and outside into a wall of noonday heat.

On the sidewalk he squinted north, then south through the glare, and spotted Floyd about a block up Broadway, his tiny outline wavering in the heat, just short of Sixth Street. Floyd rounded Sixth before Decker—who preferred not to run—could catch up to him, and disappeared into the lunchtime jam in front of P&G headquarters. Decker soon spotted him again. Like Moses parting the waters, Floyd cut a swath through a sea of olive and beige summer suits.

Decker smiled and fell into step alongside Floyd. A moment later the old man turned, and his gentle blue eyes flashed like a kid's. He offered his small, sticky hand.

"Ain't you a sight for sore eyes. I done thought you'd forgot who I was."

Floyd was only in his late fifties, but he looked at least twenty years older than that. His weatherbeaten face reminded Decker of a parched river bottom—the clay-colored skin creased and folded into a patchwork of odd geometric shapes. Excited as he was, Floyd's greeting to Decker was spoken barely above a whisper. He was, in almost every sense, a true Southern gentleman.

"Sorry I missed you at the office," Decker said. He was still a bit breathless from his pursuit. "Listen, do you mind if we step out of this heat?"

"It'd be mighty sensible."

They went to a combination lunchroom-bakery across the street, where the hostess seated them all the way at the back, next to the dirty dish tub and kitchen door.

Floyd hadn't changed much since Decker had seen him in the fall, not even his clothes. He wore the same navy knit cap (only rolled now above the ears), the same grimy, tattered blue jeans, the same faded flannel shirt. Only his denim wind-breaker had been sacrificed to the 90-degree heat.

Floyd's pungency became more apparent in the confines of the restaurant, giving Decker an excuse to light up. He brought out his pack of cigarettes and saw the hungry look in Floyd's eyes. He patted one out and offered it.

"Why, thanky," Floyd said, and pinched the cigarette between two darkly stained fingers. Like a farmer's, his nails were cracked and encrusted with dirt, the knuckles scarred and creased. Floyd bent forward for a light from Decker's Bic, then leaned back to take the smoke deep into his lungs. "My, my. Can't tell you what a treat this is, Mr. Decker. Ain't had nothin' but rolled in a coon's age."

"Floyd, I've told you a million times. Call me Rick."

"Sorry. I guess it's a habit I picked up way back in grammar school. Had to call the teacher mister this or ma'am that, or they'd come and whack you right upside the head."

"You know, Floyd, when your story came out, a lot of people called the paper and wanted to give you things. One guy was offering a job on his farm in Indiana. I tried like hell to find you."

Floyd looked puzzled and a touch indignant, as though he'd left a forwarding address with the post office and never gotten his mail. It was one of his better performances. "Well, now, I remember distinckly tellin' just about ever'body I was goin' up north to work on a fishin' boat in Lake Erie. Nobody tol' you that?"

Decker shook his head, playing along. He remembered now. The weather had turned to freezing the week before the story had run. Floyd had taken refuge at the Salvation Army halfway house, had even signed up for the seven-day dry-out program. But he was kicked off the premises a day or two later after a bottle was discovered in his room. The major in charge had no idea where Floyd had run to.

"I didn't have no chance to see it, mind you, but I heerd it was quite a nice write-up you done give me in the paper," Floyd said. "It was hangin' in the shelter lobby for quite some time, I understand. A lot of the fellers there still remember, too. Yessir. I do appreciate what you done."

The waitress came—a tall, nervous young woman with her

dark hair up in a bun. She stood a safe distance from the table.

They both ordered large iced teas with lemon. Decker asked for a tuna on whole wheat and a bowl of vegetable soup, Floyd for a grilled cheese and a side order of French fries. The waitress wrote it down without looking at either of them. She gathered up the plastic menus and quickly disappeared.

If Floyd had any inkling of how most people reacted to him, he never showed it. Decker had never seen the man in anything but high spirits.

"So what brings you back to town, Floyd?"

Floyd took a deep draw from his cigarette, crinkling the dirty crow's feet at the corners of his eyes with the intensity of the effort.

"Just passin' through, I guess. I had myself a nice home down by the river fer a while. Found this big drain pipe I could crawl into and keep the bugs off and all. But then some kids started comin' round. I decided to git and find some other place. That's when a friend tol' me about the old subway tunnel. You familiar with that atall?"

Decker nodded. "Sure, the city built it, never used it." It was true. Four miles of tunnel, three or four completed stations, most of it under Central Parkway. The project had been launched in 1916 by the infamous "Boss" Cox and his Republican machine. It was delayed by the war, then mired afterward in double-digit inflation. By the late twenties automobiles and parking lots had become the future and the subway was closed and sealed.

"Well, now, I don't know nothin' 'bout the history of it, but it do make for a nice house. Real dry and cool in there, even in this god-awful heat. And nobody to bother you, either, 'cause there ain't many knows about it. A black feller over to the shelter showed me how you could git inside after I give him some of my bottle. You know how them two tunnels open up out there along Central Parkway, just shy of Hopple Street?"

Decker nodded again. If you were looking, you could see the

openings as you drove north on I-75—two big metal doors where the curved retaining wall came to an end.

"But I thought the entrances were sealed," Decker said.

Floyd grinned. "Oh, they're sealed, all right. You just got to know where to look. Somebody done hammered a rabbit hole through the cement. It's down behind some bushes and dug so low to the ground not even the city crews has seen it."

The waitress came and plunked down their iced teas and disappeared again, rubbing her nose as she sped away.

Decker decided it was time to get down to business. "I understand you have some information for me, Floyd."

"Well, now, I don't know. But there's somethin' mighty strange I seen the other night. I figured I'd come tell you first, seein' as how you done such a good job of writin' me up in your article and all."

Floyd had never asked him for money before, but now, Decker sensed, that was about to change. "I should tell you, Floyd, I'm not authorized to pay anyone for information."

Floyd shook his head. "Believe me, I ain't lookin' for no handout. No, sir. This is just somethin' I feel like I got to git off my chest." Floyd took a drag on his cigarette and settled back in his chair. Suddenly the mask of grinning folksiness was gone and there was a tight, haunted look in its place.

"Seems most ever'body's talkin' about this Injun they found dead back behind the shelter. The one they say got the bubonic plague." Floyd pronounced "bubonic" correctly. It showed how much talk was on the street already.

"There was a feller at the recyclin' center this mornin' seemed to know ever'thin' about it. He told me he read an article in the *Eagle*. Well, I ast him, I said, 'How'd they know this feller that died was an Injun?' And he said, 'Well, the story says they found all this Injun stuff—powder and sticks and jewelry and such he kept in a gunnysack.' Then that got me to thinkin'."

Floyd smiled a little nervously and looked around for a place to drop his cigarette ash, which was as long now as the rest of his cigarette. Decker pushed the tray over.

"Like I said, this got me to thinkin' 'bout somethin' I seen a couple a nights ago down in the tunnel."

"The tunnel where you've been sleeping?"

"Yes, sir. Until the other night, that is. What I seen give me such a case of the willies I ain't been back there. No, sir." Floyd paused again to savor his cigarette. He could match Hitchcock for building suspense.

"Floyd, are you going to tell me what you saw, or do I have to give you a whole pack of cigarettes first?"

"Now just gimme a second here to recolleck my thoughts a little. You Yankees. Always in some fired-up hurry. Like I was sayin', I was down in the tunnel a couple a nights ago, sleepin' off a mighty good drunk. You see, that was after I found a perfeckly good pair of 'lectric hedge clippers in a dumpster earlier that afternoon."

"Floyd, what does any of this have to do with hedge clippers?"

". . . Nothin' at all wrong with them clippers, 'cept somebody cut right into the cord, probably by accident, so they just throwed it out. Hell, I took a tiny bit of 'lectric tape, wrapped it around once or twicet, and sold the damn things for ten dollars to some old lady cuttin' her forsythia bushes in Newport. Them clippers worked just like new."

"Okay, you sold the clippers, you bought wine, you got drunk . . . . Then what?"

"I had myself a good drunk. Wee doggies! I was on that night train to heaven, I tell ya. Didn't share none of it with nobody. Just sat there out by the highway and watched the cars go by, and when I was good and tired, I crawled through the rabbit hole into the tunnel and slept it right off."

Floyd stamped out his cigarette in the ashtray, but before he could start again, the waitress came with their plates. She quickly set them down and slipped the check under Decker's napkin.

78

Decker checked his watch.

"Well, now, I'm gittin' to the important part," Floyd said. "You see, later that night—and I think it was night 'cause I din't see no light comin' through the rabbit hole—I wake up to answer Nature's call and I heerd this moanin' a ways down the tunnel."

"Moaning?"

"Yeah, real low and eerie-like. 'Nuff to set my teeth on edge."

"So then what?"

"So then I nearly pee my pants tryin' to find my pack o' matches. I finally git hold a one and strike it, and I'm lookin' first down one direction, then down t'other, and I don't see nuthin' atall at first. I sit real still until I hear it again—that awful moanin' sound—and now I know where it's comin' from. It's down past the rabbit hole and on the other side of the divider. You see, there's two sets of tracks down there, with a wall in between, only there's these openings 'tween the walls you can kinda scootch sideways through. So I light another match and start my way over there, real slowlike, 'cause I can't see but three or four feet in front of my face. But come man or ghost, I got to know what's making that noise down there. This moanin', you see, is real steady, like some kinda chant."

"An Indian chant?"

"I'm gittin' to that. Just hold your horses now. So then I crawl through the divider and, sure enough, I see somebody layin' beside the tracks about ten or fifteen feet away. I make sure he's not movin' or comin' at me, and then I start inchin' closer. Step by step. I ain't too scared now, 'cause the moanin's stopped, you see. So I get right close to this feller's face and light another match, and I see he's havin' a fit. His eyes are rollin' back into their sockets and he's ashakin' from head to toe."

"Did you go for help?"

"No, sir, I'm sorry to say I din't. I just figured he was havin'

79

the good ol'-fashioned shakes. Git 'em all the time myself. You just ride 'em on through and pray for another day."

Decker was skeptical. "And you think this man was the Indian who died."

"Well, not exactly at the time. You see, there's a lot more to this story. Anyway, I went back to the little bed I'd made up with my jacket and some newspapers I'd piled up level-like on the ground, figurin' what we both needed was to sleep things off. I conked out just as soon as my head touched ground, and I stayed like that for I don't know how long. But when I come to again, I hear voices in the tunnel. Diff'rent voices. Down near where the Injun is layin'.' "

Decker pulled out his notebook and started scribbling.

"You gettin' all this down?" Floyd asked. He nabbed a French fry from his plate and bit off an end of it and chewed it around. He wasn't much into solid foods.

"Just keep talking," Decker said.

"Okay. So I figure these voices are either maintenance men come to kick people out of the tunnel, or teenagers up to no good. So I lay there just as still as I can be."

"Could you see them at all?"

"Not hardly. It's pitch-dark in them tunnels even durin' the day. They had flashlights with 'em, though, and the light was bouncin' all around the walls. But what I did see has got me to thinkin'. You see, these two fellers picked up that Injun and started draggin' him down the tunnel."

"Dead or alive?"

"I figured he was dead, see, 'cause he weren't kickin' or fussin' or nothin' like that. They just had 'im by the arms and were pullin' him down the tunnel like he was a big sack o' 'taters."

"And after they left the tunnel?"

"Well, now, that's what's so strange. They din't go back out the rabbit hole at all. They went right past it, and just kept on goin' down the tracks toward town."

"You mean downtown?"

"Yep."

"And you didn't see these men after that?"

"Well, let me finish now." He took a swig of tea and made a sour face. Decker pushed the bowl of sugar packets Floyd's way and watched in amazement as he ripped and emptied four packets at one time into his glass. The granules dropped like sand to the bottom.

"So after they hauled the Injun away, I started for the rabbit hole, figurin' I better skidaddle or they'd do the same business on me. But then I guess curiosity got the best o' me, and on the way out, I just had to nose around a little where the Injun been layin', you know, to see maybe if he left a bottle or some change behind. I light up a match and there I see this old gunnysack alayin' there. I open it up and inside there's these little pouches of sand and some painted sticklike things and then, way down t' bottom, all this Injun jewelry. Rings and necklaces and earrings and things. God a'mighty, I thought, I done died and gone straight to heaven.

"So I'm about to pick up the sack and fling it over my shoulder when I hear one of the two men comin' back up the tunnel. He's cussin' like a crazy man, ever'thin' is fuck this and fuck that, I guess 'cause he forgot to bring the sack with 'im. That's when I head straight for the rabbit hole, figurin' I can scootch out before he spies me. But damned if his flashlight don't pick me up, the light shinin' smack dab in my eyeballs, and he shouts and starts acomin' at me. So I drop the sack and hightail it, and before he can catch me, I'm outside and hidin' in the brush and layin' low again.

"Second or two later both of 'em come out of the rabbit hole lookin' for me. But I'm hid real good, you know, down under some dried-up weeds and honeysuckle vine. I cain't hardly see, but I can tell the one feller's quite a bit bigger than the other. The big guy says, 'Forget it. He's probably just some old wino.' And the smaller man says, 'I don't like it. He done seen too much.' And the big feller answers, 'Have it your way. But we gotta get in before the kitchen opens.' The other one, he looks around a little more, and finally he says, 'To hell with it.' So they both go back through the rabbit hole, and that's when I done git."

"Wait a minute. What did the one man say again—'Before the kitchen opens'?"

"Yes, sir. 'Got to get in before the kitchen opens.' "

Decker didn't know what to make of Floyd's story, or for that matter, whether he could be trusted. Floyd had told him whoppers before, albeit on a much smaller scale. And to make matters worse, he admitted he'd been sleeping off a drunk at the time. Still, there was a strong ring of truth to the details. Besides, why would Floyd come calling with a wholly made-up tale? Unless, of course, someone had put him up to it.

"Have you told anybody else what you saw?"

Floyd pushed out a dry, cracked lower lip and shook his head. "No, sir. I don't like dealin' with no police."

"Did you get a good look at these two men?"

"I told you—it was too dark."

"Did they leave anything behind?"

"I din't stick 'round long 'nuff to see. I just hit the road and headed straight down to the river. I figured any place got to be safer than that tunnel."

Decker tried a spoon of his soup, pushed it aside. Stone cold.

"I can fix you up some nice stew down at the camp," Floyd said. "I got me a bunch of things down there a feller gimme over at the Castellini warehouse—a nice big head o' cabbage and some carrots and some wax beans. They was going to throw it all out."

Decker said maybe another time. "Floyd, there's got to be some way to identify these guys. Did you see what kind of car they were driving?"

"Well, now you mention it, I do remember seein' a Lincoln parked down the hill, just off the highway. One of them big long jobs, you know, with the little opry winders in back."

"Do you remember the color?"

"Not exackly. It was a dark color, though. Maybe brown."

"But you're sure it was a Lincoln."

"Oh, my, yes. I always wanted one myself." Floyd grinned; Decker wasn't sure if he was being facetious or not.

"And you're certain it was theirs?"

"Now I don't know fer sure, but there ain't too many people leave their luxury sedans by the side of the road at five in the mornin'."

Decker shut his notebook and picked up his tuna sandwich. It was mushy now and oozing mayonnaise over the sides. He took a bite anyway. Floyd was inspired to try his grilled cheese, daintily bit off a corner and set it down again. He chewed uninterestedly, like a teenager.

"It's quite a story, Floyd. But I can't figure it. Why would these two guys carry the body down the tunnel?"

Floyd shrugged, sipped his tea. "It was just somethin' I seen, you know." He eyed Decker's cigarettes on the table— long enough for Decker to get the message.

"Take a couple."

"Why, thanky." Floyd slipped an extra into his shirt pocket.

Decker wondered if Floyd had succumbed to all the local legends about the abandoned subway—it was a haven for runaway teenagers, an underground church for Satanists, a bustling underworld of bums and bikers, pimps and dealers. Like most urban myths, it was hard to separate the facts from the fiction.

Decker was trying to imagine what four miles of empty tunnel would look like when another idea hit him. He dropped his sandwich on his plate. "Floyd, can you take me there? To the rabbit hole?"

Floyd grinned and glanced down at Decker's cigarettes. "It'd be my pleasure," he said.

8

"Without a doubt, this is the most RIDICULOUS damn thing you've ever talked me into, Decker."

"Save your breath, Rebo. We'll get you out," Decker said, only to hear himself mocked in a higher pitch by the tunnel's echo.

Decker and Angie were on their knees pawing and scraping like schnauzers into the hard-packed earth under Rebo's back. They were both sweating in the tunnel's cool, stagnant air. Minutes before, Floyd, then Angie, had slipped easily through the hole in the concrete wall. Decker the same, although he was seized by a moment of claustrophobic panic when he first went under the wall, his nose scraping the chipped concrete above his face.

At six four, 260 pounds, Rebo was another matter. He squeezed through to mid-torso, then stuck, leaving his head and arms just above the hole. He hadn't the leverage to lift himself.

"Look at it this way, Rebo," Decker said. "You've got an incentive to start dieting." Angie laughed.

"I've got an incentive to punch you silly," Rebo said.

Rebo was the *Eagle*'s best photographer, and Decker had

recruited him on his day off with the promise of secret passageways and the chance for some Pulitzer Prize-winning photos. But now Decker was beginning to worry. If they couldn't get Rebo out of the hole, they might all be trapped.

Angie giggled under her breath as she dug and scooped, trying to restrain herself for Rebo's sake, but helpless against the absurdity of the situation. Floyd, on the other hand, was unusually silent. He was standing off to the side, illuminating the scene with a brand-new, heavy-duty flashlight, one of two Decker had bought for the occasion.

Rebo turned his head toward Floyd. "Would you please get that damn thing out of my eyes." Floyd snapped off the light.

"Floyd!" Decker was losing patience with the whole bunch. "We can't see what we're doing!" The light snapped back on.

"Quit the goddamn digging and just pull me out!"

Decker turned to Angie "All right, let's see what we can do."

Rebo crossed his arms over his head, and Decker and Angie each gripped a meaty forearm. Floyd retreated a step or two, as if Rebo might pop out of the hole like a giant cork.

"On the count of three," Decker said. "Okay? One, two, and . . . three!"

A collective grunt echoed up and down the tunnel.

"Keep pulling!" Decker shouted. "Keep pulling! We got 'im!"

Rebo's chest was showing above the hole now, but then Angie lost her footing in the dirt and dropped sharply to her blue-jeaned bottom. She started laughing and couldn't stop.

"Oh, sure," Rebo said. "You think this is funny, don't you? Downright hilarious."

"I can't help it," Angie said, giggling again. "The whole thing is just so freaky. I feel like Alice in Wonderland."

"Yeah, and I'm Humpty-Dumpty. Just get me the goddamn hell out of this hole!"

Decker tried to be upbeat. "I think one more pull will do it." The echo teased him again.

"Forget it! I'll do it myself."

Rebo splayed his hands on the ground, his elbows pointing almost straight into the air, then took a deep breath and pushed. He growled as he pushed, long and low, ending with a mighty roar of exhaled breath that reverberated through the tunnel like the blast from a diesel horn.

"By God, one more time," he said. Another growl and his legs and feet came kicking through the hole. Angie cheered while Decker helped him up.

"You hurt at all?" Decker asked. A quick inspection showed only minor wear and tear on Rebo's blue work shirt and jeans.

"Never again, Decker. Do you hear me? Never again!" But his voice had returned to its normal gruffness, and Decker knew he had already softened. Rebo ran his fingers through his dreadlocks, shaking out bits of dirt and gravel, clicking the brass beads in his hair. It sounded like somebody walking into a gypsy parlor.

"Now, dammit, let's get this crazy shit over and done with. Where's my gear?"

Floyd beamed the light on a large black camera bag in the middle of the tunnel floor.

Decker snapped on his own flashlight and looked down the tunnel as far as he could see. There wasn't much there for the eyes to feed on—a smooth bore of gray cement spinning tighter and tighter into the distance, ending in blackness at the outer limit of the beam. There were no steel girders. No rivets. Just a continuous shell of reinforced concrete. A surprisingly modern design for 1916. Even more surprising, Decker found the walls and ceilings intact—no cracks or water leaks or mold. Hard to believe after more than seventy years.

The floor, too, was bone-dry, covered with a fine layer of silvery-gray dust. You could smell it in the air. Desiccated, dead. Like the insides of a mummy's tomb.

In a way, Decker was disappointed that the tunnel had failed to live up to its mythology. He saw no signs of rats, of bikers, of runaway teenagers or underground Satanists. Still, in its drab monotony, there was an eeriness that wormed itself into the imagination—like the timeless quality inside a cathedral vault, or the dead calm just below the surface of the sea.

Rebo was the first to break the silence. "All right, Floyd. Show us where you found old Geronimo."

Floyd shuffled up the tunnel with his flashlight, kicking up small clouds of dust that billowed and swirled in his beam. With his small shoulders and loose gait, he looked comical and a bit sad. He stayed dead center between the concrete rail supports. When he had walked about ten yards, he stepped over the left support and poked his flashlight through a break in the dividing wall. The breaks appeared about every twenty feet along the wall, just wide enough for a man to slip through sideways.

" 'Bout here, I think," Floyd said, disappearing into the other tunnel. The others followed, single file.

"Sure 'nough," Floyd said. "You can kinda see where he was thrashin' in the dirt."

They converged on the spot, Decker holding the second flashlight and Angie a bit too close by his side. He bristled each time her arm brushed against his, thinking it might be some other part of her anatomy. She had shown up braless for the evening's adventure, a white T-shirt stretched over her small, perky breasts.

Rebo had brought his own light source—a large, hand-held flash. He popped the light, and the tunnel was as bright as day for a second or two.

"See anything?" Decker asked.

"Yeah, a lot of goddamn dirt," answered Rebo.

Angie took Decker's flashlight and redirected the beam up the tunnel. "What's that?" she said. Something small and flat glistened in the circle of light a few yards ahead. She handed Decker the flashlight, careful to keep the target fixed, and went to inspect.

"Oh, wow," she said. "It's a Twizzler bag."

Rebo laughed. "Keep it. Maybe there's fingerprints."

"There might be, dammit," Decker protested. The troops weren't being serious enough about their mission. "Here. Put it in this bag." Decker had stuffed his back pockets with Ziploc sandwich bags, for collecting bits and pieces of evidence, just like in the movies. Angie dropped the wrapper in the bag, zipped it, and handed it back to Decker.

"Exhibit A," she said.

"All right," Decker said, "let's have another look."

Rebo lit the scene again, and this time Decker saw what he was looking for—footprints. The trail began just beyond the spot where the Indian had lain and led down to the next opening in the dividing wall.

"Look at this." Decker spotted a print in his beam.

"Looks like a boot," Rebo said.

An outer sole of tooth-shaped blocks surrounded a pattern of bars and X's.

"Let's get a picture, Rebo."

"How do we know it wasn't left by a maintenance worker?"

"We don't, Rebo. But take a picture anyway."

"Yes, sir, your excellency. Anything you say."

Angie tugged at Decker's elbow. "I think Floyd is on to something."

Not far behind them, Floyd was on his hands and knees, prodding a patch of loose dirt with his index finger.

Decker joined him, squatting for a closer look while Angie hovered just above his head. Decker could feel her warm breath on his crown.

"I cain't be sure," Floyd said. "But it looks like somethin's maybe buried down here."

Decker handed Angie his flashlight and began to help Floyd with the digging. The hole was centered between the rail supports, no wider than a gopher mound, but appeared to be deep. The edge of the hole was serrated, like the rim of a bottle cap, as if someone had repeatedly stabbed a knife into the ground to make a circle.

The dirt was dry and full of small rocks. It took them several minutes to dig down half a foot or more. Impatient for results, Decker clawed his fingers deep into the hole. He was grabbing a handful of dirt when he felt a sharp sting in his right middle finger. His arm recoiled, pain shooting like a hot current all the way to his elbow.

"Are you all right?" Angie was crouched next to him.

"There must be broken glass down there," he said. He examined the finger under his flashlight. It was a puncture wound, deep into the soft pad of his fingertip.

"Let me see, Rick."

She grabbed his open hand, straightened the fingers with her thumb.

"It's just a scratch, Angie."

He tried to pull away, but she elbowed him and held on. While she looked, the fingers of her other hand fell lightly across the inside of his forearm.

"I don't know, Rick. It could get infected." She pulled the bottom of her T-shirt from her jeans and started daubing the wound.

"It's all right. Quit mothering me." But he didn't pull away. It surprised him how attuned he was to her touching him. How much, perhaps, he had wanted the contact.

"What about tetanus, Rick? Shouldn't we get you to a doctor?"

"I've had all my shots," he fired back, then on further reflection, "I think . . ."

"Great," Angie said. "That's just great."

Floyd spoke up in his calm, faraway voice. "Ya know, I knowed a feller once cut his finger like that on a rusty tomato can. Two days later, he come down with blood pois'nin'." Floyd snapped his fingers. "Died just like that."

Angie wailed, "Rick, listen to me . . ."

"Forget it. I'll see a doctor later." But he was, in fact, worried now. He strained to remember his last tetanus shot. Maybe it was after that canoe trip on the Little Miami, when he cut his foot on the river bottom. That was at least ten years ago.

Angie kept after him. "When your jaws lock up, just grunt, okay?"

Decker grunted an affirmative; Angie punched his arm.

Rebo returned just as Floyd scooped away the last of the loose dirt. They could see a reflected gleam at the bottom of the hole, about ten inches down. Floyed carefully brushed around the object with his fingertips.

"It's a syringe!" Angie cried out. Decker shivered. It was buried at about a 45-degree angle, the needle jutting upward from the dirt.

Rebo started snapping pictures.

Decker thought immediately of Murdock—someone who had easy access to syringes and, yes, dangerous microbes. His hatred of the man built with every throb of his wounded finger. He only hoped now he'd live long enough to expose the bastard.

Floyd continued to widen the base of the hole around the syringe, removing a pinch of earth at a time and piling it around the edge. He had the experienced touch of a forager. When the syringe was more than half exposed, he plucked it loose and laid it on the tunnel floor where everybody could see it.

"You think it was a sedative?" Angie asked.

"Maybe," Decker said. "Or maybe it was used to inject the Indian with plague." In his mind's eye, Decker saw the Indian's contorted face, and felt the hair on his neck stand on end.

"Rick, we're getting you to a doctor." Angie's voice was firm.

"*After* we check out the tunnel," Decker said.

"Would you two quit your fussin'," Rebo said. "It sounds like a bad Western. Now goddammit, Rick, this story isn't worth dying for."

"Listen, if it is plague, I've got at least twelve hours before the first symptoms show. Now everybody shut up."

But while the others examined the syringe, Decker inspected his finger again. The blood, mixed with dirt, had turned dark and was beginning to harden inside the puncture. He splayed his fingers to tighten the skin, then used his other thumb to reopen the wound until a thick drop of blood beaded on his fingertip and dripped over either side. He'd read somewhere that bleeding a cut would prevent tetanus. He hoped it worked for plague, too.

"So what do we do with the syringe?" Angie asked.

With his good hand, Decker pulled another bag from his back pocket and gave it to Angie.

"Exhibit B," she said, and gingerly picked up the syringe by its plunger and dropped it in the bag.

Decker pulled out a handful of Ziplocs. "Here. Triple bag it. We'll put it with Rebo's things."

Floyd's tale gained more credibility with every step they took. Crossing over to the other tunnel, they found footprints on either side of the rail supports, and, between them, two wavy grooves where the Indian's feet must have dragged in the dirt.

They set out single file, Decker out front, Angie behind, then Floyd and, finally, Rebo, whose heavy tread was dogged by the swoosh of his camera bag rubbing against his jeans.

Decker squinted ahead into the recesses of the tunnel, as far as his flashlight could reach. For a long way, maybe a quarter of a mile or more, it seemed a straight shot.

After twenty minutes of trudging through the dust and the gray monotony, they still hadn't reached the first subway station at Liberty Street, a half mile from their destination. Decker was growing impatient with the group's slow pace, but he knew if they picked it up, Floyd would be left behind.

"Hey, know what we forgot?" Angie said.

"No. Now what?"

"Beer. We should have brought a backpack full of beer. My throat feels like I've been cleaning chalk erasers all day."

"Chalk erasers?"

"Yeah, remember how in grade school you'd take two erasers and pound them together, and you'd get chalk dust all over everything?"

"Yeah," Rebo said, "and it always went right up your nose. Tickled like hell."

"Right," Angie said. "And if you didn't get a drink of water right away, you just knew you were going to die."

"Okay, dammit," Decker said. "Next time we go exploring subway tunnels, I'll bring canteens."

"Beer would be better."

"Damn straight," Rebo said.

Floyd agreed, "Oh, Lordy, yes."

"I hate to tell you this, Angie, but the first subway station isn't in sight yet. And even then it's another half mile to Race Street," Decker said. "Think you can make it?"

Angie shoved him from behind. "Are you kidding? I was Rogers *and* Clark in a previous life."

A hundred yards ahead, the tunnel began to veer left. Decker felt reassured. If he remembered correctly the old engineering map he'd found in the *Eagle* morgue, they were very close to the Liberty Street station. In a minute he had his answer. When they rounded the bend, the right side of the tunnel dissolved into blackness where the platform began.

Angie broke into a railroad conductor's falsetto. "Next stop, Li-i-i-i-berty Street. D-e-e-e-part here for Yoon-yun Station, Mu-u-u-u-sic Hall, a-a-a-and the scenic West End slums . . ."

"Keep it up, Lapola," Rebo said. "Keep it up."

The platform was chest-high and stretched the length of a good-sized swimming pool. From one end of the platform to the other, fifty-gallon water barrels were stacked four high against the station walls. The barrels were made of tin and cardboard, each stamped with the Civil Defense logo—three yellow triangles against a black circle. Some of the barrels had been damaged, apparently by vandals, and scattered across the platform floor.

"What is this place?" Angie asked. "A toxic waste dump?"

"No, the county uses it for a bomb shelter," Decker said. "We did a story on it once."

"I'd rather be incinerated than live in this dump," Rebo said.

Decker beamed his light on his wristwatch. "It's six thirty now. We should make Race Street by six forty-five or six fifty. Should we take a break now or keep moving?"

The consensus was in favor of moving on.

Rebo groaned as he picked up his camera bag. "I'll tell you one thing, though. When we get out of this godforsaken place, I'm buying myself the biggest goddamn pitcher of beer you ever saw."

"My sentiments exackly," Floyd piped up.

The farther they walked in the tunnel, the more the walls, the gloom, the stagnant air seemed to press in around them.

Ten minutes later—and almost an hour from when they had left the rabbit hole—the tunnel curved again to the left, much more sharply this time, and Decker knew they were just a few blocks from Race Street. Directly above them, Central Parkway swung east around the YMCA building and into downtown. At that moment, Decker knew, the parkway was jammed with late rush-hour commuters driving home to their families in Clifton, Northside, and Western Hills, each driver sealed in his car, strapped in his seatbelt, and lost in music or thought or the chatter on the radio. And yet below, separated by a few feet of asphalt and concrete, there was only silence in the tunnel. Decker wondered if the dead, sealed in their graves, listened to the silence and dreamed, too, of what lay above.

When they rounded the curve, the black void of the station appeared on their left, just a block or two away.

"This is it," Decker announced. "Race Street station."

There was a whoop and holler from Angie, and a grumbling assent from Rebo.

Decker checked the tunnel for footprints again. They were still on either side of the rail supports, still headed for the shelter.

Decker ignored the station platform and began an immediate inspection of the tunnel's southern wall. He expected to find an opening of some kind—a trapdoor or a hole punched through the cement—directly into the basement of the shelter. But there was not even a crack, only the smooth, careful work of the men who had built the subway.

"I can't believe it," he said to Angie.

"Could there be something farther down?"

Rebo was more interested in the station platform. He flashed the dark space with his strobe. "Hey, gang, check this out. It's *huge.*"

From the tunnel floor, the station looked as cavernous and gloomy as a sunken freighter. It was half a football field long, the length split in two by a double staircase in both directions. At the top of stairs was a smaller platform, fed on either side by stairs leading up to the street. Like the rest of the tunnel, the cement was perfectly preserved. All that was needed to bring the station to life were lines of weary commuters reading newspapers and glancing impatiently at their watches.

"All right," Decker announced. "Let's take a look around. The shelter starts here at Race Street and follows the tunnel wall east along Central Parkway to Vine. Any connection between the tunnel and the shelter would have to be somewhere within this next block."

"Look," Angie said, grabbing Decker's hand and spotting the flashlight a few yards up the tunnel floor. "You can see where they all of a sudden stopped."

It was true. There was a messy circle of footprints about a third of the way down the station. Beyond that point, the tunnel floor was untouched, as pristine as a country lane under fresh-fallen snow.

"It looks like they were dancing," Angie said.

"But then what?" Decker said, beaming his light over to the tunnel wall. "There's no hole. Nothing."

"Well, I'll be," said Floyd.

"Are you sure this is the spot?" Rebo asked.

"By every map I've ever seen," Decker said. "Hell, you can stand in front of the men's shelter and see where they sealed off the entrances to the station."

Angie moved to the wall and started running her hand over the concrete in fanlike motions.

"What the hell are you doing?" Rebo asked.

"Feeling for wet cement."

"Oh, come on, Angie," Decker said. "These guys wouldn't have time to replaster a hole."

"They could have come back later."

Angie turned her attention to the platform. "What about that other wall?"

"You mean underneath the platform?"

"Yes."

"But the shelter's on this side of the tracks. Why would they bust through the platform?"

"Who knows? Maybe they tunneled underneath the tracks."

Decker shrugged. "All right, what the hell." He scanned the length of the platform wall, with Angie following right behind. Again, the concrete was untouched.

"No holes. No wet cement. Nothing."

"Maybe they took the stairs up to Central Parkway," Rebo said.

"Then how could they have dragged the body into the shelter without being seen?" Decker was losing his patience again. "That had to be their plan."

"Well, then, the story doesn't add up," Rebo said. "I don't know how two men and a body disappear into thin air." He looked down to where the prints stopped dead on the tunnel floor. "It's like 'Beam me up, Scottie,' and they were outta here."

Floyd spoke up softly in his own defense. "I only know what I seen."

"Don't worry, Floyd," Decker said. "Nobody's doubting your word." Although a part of him was now. But what about the footprints? The syringe? Or was the whole thing somebody's elaborate hoax?

Decker took a deep breath and traced his flashlight along the tunnel wall one more time. It seemed thick, impenetrable, as seamless as the truth itself. "I don't know," he said. "Maybe there's a secret door or something."

Angie clapped her hands and shouted, "Open Sesame!" Nobody laughed.

"Come on, Rick." Rebo picked up his camera bag and slung it over his shoulder. "I think all this dust is starting to fry her brain."

9

The emergency room was small and very cold. Cold white walls. Cold white light. Cold sterilized air. Decker would have shivered except that Janet was holding his hand. His whole body seemed to radiate enough warmth from that one point of contact.

He was sitting on the edge of the examining table, shirt off, bare feet dangling, the white sanitary paper crumpled beneath his jeans. She was standing in front of him, so close he could smell the freshness of her hair. Her left hand was locked around his right wrist, bracing his palm just below her breast. He could feel the slow rise and fall of her breathing.

There was something easy, simple, safe about being with Janet this way. As a doctor, she was warm and tactile, not just a logician, but also a woman, resonating to a deeper vibration. Neither of them felt the need to talk. After the nerve-wracking trek through the tunnel, he was now buoyant and relaxed.

She placed her fingertips just under the knuckles of his right hand, then probed the injured finger with her thumbnail. Her touch was light, careful, efficient.

"It's deep," she said matter-of-factly, "and loaded with grime." He nodded, a little wary of what she might do next.

"I'll have to bleed it a little," she said. She tightened her grip on his hand and pressed her thumb down sharply on the fingertip, breaking and separating the dirt-encrusted skin. It stung for just a moment before a small bead of blood, the size of a tear, oozed out and coated the pain.

"That should help clear it," she said. Her blue eyes looked into his for a moment—clinical, concerned. Yet there was something else there, too—just for him—tinged with regret.

She turned to the cart next to her, where she had arranged all the things she would need—gauze pads, Q-tips, a clear plastic cup half-filled with Betadine solution, an assortment of sutures and needles in different sizes, and two syringes placed side by side on a stainless-steel tray.

Still bracing his hand, she reached for one of the gauze pads, dipped it in the molasses-brown Betadine, then swirled it over the cut. It turned his fingertip orangish-brown. She tossed the used gauze at a nearby trash basket, missed, picked up a Q-tip and dipped the end of it in Betadine.

"This will sting a little," she said.

"Just a little?" He winced, but resisted the impulse to pull away as she probed deep into the cut. It started to bleed again, more profusely this time. A trickle of blood ran down the end of his fingertip and spattered onto the pristine white of her lab coat, just about where her belly button was. He didn't tell her. Let it soak in, he thought.

When the wound was clean, she pressed gauze around the fingertip, held it there a moment, then lifted it to see if the cut was clotting properly.

"It's mostly a puncture. I doubt you'll need stitches." There was a tinge of sarcasm in her voice. She wrapped the cut again and told him to hold the gauze there and elevate his hand.

He did, extending his middle finger in a familiar obscene gesture. "Like this?" She smiled for the first time. He felt triumphant.

"When are you coming home?" he asked.

She dropped her eyes and reached for one of the syringes.

"Let's do your tetanus booster first."

"Hell, why not? Just put it on my bill."

She dipped another gauze pad and swabbed it in lazy circles over his upper arm. Then, just when his arm and shoulder were starting to feel relaxed and unhinged, she zapped him with the needle. It was over before he could wince.

She smiled. "Have to be cruel to be kind."

"Easy for you to say."

She picked up the second syringe, eyed it against the ceiling light and spritzed a small stream of the clear liquid into the air.

"All right, Mr. Decker. Kindly slide off the table, face the wall, and drop your pants."

"You're kidding?"

"Would you prefer hepatitis?"

He did as instructed. "You realize this is the most attention you've given this part of my anatomy in a long time."

His answer was a sharp jab in the left buttock. It stung a second and was over, and then he felt a dull ache spread through the muscle where the sting had been.

"All right, Mr. Decker. You may make yourself modest again."

He pulled up his pants, zipped and fastened his belt while she went briskly around the room straightening things. There was a slight nervous energy to her movements, an overcompensation. He could tell she'd already put in a long day.

"Quick and painless," he said. "You're a real pro, Doc Shoemaker, you know that?"

"I only wish I had a shot for AIDS."

Decker stopped dressing. "But the Indian's blood work was negative for AIDS, right?"

"Right."

"Then I'm not worried."

"Easy for you to say."

He laughed without much conviction, then reached for his shirt on the door peg. "Not to be redundant, but have you thought about when you might be coming home?"

"Yes, I have." She was pushing the supply cart back into position against the wall.

"Good—would you like to expound on that?"

"I don't think this is the right place or the right time, Rick." She was standing by the door now, poised for a quick exit.

"All right, then, how about dinner tomorrow? You name the place."

She pulled a prescription pad from her coat pocket and started writing out an order. "I can't. I'm working second shift."

"Then let's do lunch."

She tore off the sheet and handed it to him. "Make sure you stop at the pharmacy window on the way out. You need to start the tetracycline today. Five hundred milligrams, four times a day. Finish the entire bottle. That will take about two weeks. During that time, I recommend that you abstain from alcoholic beverages and avoid exposure to the sun."

"No alcohol?"

"Would you rather die of plague?"

"Maybe," he said. He was rewarded with her smile again. "Come on," he cajoled, buttoning up his shirt. "Let's do lunch tomorrow. Or even breakfast." He feigned excitement over the idea. "That's it! We'll do a power breakfast, just like the yuppies in L.A. Five A.M. at Perkin's Pancakes. How does that sound?"

She laughed a little, almost the Janet he remembered again. Then she sighed and folded her arms. "Do you think we're ready to talk, Rick? I mean really talk about things."

"I'll bring notes."

She smiled again. "Okay. I'll meet you at Arnold's at noon."

"You got it."

As she turned and walked out the door, the last thing to fix in his memory was the small red stain on her lab coat.

* * *

100

Bradford Stuart Wolters, M.D., was the straight-A geek everybody knew in college, only grown up now and a little less impressed with the fact that he'd scored a perfect 800 on the math portion of his SATs. Decker had arranged to meet Wolters, the head of the CDC investigative team, in his suite at the Vernon Manor Hotel at 7:30 Wednesday morning—the only time Wolters said he could allow more than ten minutes out of his busy day. When Decker arrived, Wolters was already at his desk, dictating memos for his staff into a small tape recorder. He was fully dressed for the working day, including a tan blazer made of some stiff, synthetic material, and a tightly knotted Harvard tie.

Wolters was thirty-five, but with the exception of his thick brown mustache, which he stroked and ruffled like a pet during his more thoughtful moments, he looked for all the world like a pock-faced teenager. He was a small, nervous, precise man, the kind that gave everyone who dared talk to him the impression they were beating around the bush. As he listened to Decker, he slouched in his stuffed chair, tapping his fingertips just in front his nose.

Decker kept it short but didn't rush. In a minute or two he had summarized for Wolters all the things Floyd claimed to have seen in the old subway tunnel, and what the search party had found there the day before.

"Do you have the syringe?" Wolters asked, sounding more skeptical than interested.

Decker nodded, reached into his carrying case, and handed over the triple Ziploc bag.

"I thought you might like to test it."

"Test it for what?" Wolters said, slouching again. He started turning the bag one way and then another, peering through the plastic as though a rare species of insect were inside.

"Well, for drugs. Or maybe plague bacillus."

Wolters cocked his head as if to say you must be kidding. "The body was found three days ago, Mr. Decker. The chances are exceedingly slim that any bacilli would still be alive."

"What about testing for a sedative?"

"What kind of sedative?"

Decker had interviewed plenty of arrogant doctors in his time, and usually knew just how to stroke their inflated egos, but Wolters' platonic baiting was too much. He started gathering up his things. "I'll stop wasting your time."

"Now-now-now," Wolters said, returning to his ramrod posture. "I'm not trying to be difficult here, Mr. Decker. I simply want you to be more precise. In my experience lack of precision is the greatest failing of your—ahem—profession."

Decker settled in again. "Okay. Precision. As I told you about three and a half minutes ago, we think the Indian may have been sedated."

"Yes, in order to incapacitate the victim until the infection could take hold and kill him. Rather fantastic, I would think, don't you, Mr. Decker?"

"Is it any more fantastic than an Indian showing up in Cincinnati with plague?"

"Not if you look at the geo-ethnic history of the disease. The vast majority of plague cases in this country has occurred among Indian populations in the Southwest. Frankly, Mr. Decker, I would be far more suspicious if the victim had *not* been an Indian.

"As for this," he said, holding up the Ziploc bag by its seal, "I know of no sedative that, administered in a single dose, would work for a twelve-to-twenty-four-hour period."

"But there may be other syringes down there."

"Perhaps. But one syringe isn't conclusive evidence, now is it?"

The "now is it" was said with such haughty condescension that Decker came close to leaving again. Instead, he turned to a familiar ploy.

"Dr. Wolters, let me explain to you why I'm here. I've already contacted the police with this information, and they tell me it's a matter for the coroner. I go to the coroner, and he tells me not to waste his time. I'm here because you're the only person in this town who has both the medical expertise and the objective viewpoint to help us out."

Wolters seemed untouched by the flattery. "Why not go to the logical place—the health commissioner's office?"

Decker smiled. "We have reason to believe the commissioner may not be unbiased in this case."

Wolters stuck out his lower lip, started another round of finger-tapping. Decker couldn't tell if he was interested or just impatient.

"Mr. Decker, this whole scenario you paint is farfetched, to say the least, and probably not worth my time. But there are several things that can be done with a minimum of time and effort. Yes, I can have the syringe cultured for plague bacilli and tested for the full range of sedatives and narcotics. Mind you, even if there is a positive finding, the evidence would be circumstantial at best, but a negative result might at least allay your suspicions. Secondly, I can inquire at the coroner's office as to whether any drugs were found in the victim's body. If both avenues fail to turn up any evidence of foul play, you must promise me one thing."

"Of course," Decker said, surprised by Wolters's sudden turnaround.

"That you and your paper drop your witch hunt against Dr. Murdock."

"I'm not aware of any witch hunt, Dr. Wolters."

"Will you promise?"

"There's nothing to promise."

"Then there's very little sacrificed on your part. Am I correct?" Wolters smiled for the first time, a tight, weasel-like little grin.

Decker snatched up his carrying bag. "Have it your way."

It was 8:15 A.M. when Decker nabbed the last parking space in the alley beside the *Eagle* building. When he stepped out of the car, he yawned so violently he almost pulled a tendon in his neck. It had been a rough night without Janet. Finding the king-sized bed cold and empty, he had foregone the bedroom air conditioning and sacked out on the basement sofa, where he twisted and turned on soft, sweaty cushions until daybreak. At 6:45 he had dragged himself up, showered and shaved, and had gone straight to his appointment with Wolters. He decided now to treat himself to a breakfast special at Fausto's: scrambled eggs, thick-cut sausage patties, and hash browns with chopped onions and green peppers, a combination guaranteed to get his blood pressure up and his heart pumping.

Fausto's was across Broadway from the *Eagle* building, the standard friendly dive with Formica countertops, red stools, and cheap paneling. But Fausto kept the place spotless, and his plump wife, Theresita, who never came out of the kitchen, worked high-cholesterol magic on the grill. There were framed portraits of JFK and Pope John XXIII above the cash register, and plastic flowers on every table.

Fausto set hot coffee in front of Decker the moment he sat down at the counter, said a quick, "Good-a mornin'," scribbled down his order on a plain white notepad, and raced to the kitchen window. Fausto was a man of few words in the early morning. It was his busiest time of day.

Decker lit a cigarette and opened his copy of the Cincinnati *Times*. The morning competition had done little to advance yesterday's story. There was a short piece on the metro page saying the Health Department was cooperating with federal authorities to determine the identity of the plague victim. Murdock was quoted as saying the Indian was either Hopi or Navaho, based on the artifacts found on his body at the time. But so far, no one in the Southwest Indian reservations had reported a missing elderly man. Besides, as an official at the Bureau of Indian Affairs put it, "many Native American men experience transiency at one time or another in their lives."

Decker put his paper down and lit another cigarette. He felt at ease among the familiar clatter at Fausto's. Theresita served up two steaming plates of hotcakes at the kitchen window and shouted in Italian to Fausto, who came running. Decker waved to Theresita, but failed to get her attention. She looked even surlier and more harried than usual. Something else was different, too.

When his order came, he asked Fausto, "So where's Gertie this morning?" Gertie was an old homeless woman, as skinny as Theresita was fat, who sat at the end of the counter drinking cup after cup of free coffee and mumbling politely to herself. If you said good morning, Gertie stopped mumbling long enough to smile and nod back.

Fausto lowered his eyes and clattered the breakfast special in front of Decker. "She no come here-a no more," he said tersely. He grabbed Decker's coffee cup and refilled it from the big metal urn directly behind him, slopping hot liquid over the sides and into the saucer.

"Why not, Fausto?"

"Because I-a say so." Fausto deposited the cup and was gone in a flash again to pick up another order at the kitchen window. Decker's curiosity was piqued now. Besides, it might be a good idea to question Gertie. That is, if she was having one of her more lucid days.

Decker ate his breakfast and waited for Fausto to return to the coffee machine. "What happened, Fausto? Did you and Gertie have a fight?"

"No-a fight. I tella her she no welcome in my place."

"But, Fausto, I thought you liked Gertie." Decker certainly did; she gave the place a genuine urban touch.

Fausto jabbed a full cup of coffee at Decker's *Times*, sloshing some on the B section.

"I like-a Gertie, all right, but I have-a customers complain when they read-a the paper."

"You're kidding?"

Fausto shook his head and disappeared to deliver his coffee. Decker finished up his hash browns with more ketchup and waited until Fausto returned to collect his plates.

"Fausto, the chances of Gertie making anybody sick . . ."

"I know. I know whatta the health commissioner say. But if I lose-a customers, I no pay-a the rent."

"But, Fausto, she's an old woman."

Just then Theresita shouted from the kitchen window, louder and sharper than usual.

"I know, I know. You and Theresita—justa like. But I runna a beezness here, not welfare okay?"

There were few surprises at the meeting in Farlidge's office that morning. Farlidge was skeptical of Floyd's story, but was willing to wait and see what Wolters learned about the syringe. Farlidge was far more excited about what Decker had observed at Fausto's diner: it looked like the beginning of a plague hysteria. He assigned Angie the piece—"I think Sally Beth would want you to really effort this, Angie"—then instructed Decker to follow up on the *Times'* latest story.

At least, Decker thought, he hadn't asked for another Cody Blair story. But when Decker returned to his desk and was about to call the local FBI office, Farlidge appeared, note in hand.

"Put that follow on the back burner," he said, beaming with excitement. "I've got something a lot more interesting here."

Farlidge handed him a yellow Post-it note with a name and address in Sally Beth's crisp, no-nonsense script: "Dr. Harv Sutton, 829 Grandin Road."

"Sally Beth says she knows for a fact they'll be filming the Cody Blair movie there this morning. She wants you on the set. You can reach Dr. Sutton's wife, Polly, by phone right now. It's in the book."

"So what's the angle here, Ron? Rich doctor's wife opens estate to homeless filmmakers?"

Farlidge stuffed his hands in his pockets and smiled. "You know, Decker, I wish I could de-program that attitude of yours. It would make my job a lot more pleasant."

106

"They could always send me to Delta headquarters for some reeducation, couldn't they, Ron?"

"Just get me this story by six tonight. Sally Beth wants it for 1-A."

"I'll be sure to effort it."

The crescent drive in front of 829 Grandin Road was lined with a convoy of tractor trailers and Winnebagos for the cast and crew of *Young Obsession*, the working title for Cody Blair's latest film. Decker parked his car across the street from the house, but failed to see Polly Sutton, who had promised to meet him there at 10 A.M. He started toward the house, but was stopped short of the driveway by a college kid with a flattop and a yellow armband that said "Security."

"Yoo hoo! He's all right!" Mrs. Sutton called out. She suddenly appeared from the line of trucks, dressed, it seemed, for a day of shopping and luncheon with the girls in a bright red silk dress and gold jewelry. She was fortyish, pleasant, and well-preserved—Donna Reed, but with a larger allowance from her husband.

"He's a friend of the family's," she said to the guard, then took Decker by the arm.

She sneaked him through the back of the family manse, a sprawling white frame with a fireplace in about every room. It reeked with the musty smell of old money. They stepped quietly into the main living room where the filming was taking place, but Decker soon learned from a sound technician that Cody had already left for the day. He was beginning to wonder if the actress really existed, or if she was the product of the town's collective imagination.

"Oh, dear. I think she might have gone to Saks," Mrs. Sutton said. "She told me yesterday she needed to pick up a few things."

Decker decided to stay awhile and watch the filming. The Suttons' living room was jammed with lights and camera

107

equipment and an army of Southern California types in baggy chinos and designer T-shirts. They kept doing the same scene over and over again. It was an argument between Cody Blair's wrong-side-of-the-tracks lover and her preppy dad. Decker recognized the lover as a current teen heartthrob. He was being touted as the new James Dean, a sad-eyed rebel whose adolescent horniness passed for what critics liked to call "coiled tension." Dad was a distinguished character actor whom Decker had seen dozens of times—he could never remember the name.

To end the scene, Dad threw his gin-and-tonic into the heartthrob's face, but lover boy caught most of it in his open mouth and spat it back. Decker wasn't sure if it was supposed to be funny or not. Maybe it needed a laugh track.

On the late morning drive back to the office, Columbia Parkway was a monotony of blanched grass and trees under a hazy sky. The drought had become the great equalizer, rendering the world in barely distinguishable shades of pale yellow, pale brown, pale gray.

Decker rolled down his windows and let the air roil around the insides of his Dart. The wind blew hot across the back of his neck, sandblasted his cheeks, burrowed its hot fingers into his scalp. None of it bothered him anymore. In the last day or so, the drought had become a part of him, a coppery staleness in the mouth, a deep weariness in the bones, as though he had been sucked dry from the inside out. He was beyond impatience now. He simply accepted as fact that it would never rain again. In the name of the Father, the Son, and the Greenhouse Effect. Amen.

Lunch with Janet was less than an hour away, and Decker tried to think through all the things he wanted to say to her. He *could* change, he'd show her. First of all, he'd quit his job—just as soon as the plague story panned out—and try his hand at free-lancing. Maybe then he could give up the cigarettes again and cut down on his coffee and beer. He'd become another man—relaxed, purified, in touch with his feelings. They could start spending time with each other again.

He was back downtown by 11:20. Now it was just a matter of finding a place to park, running up to the newsroom to give Farlidge the bad news about Cody, and he could slip away to meet Janet. But as he cruised the meters in front of the *Eagle*, he saw Angie rocket out of the revolving doors in heels and a miniskirt and run for his car. He stopped and she stuck her head in the passenger window.

"What's up?" he said. "You look like Farlidge asked for a date."

She was breathless. "Bart just called from the cop shop. They found another body."

"Where?"

"Down by the river."

10

According to Bart, the body had been found by a fisherman along the riverfront, just below the stadium parking garage and east of the Suspension Bridge. It wasn't an easy part of the riverfront to get to, but Decker remembered a pedestrian access from the ground-level of the garage. He and Angie drove the seven blocks to the stadium and paid three dollars to get into the garage, only to find a police cruiser blocking the river access.

"No problem," Decker said. He pulled out of the garage, turned right on Pete Rose Way, and took another right down a narrow access road between the stadium and the coliseum. The road led to the public landing, a cobblestone bank where free parking spaces had been laid out for use whenever the river was low. Decker had never seen more than two or three rows of cars jammed onto the landing, but that morning there were seven rows, all the way down to where the cobblestone disappeared into the cracked mud of the riverbed. The river itself was another ten feet from the edge of the landing. It was the color of vending machine coffee, heavy on the creamer, and seemingly immobile, save for a thin, turbulent current through its shrunken middle.

Decker found an empty space in the last row and parked.

When they got out, the sun was high and the air was as thick and rancid as week-old fish chowder. Angie held her nose. "Did somebody pull the plug?"

The drought had tipped the delicate balance between man and river firmly in favor of man. The lower reaches of the riverbank were littered with debris—big clumps of driftwood speckled with plastic bottles, jugs, cups, burger boxes—all the refuse the mighty river used to swallow whole, but now, in its weakened condition, could only regurgitate along its shore.

They started up the slanted cobblestone to a narrow walkway, just below the stadium floodwall. Decker glanced at his watch. It was 11:35.

"Damn," he said. He picked up the pace.

"Damn, what?"

"I should have called Janet."

"So call her when we get back."

"We were supposed to meet for lunch."

Angie let out a soft little, "Oh." She was looking straight ahead. "You mean *that* kind of Janet."

Decker checked his watch again. All was not lost. He could pop into Arnold's on the way back to the newsroom and explain to Janet in person. With any luck, he and Angie might still make final edition.

They could spot the official gathering a quarter mile or so downriver, past the stadium and the public docks. Decker had picked up the pace another step or two when Angie pulled him by the arm. "Have you taken up power walking by any chance?"

"I'd run if you weren't wearing those ridiculous heels."

"Well, excu-u-se me. Next time I'll wear a jogging suit to work."

Angie was decked out like an MTV princess. Black heels, black miniskirt, a white tank top that didn't quite reach her navel. She was carrying a black leather cinch bag over her shoulder.

"Whoa, Flash! Aren't we missing something?" Angie

pointed down the bank to an old black man fishing from the tailgate of a station wagon. He was holding a cane pole across his lap and his eyes were fixed on a small red bobber just beyond the river's edge.

"So?"

"So, dummy, think. He might be the guy who found the body."

They left the walkway and started down the bank. It was no longer cobblestone but a crunchy mass of gravel, tiny shells, and silt. "Wait a second," Angie said, clutching Decker's arm for balance. She reached behind and slipped off one heel, then the other, and started walking barefoot.

"What about your stockings?"

"What stockings?"

The old man hadn't taken his eyes off the bobber. There was a coffee can of dirt and worms beside him on the tailgate and a beat-up tackle box at his feet.

Decker said a friendly good morning. The man replied with a quick "mornin' " without turning his head.

"Could you help us with something, sir?"

The man turned to look at them, a little surprised.

"That all dee-pend on what kind of help yo' need, now don't it?" He smiled as he said it, snags showing. He was a thin man with a thin brown-yellow face and a sparse white goatee. He wore an L.A. Dodgers ball cap, about as anathema a piece of clothing as a person could wear in Cincinnati.

Decker continued to do the talking. "We're reporters from the *Eagle*. We were wondering if you were the one who found the body just up the way there."

"Nuthin' to find."

"What do you mean?"

"Smelled so bad a blind man coulda found it."

"Did the police talk to you?"

"Oh, yeah. I tol' 'em everything I knowed. Weren't much to tell. I got here about ten. Put my line in downriver there just below them trees, then started smellin' somethin' real bad—I mean REAL bad, like rotten potatoes, you know—and I started lookin' around. That's when I found him layin' up there by them woods, right next to a drainpipe. Some poor old hobo, I s'pose. I walked up the tunnel there into the parking garage and tol' somebody to call the po-lice."

The man pulled a little on his line to keep it tight. The bobber was ramrod straight in the stagnant water.

"Did you notice anything unusual about the body?"

The man grinned. "Unusual? I'd say bein' dee-ceased is mighty unusual."

Angie elbowed Decker.

"I mean, were there any signs of violence or maybe a struggle?"

The man shook his head. "I knowed one thing right away, though."

"What's that?"

"That man been eaten up by rats."

Angie groaned. "You could tell?" she asked.

"Oh, yeah. I done lived around enough rats in my life. I know when I see a rat bite. They take dainty little nibbles, up and down, up and down, just like some ol' woman eatin' an ear o' corn." He demonstrated with what was left of his front teeth.

Angie tugged at Decker's elbow. She was looking over her shoulder now. A stretcher was being trundled down the river-bank from the stadium garage. "We better get going," she said.

"Can I have your name, sir?" Decker asked.

"Orvis Johnson. That's O-R-V-I-S." He spied Decker's notebook as he wrote it down.

"And your address?"

"Don't worry 'bout no address. You got my name there. Folks know who Orvis Johnson is."

Angie was tugging again. "Okay, okay," Decker told her, then to Johnson: "And a phone number, sir, in case we need to reach you later."

"You need me, I be right here."

* * *

The police were standing in a semicircle, about a half dozen of them, facing downstream with their backs to Decker and Angie. Some were holding handkerchiefs over their mouths and noses. In another step or two along the walkway, Decker and Angie knew why. The stench cut through even the rank air along the river. It was just as Orvis had described it, sickly sweet, like rotten potatoes. Angie clapped a hand over her nose and honked, "How we gonna innerview pipple li' thith?"

"Please?"

She removed her hand—"I said, 'How are we going to interview people with this smell?' "—and quickly pinched her nose again.

"What smell?" he said. Angie jabbed his upper arm. "Be honest. Are you up to this?"

"Of course, she said. You think I haven't seen a dead body before?"

"Yes."

She grinned. "You're right. But no way I'm going to miss my first."

They left the walkway and started down the silt and gravel. Angie carried her shoes again.

"Remember," Decker said, clamping a hand on her cool, bare shoulder. "You can bail out anytime. I'll meet you back at the car."

They stopped just behind the line of police, where Decker expected to be challenged, but the cops were too engrossed in the proceedings to notice. The body—what they could see of it—was lying in muck about five feet from the river's edge, not far from the base of the stone tower supporting the Suspension Bridge.

Four men were crouched around the victim—two coroner assistants wearing masks and white jumpsuits, along with Wolters, who had donned a surgical gown for the occasion, and a fourth man, Wayne Plaxton, the Health Department's rat control expert, whom Decker remembered from the press conference. Wolters was holding forth, talking rapidly, while Plaxton and the two assistants obediently nodded. They looked like dashboard bob toys.

Off and on, Wolters pointed to a sewer pipe that opened on the riverbank a few yards upstream from the body. It was a big cement pipe, large enough for a man to crawl into. The mouth of the pipe was dry. Even the moss around the rim had been scorched brown.

Just beyond the body, underneath the Suspension Bridge, was a stand of bleached-out willow trees, their tops rustling in the downdraft from the bridge traffic. The cars made a sad kind of droning on the metal grates, a monotonous, steely hum. A mantra for the city.

Decker looked at his watch—11:50—and back to Wolters, who was still delivering his sermonette. At this rate, he'd miss Janet altogether. Then, a minute or two later, a third coroner's assistant came with a body bag, and Wolters and Plaxton stepped away from the body, exposing it to view.

Angie slapped her hand over her mouth. The right leg of the body was stripped below the knee, the bone gleaming white in the sun. Most of the face was gone, too; only the beard and long hair were still intact. What remained of the body was covered in a tangle of trash bags and rope. It might have been something coughed up by the river.

Decker knew instantly who it was.

"It's the Glad Man," he said. Angie flashed him a quizzical look. "I'm sure you've seen him," Decker said. "The old man who ties trash bags around his legs. He's downtown all the time. Pushes a grocery cart around."

Angie rolled her eyes and nodded.

A coroner's assistant unzipped the body bag, spread it on the ground and then all three assistants carefully rolled the bloated remains onto the bag and sealed it. One of the cops, an older man with gray sideburns, rattled a stretcher cart down the gravel to the body.

While the assistants loaded the body, Wolters signaled to the police, who slowly gathered around.

"Well?" Angie asked. She was putting her shoes back on. "We want Wolters, don't we?"

"Not yet," Decker said. "It's all in the timing."

Plaxton and the coroner assistants pushed the stretcher up the bank, wheels wobbling and rutting through the gravel, while the cops and Wolters stayed behind.

The older cop who had brought the stretcher started toward Decker and Angie, beating the air with his hands. "Move along now. We're securing this area."

"I'm waiting for Dr. Wolters," Decker said.

The cop smiled as he approached, but he was all business. "You a reporter?"

Decker nodded.

"You can talk to the doctor later. Let's get moving."

"I need him now. I'm pushing a deadline."

"Listen, pal, we're all pushing deadlines. Now clear the area or I'll have to take you in." The cop was about to get physical when Angie started waving her shoes over her head, crying out in a phony singsong voice, "Oh, Dr. Wolters! Yoo hoo! Excuse us, Dr. Wolters!"

It was embarrassing for Decker, but it worked. Wolters came trudging over the gravel to find out what all the commotion was about.

"This reporter here says he wants to talk to you," the cop said to Wolters. "You know him?"

"Yes," Wolters answered matter-of-factly, "it's fine." The cop tipped his hat good-bye to Angie. She curtsied in return.

Wolters' surgical gown was folded in quarters and draped over his forearm like a waiter's towel. He seemed in far better spirits than he had been earlier that morning. His blue eyes were twinkling. Nothing like a good post-mortem to get the juices flowing.

"Well, Mr. Decker, you certainly get around."

"You're not doing so bad yourself."

Decker introduced Angie as "his assistant," and got a scowl in return before she extended a hand to Wolters.

Decker got to the point. "Was it plague, Dr. Wolters?"

Wolters lost the twinkle in his eye. He started to answer, then stopped. "Could this be off-the-record?"

Decker shook his head.

"Then it will have to be background. I can't be quoted."

"And I'm sorry. We can't use unnamed sources in the *Eagle*."

Wolters pinched his mustache. "I'll let you quote me on two conditions. One, that you get further comments from Dr. Murdock, and, two, that you make it clear that I was here at his request."

"If that's the case," Decker said, "no problem."

"All right, then. Yes, the body we found here appears to have been infected by plague. But that may not have been the immediate cause of death."

Decker and Angie looked up simultaneously from their notes. "Then what was?" Angie asked.

"It's a rather tangled situation. I'm afraid we won't have all the answers until the autopsy is performed. But we do know this man was in very bad shape even before he was infected. His lower left leg, for instance, was almost completely gangrenous."

"Which explains the smell," Decker volunteered.

"Yes—the necrotic tissue produces a rather distinctive odor."

"How long has he been dead?" Decker asked.

"Based on our initial exam, not more than twenty-four hours."

Angie spoke up. "A fisherman down the way told us he thought the body had been eaten by rats."

Wolters nodded solemnly. "Most likely after death."

Wolters took a deep breath and tugged at the corner of his mustache. He seemed to be wrestling with something. Finally he said, "That's really all I can give you right now. Good day."

Decker and Angie checked their notes as he walked away.

"Not much, is it?" Angie said.

"Enough. We'll throw in lots of background."

On the way back, they found Wayne Plaxton crouched near the sewer pipe. He was touching his fingers to the moist silt just below the opening.

Decker was in a hurry to get back to the car, but Angie stopped him. "Come on. Just a couple of quick questions."

It took a while before Plaxton noticed Angie and Decker standing behind him. He suddenly stood up.

"Find anything interesting?" Angie asked.

Plaxton broke into a sheepish smile, a kid caught red-handed playing in the dirt. He hitched up his trousers over a round, soft belly. He was a big, doughy-looking man, classically out of fashion in a shortsleeve shirt, fat shiny tie. The kind of guy you could trust.

"You two with the press?"

Angie introduced them both, calling Decker her "posse." Decker extended his hand, but Plaxton declined. He was wearing rubber gloves.

"You might as well know what's going on. You'll find out eventually anyway," Plaxton said, a true man of the Enlightenment. He pointed to the ground just in front of his feet. "Take a look at the mud between here and the riverbank."

Angie squatted down, hugging her knees for better balance. "There's like lots of little scratch marks," she said. "Like somebody dragged a rake across it or something."

"Try rats," Plaxton said. "What you're looking at are the paw prints of hundreds, maybe thousands of rats."

Angie sprang from her squatting position. Decker's eyes followed the trail. The scratch marks fanned out wider and wider as they neared the river.

"Oh, we're quite safe now," Plaxton said. "They won't come out until night."

"For what?" Angie asked.

"The water, of course."

Decker shivered as he imagined the scene—thousands of black, squirming rodents pouring from this open pipe, swarming down to the river under the cover of darkness. If you listened closely at night, maybe you could hear the sound of thousands of tiny tongues lapping.

"This isn't like normal, is it?" Angie asked. "I mean, don't they usually stay down in their little holes?"

"Yes, but they're very adaptable little creatures." Plaxton smiled with heartfelt admiration; he loved his work. "With this drought, you see, even the sewers have dried up. And with the fumigation going on at the men's shelter, they've had to find a new source of water."

Decker nodded to where the Glad Man's body had been found, a yard or two downstream from the pipe. "I guess he was in the wrong place at the wrong time."

"Yes—and in no condition to get away."

"Why not?" Angie asked.

"He was nursing a gangrenous leg. I doubt he got very far."

"So you think he was alive when the rats attacked," Decker said.

Plaxton nodded.

"But Dr. Wolters told us he was probably already dead," Angie said.

Plaxton looked surprised. "He told you that?"

"Yes. Just a minute ago."

"Well, I'm no medical doctor, mind you. Just a Ph.D.," he said quietly, then added, "You're not going to quote me on this, are you?" He looked a little frightened now. The high school nerd about to be sent to the principal's office.

"Don't you think the public should know?" Decker said.

"It's not my place to say," Plaxton said. He folded his arms over his belly and squinted out over the glare of the river.

"Whose place is it?"

"Dr. Murdock's."

"Dr. Murdock doesn't seem too concerned about where the homeless spend their nights," Decker said. He could see the

119

conflicting impulses raging in Plaxton's face: job security, maybe even his loyalty to Murdock, fighting against something. Maybe his social conscience.

Decker pushed. "What do you think the city should do about the men's shelter?"

Plaxton looked out over the river again, eyes narrowing in his plump face. You could see him mustering courage. "You know what gets me?" he said.

"No, what?"

Plaxton nodded across the river, toward one of the trendy riverboat restaurants tethered to the shore. "Over there you got businessmen on expense accounts eating twenty-dollar steaks and thirty-dollar lobsters and thinking nothing of it, while here," he said, pointing to the stand of willow trees, "you got men can barely keep their body and soul together."

Plaxton looked down at Decker's notebook. "I shouldn't say this, but I will anyway. And you can quote me on this. I think this city needs a temporary shelter for the homeless. And the sooner the better."

"What about Longview?" Decker said. "Aren't they sending men up there?"

"They won't stay put. It's too far from their normal haunts," Plaxton said. He pointed to the willows again. "There's a whole camp of them back there in those trees and bushes right now. That means you've got three things down here that just don't mix from a public health standpoint. You got plague. You got rats. And you got men living in close proximity to rats. If somebody were systematically trying to rid this city of its homeless, they couldn't devise a better plan."

Angie spoke up. "Don't you have a say in whether the shelter is closed?"

"Yes. Some," Plaxton said. "But when you get right down to it, this is Dr. Murdock's show. Now you go and talk to him."

11

Hang on." Decker stomped on the gas pedal. The slant six hesitated, sputtered, then finally synchronized and roared as the Dart passed under the yellow light at Fourth Street. The air downtown seemed full of baked grit that bit into the back of his neck.

"Boy," Angie said, "we're talking life-or-death lunch date."

"I'll drop you in front of the *Eagle*."

"No need to stop," Angie said, tugging at her miniskirt. "I'll just open the door and sort of, you know, tumble out."

Decker's watch showed 12:15. Janet had to be at work by one. She'd be fuming, and he couldn't blame her.

He missed two of the next three lights on Broadway—thanks to slow-footed pedestrians—then beat another yellow at Eighth and nearly overshot the *Eagle* building before hitting the brakes. Time of arrival: 12:20.

Angie swung her bag over her shoulder, popped open the door. "Thanks for the ride, pal. And to think I'm not even maimed!"

"Tell Stein I'll be up in five minutes. Start plugging in your notes and playing with a lead. Something like: 'The city's second plague victim may have been found today . . . blah, blah, blah.' Okay?"

"Anything you say, boss." She blew him a kiss through the open window.

Decker hit the gas and, almost simultaneously, the brake. The Dart shivered back and forth. Traffic screeched, horns honked.

Janet was standing in the shade just outside the *Eagle*'s revolving door, gripping her lab coat in both hands. Not gripping. She looked like she was strangling it. Angie breezed by her in the miniskirt, spike heels pounding out a staccato racket.

He snapped on his emergency flashers, dashed around the car. His whole face was in a sweat when he reached Janet. She hadn't moved.

"Look," Decker said, talking faster and louder than he had wanted to, "I'm sorry I'm late. They found a body on the river this morning, and I didn't . . . There just wasn't enough time to call. Listen, I'm sorry. Can I drive you back to your car?"

Janet started walking away. "You're the one who wanted this lunch." He trailed after her.

"But, Janet, I can't. I've got twenty minutes to crank out a story for the final."

She stopped and stared. She was calmer now, icy. "Then forget it," she said. "It won't be necessary."

"What won't be necessary?"

"I can walk to my car." She started up Broadway again. He kept after her, knowing it was stupid.

"Janet, you can't possibly think . . ."

She turned and glared, all heat now. "I don't think anything, Rick. If you'd like to try getting together again, call. You know how to reach me." She flung the lab coat over her shoulder and started up the street again, holding her head high.

Decker stayed behind, his heart squeezing inside his chest. Why was his whole life suddenly out of control?

* * *

In the newsroom Angie was sitting at his computer with Stein bent over her shoulder peering at the screen. Stein was all smiles as Decker entered the cubicle.

"You two landed quite a scoop. Angie already has half of it written."

"Good," Decker said, although he wasn't sure he meant it. His head seemed disconnected, spinning somewhere just above his neck. He knew he had to shake it; there was work to do. He'd call Janet later and explain. It was all very silly, really, like some forties screwball comedy. He pushed aside the clutter on his desk and sat down—Angie had his chair—and started scanning his notes.

"So what's our lead?" he asked.

Stein read aloud while Angie continued to write. "The body of a homeless man—possibly the city's second victim of plague—was discovered late this morning in the mud flats below the Suspension Bridge.

"At least one health authority fears that other homeless men now camping on the river are at high risk of contracting plague, and has called for the creation of a temporary shelter to replace the one closed by Health Commissioner Reginald X. Murdock early this week. . . ."

"Not bad," Decker told Stein, knowing it was better than "not bad." "Does she have the fisherman in there?"

Angie answered this time. "Yep, and all the gory details. The smell. The gangrene. The killer rats from hell."

Stein nodded, smiling. He was clearly impressed.

Decker flipped through more notes. "All right, what about our promise to Wolters—have you got that?"

"What promise?" Angie said. Her fingers worked over the keyboard in quick, soft ripples.

"That we mention Murdock dispatched him to the scene, remember?"

"Gotcha."

Stein excused himself. "I'll let you two have at it. Catch you in ten minutes, okay?"

Decker pulled up his straight-back chair next to Angie. She was leaning forward from the hips, legs crossed. A black high heel dangled from her raised foot like a comma.

"Did you work in Plaxton's theory about the sewers?"

She nodded, still typing. Decker read what was on the screen. She already had a good fourteen, fifteen inches. It was clear, concise, filled with all the dramatic details Decker would have included, like the rat prints in the mud. He hadn't seen anyone so fast, so accurate in years. Not since Turk.

He looked a moment at her profile. No sign of tension in the fresh young face. Just a relaxed concentration—eyes shining, skin glowing, lips puckered ever so slightly. She was a kid intent on having fun.

Decker reached the end of his notes, then realized something. "We've got a hole."

"Where?" Angie stopped typing.

Decker jumped back to his desk and picked up the phone. "We need Murdock's response to Plaxton. About the temporary shelter."

He punched in the number and waited for the calm, cheery voice of his secretary.

"I'm sorry, Dr. Murdock is in conference at the moment."

"Could you possibly interrupt?" Decker said, straining to be polite. "We're on deadline."

"Please hold." He was cut off and, instantly, the *Nutcracker Suite* started playing in his ear. The Dance of the Sugar Plum Fairies. It sounded cool and breezy.

"I can't believe it. They're playing Christmas music."

Angie looked at her watch. "Rick, it's twelve thirty-five. Barry will be breathing down our necks any minute."

The music stopped and Murdock was on the line, his resonant baritone like a wake-up call from God.

"Yes, Mr. Decker. How may I help you?"

Decker told him about the second body, then asked if he agreed with Plaxton about the need for a new downtown shelter. .

There was a long pause. Decker braced himself.

"First of all, Mr. Decker, I would ask you *not* to print your story. No one—certainly no one in my department—has confirmed that this man was infected with plague. In fact, the coroner is only now performing the autopsy. Secondly, it is not my responsibility—nor that of Mr. Plaxton, I might add—to determine the site of a new shelter. That's the prerogative of the city zoning board and city council. Now I suggest you call them and let *me* return to my responsibilities."

"One last thing, Dr. Murdock . . ." But the line was dead. Decker held the receiver in his grip like a barbell.

"Well, at least he was quick about it," Angie said. "Where do you want the insert?"

"Right up Murdock's . . ."

"Oooh, we *are* testy today. Have something disagreeable for lunch?"

"Nothing that concerns you."

Decker shooed Angie out of his chair while he typed in the quote from Murdock. When he finished, he scrolled through the story again. It was tight, complete, accurate—except for a half-dozen spelling errors that popped up on the spell checker.

"Christ, you've got 'occurred' with one *r* and 'laboratory' spelled like 'Labrador.' Don't they teach you kids anything?"

"Little details for little minds," Angie said.

"Details, honey, are what make this profession."

Decker folded his arms, stared at the pulsing screen. "I don't care what Sally Beth says, Murdock has *got* to be involved in this mess up to his ears." He made a mental note to check with Wolters after deadline—the lab results on the syringe might be in.

"Look out," Angie said, peering through the front glass. "Here comes Stein."

Decker stuck his head above the partition. "It's on the way, Barry!"

"Forget it. We're holding the final. Channel 8 has a special report." He motioned them to follow.

Decker took a deep breath. If they were scooped, they were scooped. It was only a goddamn story—here today, garbage tomorrow.

At the metro desk, reporters and copy editors were clustered around the newsroom's official TV set—an old black-and-white portable with lousy reception.

Decker and Angie arrived in time to find the station's female anchor standing live on the steps of St. Peter in Chains Cathedral. Decker tried to ask what was going on, but was immediately shushed down. The older male anchor was on his throne in the Channel 8 studio, cross-examining his cohort at the scene.

"Liz, have the authorities been able to confirm whether this was another case of plague?"

"Not at this time, Stanley. They say they'll have to conduct blood tests on the body first. But in the meantime they say they're not ruling out that possibility, either."

"Liz, I know you weren't permitted to take video equipment inside the cathedral, but were you able to talk to any of the witnesses there?"

"Yes, Stanley. Several people who were attending the noon-hour service told me basically the same story." Liz consulted her notes, a true professional. "They said the unidentified man entered the church near the end of the service. He stumbled up to the altar and cried out in a loud voice, 'God have mercy on us,' and collapsed. He then went into serious convulsions, witnesses said. Paramedics were too late to revive the man, but they did notice the swollen areas on the victim's neck and under the arms."

"And those indicate the likelihood of bubonic plague?"

"That's right, Stanley."

"Has there been any identification of the victim?"

"No, Stanley. No one is releasing that information at this time. Witnesses said the man was Caucasian, possibly in his late sixties, or older, and looked as though he might be a vagrant."

"And where are the witnesses now?"

"All of them have chosen to remain inside the church, Stanley, where Bishop Gerhardt is now conducting a special benediction for the man who died here, and for the city of Cincinnati as well."

"I'm sure we can all use a few prayers at a time like this, Liz." There was a collective groan in the *Eagle* newsroom.

"Yes, we certainly can, Stanley."

"Thank you for that informative report, Liz." Stanley swiveled in his chair and faced the camera, staring down the city's crisis with a grim but determined look.

"For those who tuned in late, I'll repeat what has happened. Less than thirty minutes ago, an unidentified man stumbled into services at St. Peter in Chains Cathedral in downtown Cincinnati, collapsed and died on the steps of the altar. Health authorities are investigating whether the man might be the city's second victim of bubonic plague. . . ."

A copy editor managed to interject, "It was probably the goddamned heat," before being shouted down.

Stanley had the final word: "Health authorities are cautioning area residents not to panic. Plague, they say, can be treated *and* cured with available antibiotics, and it does not—I repeat—*does not* pose a threat to the general population.

"Coming up on today's five o'clock report, more news on the city's plague scare. Channel 8 will have an exclusive interview with a Norwood woman who says she rode a bus from Nashville, Tennessee, with the man who may have brought plague to the Tri-State. Keep cool until then, and stay in touch. This is Stanley Lizaro, for the Channel 8 news team—"

Farlidge snapped off the set amid the ensuing hubbub. "All right, gang. We have work to do. Final deadline has been moved to one fifteen. Let's get cracking."

With the gallows humor typical of every newsroom, a reporter shouted, "God have mercy on us!" and the assemblage broke up.

Stein turned to Decker and Angie. "It looks like we have our work cut out."

Decker felt his stomach complain—the raw spot left whenever he was scooped. "Well, at least we still have an exclusive on the river death."

"Should we include the Channel 8 stuff in our story?" Angie asked Stein.

"I don't know how we can ignore it. Give the bishop's office a call and see if they'll confirm."

"What about the woman on the bus?" Decker asked.

"We'll have to see what we can do this afternoon."

The story for the final was filed at 12:52:10, according to Decker's computer screen. A minute later, with Angie on the way to lunch, Decker tried to reach Janet. He called her automatic pager, punched in his work number after the beep, waited. For ten minutes he sat by his phone, scribbling notes on his desk calendar on what he would say once she called, then finally threw his pen down and headed for Vendville.

Lunch was quick and forgettable—a rubbery, microwaved chili dog for Decker; vanilla yogurt and a heavily waxed apple for Angie. They met briefly again with Stein around 1:30. Angie volunteered to hang out at the downtown Greyhound station and see if she could track down the driver on the Nashville-to-Cincinnati run. Already Greyhound management was stonewalling, directing all inquiries to their lawyers in New York. No doubt somebody would find a lawyer to sue the company for transporting plague victims.

With Angie gone, Decker and Stein puzzled some more over Floyd's tale and the dead end in the subway tunnel.

"It's probably one of those things you miss because it's so obvious," Stein said. He was slouched down in Decker's typing chair, pushing out his lower lip with his tongue, a simianlike habit he'd developed since giving up his pipe.

"You mean like those old brain teasers we all told as kids,"

Decker said. "Remember the one where the husband kisses his wife good-bye, hops on the elevator in their apartment building, then gets stuck between the third and fourth floors. Instantly the man knows his wife is dying. How?"

Stein smiled. "Because the power went out and his wife is on a lung machine."

"You've heard it."

He nodded. "I remember another one," he said, getting into it now, "about a dead man they find face-down in the desert. He's got a pack on his back and enough food and water to last for two days. So how did the man die?"

Decker toyed with it a second, shook his head.

Stein laughed. "His parachute didn't open."

Decker groaned and reached for the cigarettes on his desk. He figured he might as well light up in front of Stein. He felt the need to be alone anyway.

Strangely, it was the image of a dead man with a pack on his back that set the pinball logic ricocheting through his brain. From pack to pack rat—*boink!* From rats to sewers—*bing!*

"Barry," he burst out, "it's the sewers!" He stopped for a quick drag on his cigarette.

"You lost me. What sewers are we talking about?"

"No, really, Barry. Listen. Plaxton says the rats came out of the sewers looking for water. That's how the little bastards got from the shelter to the riverfront. You're absolutely right, Barry. It's so goddamned obvious we missed it!"

"Whoa. Back up a minute. What's obvious?"

"There's a sewer line between the subway and the shelter!"

From the outside, the Historical Society building looked more like a mausoleum than a city museum—a windowless box of green marble slabs and prefab concrete. One more architectural nightmare from the fifties. The irony was that it had been built over the city's original fine arts museum, a grand old piece of Romanesque architecture. Decker couldn't figure it.

The lobby was two stories high, a drab space of blond furniture, dingy olive walls, and dim fluorescent lighting. Models of riverboats, canal barges, and inclines collected dust above a disparate collection of card catalogs. The place smelled of cheap floor wax and musty bindings.

Decker signed and dated the guest register at the front desk, filling in a laconic *"Eagle*—Broadway" in the space asking for company affiliation and address.

"Are you here for a book or a document?" asked a woman behind the reception desk. She was plump and vaguely distracted. Her black dye job looked deep purple in the artificial light. She neither smiled nor made eye contact.

"I'm looking for some old blueprints," he said.

"That will be reference," she said, pointing to another desk across the room. No one was behind it. The woman picked up her phone, pressed a red button. Her soft voice came booming over the PA system.

"Kevin to reference, please! Kevin to reference!"

Decker arrived at the desk just as Kevin came strolling out, past a sign that said, ABSOLUTELY NO STACK BOOKS AFTER 4 P.M.!

Kevin was a GQ wannabee—tall, thin, dressed in a white shirt, red suspenders, and paisley bow tie. He looked forty, easy, although his hair was dark and shiny and pulled back in a ponytail. He used a better rinse than the receptionist.

"May I help you with something?" He smiled, then immediately sat down and started jotting down numbers in a ledger. Decker wondered if the whole staff was trained not to make eye contact.

"I'd like to look at blueprints of the old subway."

"Are you engaged in architectural or historical research?"

"Actually, I'm a reporter for the *Eagle*."

"And you need the blueprints for . . . what exactly?" There was a slight condescending lilt in his voice.

"To look at," Decker replied.

Kevin pursed his lips, stared off to another part of the room.

"The reason I ask is that the prints are in rather fragile condition at this point, and *not* to be handled unless necessary. Perhaps you'd like to look at some old photographs of the tunnels."

"No, I need the prints. It's for a story. Now do I have to get a court order or what?"

A curtain of restraint fell over Kevin's eyes. "That won't be necessary," he said. He rose from the desk and disappeared into the stacks.

He returned in a minute or two carrying two oversized black binders in his outstretched arms. He signaled Decker to follow him to a table in an alcove off the lobby, where he set down the two binders side by side. Both were stamped in gold lettering, "Cincinnati Subway Project, 1920–27," with the one on the left subtitled "Exterior Drawings," the one on the right "Interior Drawings."

"Which do you need?" Kevin asked.

"Interior—Race Street Station."

The binding let out a sharp crack as Kevin slowly opened the cover and, with both hands, began turning one precious page at a time.

"I'm not certain these are in any kind of order," he said.

"I'm in no hurry."

The drawings were in dark blue ink on thin, crinkly paper, yellowed and waffled now at the edges. The artist's style might have been a precursor to art deco—bold lines and streamlined shapes, full of hope for a future that never happened.

"You should know that you're the third person in two weeks to request a look at these," Kevin said, still turning pages. "I'm afraid they'll never hold up to this kind of abuse."

"Really? How often do people normally look at these?"

"Never, as far as I can recall. And I've been here practically forever."

"No kidding?"

Kevin scowled. "Well, not that long."

Decker scanned the drawings as they turned. Marshall

Street, longitudinal and lateral views. Brighton Station. Mohawk Corner. Finally, Race.

"Hold it there," Decker said.

The page showed a longitudinal cutaway of the big double staircase leading down to the subway platform, and below it the track well and rail supports.

Decker shook his head. "It's not there."

"May I ask what you're looking for?"

"Sewer lines—underneath the station."

"Well, then, let's have a look at the lateral drawings."

Kevin turned the page and gasped. "My God!"

Decker looked at Kevin, who was still staring in horror at the book. "What's the problem?"

"It's been removed! The entire page! Can't you see it?"

Decker saw it. A page stub was sticking out an eighth of an inch or so from the binding. It had been cut cleanly, with a razor or maybe a very sharp pocketknife. The boldness of the tactic was chilling. So was its completeness.

"It's barbaric!" Kevin wailed. He closed the book and pressed both hands down on the cover, applying pressure, it seemed, to stop the bleeding.

"Do you remember who looked at these last?"

Kevin shook his head in disbelief. "But they were *never* out of my sight. Not for a second. *Never* . . ."

A second later he did a double-take, slapping his palm against his forehead. His voice dropped an octave or two. "Oh, my. Oh, dear. Now I remember. How could I have been so stupid?"

"Tell me."

"He asked for a magnifying glass. I went away, and he . . ."

"Who's he?"

"Good Lord, I don't know. He was big. He had muscles. He was young—and nice. I remember he was very, very polite. For some reason, he kept calling me 'sir.' "

"About how old?"

"Oh, young. Very young. I'd say under twenty-five. He looked like a football player. You know, the thick neck. Blond curls. The rattail down the back. He was handsome, really—in an homogenous sort of way."

"Homogenous?"

"Well, you know. Rather common."

Decker had his notebook out. "Did you get his name?"

"No, why would I?"

Decker let it go. "Do you remember what day it was?"

Kevin bit his lower lip, closed his eyes. "Oh, God, let's see. It must have been a week ago . . . Monday. Yes, that would be it. I only work the blueprints on Mondays, Wednesdays. And I'm almost certain it was early in the week."

"All right," Decker said. "Let's look at the register."

They crossed the room to the reception desk, where the plump woman was ensconced behind her phone equipment. Decker checked the calendar on his wristwatch and did some quick figuring. "Last Monday would have been the sixteenth, I think."

"Fifteenth," the receptionist corrected.

Decker leaned over the register as Kevin flipped back through several dozen pages of signed visitors. A surprising number, Decker thought, in just a week's time.

"Here we are," Kevin said, tracking his index finger halfway down the page. "The fifteenth begins here."

"Was it morning or afternoon?" Decker asked.

Kevin stood straight and took a deep breath. "Oh, dear. It didn't seem early *or* late."

"Around lunch then?"

"I never eat lunch."

"Good for you," Decker said.

"Let's see." Kevin went on thinking. "It might have been around one, I think. Beverly had just come back from lunch." He spoke to the woman at the desk. "Juanita, when does Bev usually go to lunch?"

"I'd say about one most days."

133

Kevin's finger started at the one o'clock listings and tracked down. More than half the names were affiliated with one of the local colleges—UC, Xavier, Mount St. Joe. Some listed major corporations like P&G. A few wrote in the names of law firms. But everyone had put down something that day.

Decker realized now it was a long shot. "The guy probably used a phony name and lied about his credentials."

Kevin looked up from the register, his mouth and eyes forming little *O*'s. Apparently the possibility of such fiendishness had never occurred to him. "Do you think so?"

Decker nodded, but started to jot down names and affiliations anyway. There were more than a dozen registered between one thirty and two. "It's still worth a quick phone check," Decker said.

"For a phony name?"

"Better than no name at all."

12

"Darrell Andersen—with an *e*," Decker said, handing his list over to Stein. "It was the only name that didn't check out. I called Xavier PR, they never heard of the guy."

"Andersen" had filled in "Xavier U." next to his name in the Historical Society guest register.

Stein was in Decker's straight-back chair, leaning back on its hind legs, looking calm and self-contained as usual. "You checked the phone book and the crisscross?"

"Yes. No Darrell Andersen—at least not with an *e.*"

"Could he have anything to do with Ted Andersen?" Stein asked.

"As in Ted Andersen, president of Crown Pointe Development?" Decker laughed at first, then saw Stein was quite serious. He was about to launch into one of his discourses on human behavior.

"Okay, Barry, let's have it."

"All right, try this one on. Imagine that a certain party has hired you to pilfer the blueprint in question. You, the pilferer, haven't been inside a public library more than, say, twice in your life—much less the Historical Society. You walk in, you gawk at the card catalogs, the exhibits, the stacks, when sud-

denly the receptionist calls for your attention. 'Sir, you'll need to sign the guest register.' You panic. You know you can't sign your real name, because you're there to steal. So you scribble in your first name, then whatever last name happens to pop into your head. Maybe it's the last name of the man who sent you there in the first place. In this case, maybe it's Ted Andersen."

"But how could anybody be that dumb?"

Stein smiled. "The librarian said he looked like a football player."

"You're serious?"

"Of course."

"You have to admit, Barry, it's pretty farfetched. 'Tireless Teddy' mixing it up with killers?"

Stein shrugged. "We're not talking about knocking over a 7-11 store. We're talking about the fate of a six-hundred-million-dollar project, and maybe the future of downtown commerce."

"But why go through all this trouble?" Decker asked. "I mean, touching off a plague to close down a homeless shelter is like tossing out the baby with the bathwater. Am I right?"

"I don't agree. You underestimate these people. They figure a few bums and winos are wiped out until the crisis is gotten under control. No big deal. In fact, all the better for downtown."

"But what if plague scares people from coming downtown?"

"Maybe. But they know what you and I and every journalist has always known, Rick. When it comes to news, people have the memory of gnats. In six months the whole thing will be history. Trust me."

They spent the next few minutes debating whether an anonymous call to Andersen, asking if he wanted more blueprints, might trigger a reaction. In the end, they decided it was sleazy and wouldn't yield anything printable anyway.

Yet at least one thing was clear now: There *was* a passage

between the tunnel and the shelter. The blueprint, if it hadn't been destroyed, would show it. Decker was sure of it.

"I'm going back into the tunnel this weekend," Decker said. "You want to come along?"

"No, thanks," Stein said. He stood and stretched and pressed his hands against the small of his back. "I think I'll leave the Indiana Jones stuff to you youngsters."

Alone again, Decker tried Janet's automatic pager again and waited. He checked his cigarette pack: only three left, and he'd just bought them on the way to the Historical Society two hours ago. He was determined not to light another; he would handle his stress like a man, confront the situation with Janet head-on. He chewed his nails instead. He was still waiting, and chewing, five minutes later when Farlidge popped into his cubicle carrying a stack of final editions. He flopped one on Decker's lap.

"Nice job," Farlidge said. "But I didn't expect Angie to get the byline."

"Why not? She wrote the story," Decker said.

Farlidge broke into his best malicious grin, probably the one he saved for sending back wines in fancy restaurants. "Are you saying you can be replaced by a copy clerk?"

"Better a copy clerk than a robot, Ron."

Farlidge stopped smiling and moved on. After a quick glance at the front page, Decker went running after him.

"Ron, what happened to our story?"

Farlidge tossed a paper on the neighboring desk and kept moving. There were two dozen cubicles in the room. "It's right there on A-1."

"But it's buried on the bottom, Ron. It won't show in the street boxes!"

"Correct. There's enough paranoia in the streets already. It was Sally Beth's decision."

"But dammit, Ron, we had it first! An exclusive!"

"Ask Sally Beth," he said calmly.

"Right—and have it go in one ear and out the other while she sits there and smiles like a lobotomy case."

Decker cut his tirade short when his phone rang. He ran for his desk. Three rings, four rings . . .

"Hello, Rick Decker . . ."

Dead. He slammed down the receiver, punched Janet's pager number again, hung up, and waited. Farlidge popped his head in.

"I might as well tell you now. I've got some more news from Sally Beth you won't like."

Decker stared at his phone, hating it for not ringing. He felt mad enough to break something. "Just say it, Ron."

"She wants to know if this latest body will cause any problems for the Cody Blair film. They're supposed to have a shoot this evening on the riverfront."

"You're kidding?"

But Farlidge was already gone.

Decker picked up the trash can next to his desk and threw it. He watched it sail out into the newsroom, where it struck with a dull thud against the nearest partition, spilling the output of his working life—half-filled coffee cups, flattened burger boxes, piles of cigarette butts.

Should he walk out now and admit defeat? Or go on beating his head against a wall?

His next emotion, he knew, would be self-pity. But he was saved from that when he spotted Angie through the front glass of his cubicle. She was almost skipping up the hallway. He smiled and she flashed him the victory/peace sign. In a moment she was sitting in his straight-back chair, too excited and full of news to notice the disgorged wastebasket across the aisle.

"Guess who I just found at the bus station?" She crossed her legs, tugged at her miniskirt. She was wearing bright-red lipstick.

"Let me think—Elvis?"

"No, geek. Try again."

Decker reached for a cigarette from the pack on his desk. His hand, he noticed, was trembling. "You found another woman who says she rode the bus with the Indian."

"Better—I found the driver." Angie's green eyes sparkled. Decker felt the old news rush.

"Good job, Ace." He was putting less sarcasm into the "Ace" all the time.

"Piece a cake. I just waited until the bus from Nashville came in, then waylaid the driver in the cafeteria. The hardest part was hanging out at the bus station for two hours. Tell me, why do they always smell like stale broccoli farts?"

"Like what?" He grappled and let it drop. "Never mind."

"And the *people* you see there—it's like *Night of the Living Dead*, you know. A way station to hell or something . . ."

"So you hooked up with the driver in the cafeteria. What did he have to say?"

"Not much. He thought one of his supervisors might be watching."

"Damn. What about the Indian? Did you at least ask if the Indian was on his bus?"

"Chill out, Rickie boy. He said he'd meet with us."

"Good. Where?"

"At *le Fausto's gourmet restaurante*. In about ten."

It was the post-lunch-hour lull when Angie and Decker walked into Fausto's. The place smelled of burnt grease, but the booths were empty and the tabletops clean. Fausto was behind the counter tidying up his old-fashioned coffee machine. Decker and Angie took the booth farthest from the door and the noisy air conditioner, with Angie sitting where she could watch for the driver.

Fausto was in a foul mood. Decker guessed he was still feeling guilty about giving Gertie the boot. He should. He came over to their booth and, without smiling or saying a word, held up his check pad to signal he was taking orders.

"Coffee is all," Decker said.

"Decaf for me," Angie piped in. Fausto gave her a distrustful look and walked away.

Decker and Angie went over their list of questions together and agreed that Angie should do most of the talking since she'd made the initial contact. They were on their second coffees when Decker expressed his doubts that the driver would show.

"Don't be so antsy, Rick. The guy promised he'd be here. I think he wants to get things off his chest."

Decker resented the wasted time, especially away from his phone. What if Janet called? What if more bodies turned up? Besides, he still had to bang out his update on the Cody Blair shoot. Which reminded him: He'd forgotten to call the film's unit publicist, Thea Swanson, before he left the newsroom. She was impossible to reach in the afternoons.

He decided to settle his nerves with a slice of Mama Fausto's homemade cheesecake. He was signaling Fausto with his order when Angie burst out, "Here he comes."

Decker turned and saw a bowling ball of a man in a gray uniform step through the door and take off his cap. There was a crescent of sweat on his stretched-out shirt just above his belly button. He seemed a little spooked until he spotted Angie, and then his eyes lit up and he rolled over to the booth.

"Clem Thompson," Angie said. "This is Rick Decker, another reporter from the *Eagle*. I hope you don't mind if he sits in."

"It takes two of ya, huh?" Clem said. He seemed a jovial guy. "I must be a mighty important guy."

Decker stood and they shook hands. Clem's grip was pudgy and moist, like having your fingers squeezed between a couple of wet sponges. He seemed about fifty, but his hair was thinning and completely white, even his eyebrows. He was smiling self-consciously, as if he weren't quite sure what was expected of him.

Angie motioned him to sit next to her, and Decker scootched back into his corner, thinking it would be more comfortable for Clem if they weren't sitting eyeball-to-eyeball.

Fausto came over with his pad again, and Clem shook his head and waved him away.

"I can't stay long," he said, setting his driver's cap on the table. He looked at his watch. "I pick up the Dee-troit leg at three-o-five, and the passengers, you know, get all fired up if you're not there right on the dot."

It was almost 2:40. "All we need is a few minutes of your time," Decker said. "Have you been reading about the body they found at the shelter here?"

"You mean the old Indian fella? 'Course I have. Saddest damn thing. Somehow I just knew that old guy was in trouble the minute I seen him." Clem looked with soulful eyes at Angie, who was nodding sympathetically in her corner. "You know how you can just tell sometimes with people? They got this look in their eye, you know, like they're being hunted or something."

"Did he seem sick to you?" Decker asked. He drew a stare from Angie for hogging the questions. Clem turned his attention back to Decker.

"No. Not at all. That's what surprised me so when I seen the stories. Boo-bonic plague. Hell, I thought that was only somethin' you read about in the history books. He just seemed a little scared is all."

This time Angie broke in. "About what?"

"I don't rightly know. It was like he was lost or somethin'. I don't think he'd ever been East before."

"Why not?" Angie asked.

"Well, for one thing, he told me he'd never seen blue mountains before."

"Blue mountains?" Decker said. "Was he drunk?"

"Not a bit, as far as I could tell. He was very dignified. You

141

could tell he was somebody important—to his people, I mean. That's why I started calling him chief. Anyway, we were coming up 75 through Tennessee, just on the west edge of the Smokies, and he all of a sudden says in this deep voice of his, 'You have blue mountains here. Very pretty.' I guess if you never seen the Smokies before, they'd look mighty blue. Specially in the mornin' hours."

Clem spread his fingers on the table. A gold wedding band was nestled in the white hair between the knuckles.

"Did he say where he was coming from?" Decker asked. He and Angie were both poised now over their notebooks.

"No, but I seen his ticket. He originated in Flagstaff."

"Texas?" Angie asked. Decker clenched his teeth.

Clem smiled. "I believe that's in Arizona, honey." Clem seemed to be quite taken with Angie, in a fatherly way.

"Did he mention why he was coming here?" Decker asked.

"That's why I decided to come and talk to you folks. You see, the old fella didn't say much, but he kept pullin' this letter out of his bag. I done told the Health Department people, but they don't seem to care much. They say they didn't find no letter on the man's body. . . ."

"The sack—was it like a gunnysack? A burlap one?" Decker recalled Floyd's description of the sack he'd found in the tunnel.

"That's right. He kept all his belongings in it. Never let it out of his sight."

"Go on, Clem," Angie said, shooting Decker another hard glance. "Tell us about the letter."

"It was a funny kind of letter. It was typed and . . ."

"He let you read it?" Decker asked. He caught the look from Angie again. "Sorry," he said. "Go on."

"Don't apologize. I just take a little time to wind up, is all. The answer is, yes, he did—after I asked to take a look. I thought maybe I could help. Like I said, he seemed lost and a little out of it."

"Like maybe crazy?" Angie asked.

142

"No, not crazy. In a little bit of a daze, I guess. I thought maybe if he was supposed to meet somebody in town, I could help him get there. But, see, here's the really funny thing. That letter had no date on it, and no address or addressee. Why, it weren't even signed."

Decker and Angie looked at each other. "Do you remember what it said?" Decker asked.

"Not a whole lot. Except there was something about a woman being real sick and needing help—a woman with an Indian name like Little Bear, or maybe Little Beaver, I can't recall exactly—and he should come quick. Now I do remember this part: They wanted him to come do something called 'The Mountain Way.' That's it, exactly—'The Mountain Way.' "

"Is that like a ritual or something?" Angie asked.

"I don't rightly know. But that's what it said."

"How did the Indian know who to contact here?" Decker asked.

"There was a phone number, written in pencil down near the bottom, but I can't remember it."

"Was it a Cincinnati number?" Decker asked.

"I couldn't even tell you that. I was reading the dang thing while I was driving."

Angie looked at her watch. "It's almost three, Clem."

"Oh, damn. I got to talking to you folks and plumb forgot."

"Can I get your age and the spelling of your name?" Decker asked.

"You ain't going to quote me in the papers, are you?"

"We can't use anonymous sources, Mr. Thompson. Angie should have told you that."

"But I'll lose my job for sure. The higher-ups don't want nobody talking 'bout this."

There was such genuine fright in the man's eyes that Decker quit pushing. "We'll keep your name out of it. Thanks for your help anyway."

"I just hope you two can find out what happened to that old

143

man. Ain't nobody deserves to die like that. Like some dog in the gutter. Especially an old man got that much pride. It's a damn shame."

Decker and Angie thanked him and Clem picked up his cap and rolled on his way. They stayed behind awhile to compare notes.

"Hey, we've got a name to go on now—Little Bear," Angie said. "Ain't that terrif?"

"Unless the name's Little Beaver, or maybe Little Muskrat. The guy didn't sound real sure of himself."

Angie smiled. "We can always look in the phone book."

"Har-dee-har. There *are* places we can check, though. There ought to be some kind of Native American group around, even in this town. An American Indian Movement chapter or something."

Decker made a note of it, then remembered something that was bothering him. "Did you see the final by any chance?"

"Yep," Angie said, stuffing her notebook back into her bag. She sat straight and let her head fall back against the top of the booth, showing off the smooth white flow of her neck. She looked contented, almost sleepy as she peered down her nose and smiled. "I figured that's why you booted your trash can."

"Tossed it," he said. "Kicking's not polite."

They both laughed, and then Angie leaned forward, holding her pixieish chin in one hand, setting the other hand near his. There was a mix of daring and vulnerability in her eyes. "How 'bout a drink together after work?"

Decker took a moment to collect his thoughts. He must have been staring. Angie retreated, turned her head.

"Sure," he said, "why not?" Her eyes came around again, sparkling this time.

"Yeah, why not?"

"Arnold's?" Decker suggested. "Say around eight?"

"Groovy."

* * *

Back in the newsroom, Decker called the Museum of Natural History and talked to an anthropologist named Bob Quigley, who gave him a number for the Ohio Valley Council for Native Americans. "It's the only Native American group in town, as far as I know," he said. "The director's name is Ray Feathers. He's feisty and outspoken, but I think he'll talk to you. Use my name if you'd like."

Decker called the number and got a recorded message, complete with Indian chant and drums in the background. He left his name and number at the *Eagle* and said he needed the council's help in locating a certain Native American woman.

In the meantime Decker called the production office for *Young Obsession* and, in a stroke of luck, Thea Swanson picked up the normally busy line. She was a woman of few words. Yes, she said, filming would continue in Cincinnati, although the director was canceling a boating scene he'd planned for the riverfront. . . . No, it had nothing to do with plague; the river level was too low. . . . Yes, Ms. Blair was on her way back to LA, having finished all her work here. . . . No, her sudden departure had absolutely nothing to do with all this plague stuff.

Decker banged in a quick story complete with phony denials, called Thea again to find out a departure date for the director and crew, added it to his story, then tried the number again for the Indian council. This time he got a real speaking person—Ray Feathers himself.

Decker dropped Bob Quigley's name and explained that he was trying to contact an Indian woman in the area, possibly named Little Bear.

Feathers spoke in the soft, halting accent of many Native Americans. His voice was almost inflectionless. "Any special reason you want to talk to this lady?"

Decker answered that she might know something about the Indian who died of plague here.

"I see," Feathers said. "You are talking about the dead Navaho who got this whole town in an uproar. Tell me, Mr.

Decker. Why is it hundreds of Native Americans die of malnutrition, poverty, and disease on reservations every day, and no one cares. But let just one die here in the middle of the city, and suddenly it's a national crisis."

"I don't know, Mr. Feathers. But I thought you might help. If we knew the man's identity, maybe we could find out why this horrible thing happened to him."

"How would I know the answers, Mr. Decker? I don't even know this Navaho woman you speak of. The way the papers and the radio people talk, they make it sound like all Native Americans are unclean people, that we spread diseases. Our council finds this whole incident a slap in the face of Native Americans."

Decker tried to get things off the political track. "What you're saying may be true, Mr. Feathers. But what I'm trying to find out is why this man left his reservation."

"Does a Navaho need permission to leave his reservation?"

Decker put his hand over the phone and groaned. Calm again, he said, "No, Mr. Feathers. But I've been told that an Indian, especially of this man's age, would not leave his home lightly. That he would consider his homeland to be sacred ground."

"Sure, every Navaho has his sacred place. But that does not mean he cannot take it with him."

"What do you mean?"

"I mean he can take the sacred land anywhere inside his head. All he needs is his memory of that land to call up the Great Spirit."

"I'll get to the point, Mr. Feathers. We have reason to believe the man traveled here to help a Navaho woman named Little Bear. Does that name mean anything to you?"

"Do you know this person's Anglo name?"

"I'm not sure what you're asking."

"Little Bear is this woman's Navaho name. Only her family and her closest friends would know her by that name. Everybody else would know her by her Anglo name."

146

"I'm sorry. All I have to go on is Little Bear. Is there any way you could ask around?"

"I can, but I don't think it would help, Mr. Decker. There are two or three hundred members in our organization, but only three Navaho. Only one I know is a woman, and her name is Roberta. She is an old woman. I am sorry. I cannot help you in this."

"Do you have a phone number for this Roberta?"

"No, I don't think you should bother her. She only came here to be with her son, who has a good position with the Air Force in Dayton."

"Could there be other Navahos in town you don't know about?"

"It's not likely, Mr. Decker. Our organization is a way for Native Americans to get help when they settle in this area. If there are Navaho around, they would contact us. We are the only place where their values and their customs would be cherished."

Decker thanked the man and left his number, just in case.

"Yes, Mr. Decker. I will help if I can."

Decker doubted it.

13

Arnold's was the closest thing in town to that high-water mark of Western civilization—the English pub. The place was dark and dingy but comfortable, with a bar just right for leaning on and a brass footrail that didn't glitter. Ceiling fans prodded the cozy gloom. There was Guinness on tap, along with the local brews, Hudepohl, Oldenburg, and Christian Moerlein. On almost any night there was a chance for interesting conversation, given the clientele of artists, would-be artists, and the city's dwindling core of young Democrats and aging hippies. What more could a person want, except maybe a golden retriever hunkered down on the floor somewhere. But the health laws didn't allow for that.

Decker arrived about ten minutes early and took up his station near the center of the bar, next to the beer tap and glass strainer. In the days before Janet, Decker had practically lived at Arnold's, insisting one drunken night that, upon his death, Jack the bartender arrange to have his ashes placed in a Moerlein bottle above the whiskey shelf. Jack nodded and said, "We'll toast your health every night."

The bar was surprisingly empty for a Thursday night—a victim of the heat and drought and the owner's long-standing antipathy to air conditioning. Decker doubted it was part of the plague scare; Arnold's patrons were more savvy than that. At one end of the bar a couple of regulars were gathered around an old transistor radio, listening to the first inning of a Reds game. At the other end was Riley, a middle-aged Irishman Decker had listened to long enough one night to learn he'd left his family and advertising job a number of years ago in order to paint and live on welfare. He was sipping coffee and eyeing potential victims for one of his lectures on mysticism and art.

Jack was on duty that night. He moved up and down the bar in his slow yet efficient way, seeming to stop almost by accident in front of Decker, where he started swiping a wet gray towel over the bartop. Jack looked more like a refugee from a sixties garage band than a bartender. He had long hair that straggled over the ears, thick Buddy Holly eyeglasses, and an eternally youthful, unlined face. He spoke the way he moved—in a kind of lazy, half-ironic monotone.

"Well. Long time no see. How's the reporting biz?"

"More of a business every day."

"You don't say." Jack smiled just a little. Stress had no place in Jack's emotional lexicon. He supplied a respectful pause, then asked, "What's your pleasure tonight?"

"Something serious. I'm in a serious mood tonight, Jack."

"In that case, may I suggest a perfect Manhattan. Straight up."

"Sounds pretty serious to me."

Jack made the best in town—rye, a touch of sweet and dry vermouth, shaken through ice and poured to the very brim of a long-stem glass. Instead of the usual cherry, he plunked in a twist of lemon and slid the glass in front of Decker, careful not to spill any of its pale gold contents.

"You should have been here last night," Jack said in his low-key voice. He might have been joking. "Big excitement."

"No kidding? Did somebody drop dead from plague?"

"Nah. Nothin' that exciting. But we did have a celebrity in here. That movie actress in town—Cody what's-her-name."

149

Decker nearly choked on his drink. "Jack, why in hell didn't you call me? I've been trying to track her down for weeks."

"I know," Jack said. "I read the papers." A young waitress in baggy cotton shorts and a white sleeveless T-shirt came to the bar, pressing her wrist against a damp forehead. She asked for a half and half—half Guinness, half Hudepohl. Jack nabbed one of the pint glasses from the strainer, flipped it right-side up in one hand and put it under the tap.

Decker was still upset. "Jack, I thought you and I were buddies."

"We are. I just like to respect a person's privacy, that's all. But I will let you in on something . . ." He handed the foaming glass to the waitress, took her money, and turned again to Decker. "She may be back again tonight, probably late. She's been in two nights in a row to hear Katie." Katie Laur was the house jazz singer, a good ol' Tennessee gal with a soft, bluesy voice and a swinging backup band.

"I doubt it," Decker said. "Her publicist says she's gone back to La-la-land."

"Well, sorry to hear that."

Decker lit a cigarette and hunched over his drink. He alternately puffed and sipped, taking his time at it as he turned over the crazy events of the day. The poor bastard on the riverfront. The botched date with Janet. The deadine panic. The interview with Clem Thompson. And all the calls to Janet, three or four at least—none returned. That was something new. She'd never been that petty before, not even after their worst fights. Janet jealous? That wasn't the Janet he knew, or at least thought he knew. But then hell hath no fury . . .

He ordered another drink.

Decker wondered sometimes if he was an alcoholic. He'd read enough of the pop literature on the topic to know he might fit one of the definitions. No, he didn't need it all the time, but there were times like these when alcohol seemed to unclutter his mind, loosen the knot between his eyes. Not that it took that much. By the end of his second Manhattan, most of the day had been erased. He was ready to start fresh—all hope sprung eternal again. In the right mood and with the right company a third or a fourth would make him buoyant, confident, in love with the whole goddamn world. If he was a drunk—well, then, at least, by God, he wasn't a maudlin one.

He was pretty far into his buoyant phase when Angie arrived, about twenty minutes late. He almost didn't recognize her. She had moussed her short red hair into a spiky, high-fashion look, and slipped into a bright green minidress—the strapless kind that clings to the torso like one long tube top. The men listening to the game snapped to as she strutted up to the bar, her tight frame perched on red heels. Even Jack raised his brows.

She moved in close to Decker and executed a quick half pirouette that ended with her back and bare shoulders arched over the bar. Then she tossed her head back in the dramatic way of old movies and said, "Dahling, at last we meet again."

There was laughter and a groan from the boys at the end of the bar. Jack sort of shook his head.

Decker applauded. "Lauren Bacall, right? *To Have and Have Not.*"

"No, dahling. Bette Davis. *All About Eve.*" Angie smiled once to her larger audience, then turned again and folded her arms on the bar next to Decker's, close enough to touch elbows. Decker shifted away.

"What would you like to drink?"

Angie had one foot up on the rail, swaying her hips back and forth just a little. Her spring was set at pelvic level and wound pretty tight. "Ohhhh, how 'bout something in a Scotch."

"Scotch and soda?"

"No, make it neat. With an ice cube or two. Just like the Dewar's ads."

Decker signaled for Jack. "The lady would like a Dewar's on the rocks."

"Two rocks," she said, holding up two fingers. "In a heavy-ish tumbler, please."

"A heavyish tumbler," Jack repeated. He clasped his hands below his chest, a priest about to launch into a sermon. He grinned at Angie. "Uh, hate to ask, but do you have an ID with you?"

Angie seemed startled at first, but quickly recovered. "It must be the hair," she said. "I've been legal practically all my life." She snapped open her small red purse, rooted among keys and makeup, and finally produced a laminated card with a wide-eyed mug shot. She handed it to Jack.

Jack looked at the card, looked at her. "Quite a difference."

"That was taken prior to my glamour phase," she said.

"So—twenty-two," Jack said, returning the card. He gave Decker a sly, sidelong glance. Decker scowled back.

They took their drinks to a small table nestled underneath the back stairway. They were just getting settled when Katie's band struck up "Bye Bye Blackbird" out in the courtyard. It came to them with a distant echoey sound.

Decker stared off toward the kitchen, Angie the front door. An awkward silence ensued. Decker wasn't sure what the point of their meeting was, especially the way Angie was decked out. She reminded him of a little girl playing dress up, trying to impress Daddy. He was more irritated than flattered.

"So . . ." Angie said finally, fingering her glass, "we're having a drink."

"Yep," Decker said. "I guess we are."

He downed the rest of his and signaled Jack for another. His third. Or was it his fourth? He plucked the lemon twist from the bottom of his empty glass and started nibbling on the end. The booze had made it soft and sweet.

Angie tried to put things on their old footing. "So what's next in our plague saga?"

Decker relaxed a little. "I'm still waiting to hear from Wolters about the syringe. Meanwhile, one of us, I would think, should head out to Flagstaff and sniff around."

"Why not both of us?"

"We'll be lucky if the cheap bastards send one."

Angie let out a small "oh" and looked past Decker to the front door again.

He hadn't meant to be cutting, but for some reason, Angie brought out that part of him. The mean big brother. "Come on. Let's go listen to the music," he said. He was already standing, feeling a little wobbly in the knees.

The courtyard at Arnold's was an airshaft, really, where the surrounding brick kept the air cool and musty-smelling at night. Candles flickered atop lawn tables. A black walnut tree, the result of some crazed squirrel's winter preparations, rose dead center from the cracked cement, its branches prematurely bare. Party lights had been strung from the tree to a covered wooden stage in the corner, where Katie and her band were playing.

Decker and Angie sat under the tree, one table away from where Decker remembered having his last drink with Turk. Katie was singing "All of Me" in a way that was bouncy and sad at the same time. She sat in front of the stage on a small folding chair, legs crossed, smiling and searching out the faces in the sparse audience. The night was still early.

Angie leaned forward, hugged her arms on the table, scrunched her shoulders. She was all angles and dewy flow of skin. She was young. "You know, I've been thinking."

"That could be dangerous."

"Seriously, about the car Floyd said he saw at the tunnel."

"The Lincoln."

"Yeah. With the little opera window in back. I was wondering, how hard would it be to find a car like that?"

Decker stuck out his lower lip. "Oh, I'd say there are probably only a couple thousand in the area." He did it again—another dig—but Angie didn't seem to notice.

"But what if we called Murdock and every partner in Crown Pointe and asked what kind of car they drove?"

"Just call and ask point-blank?"

"No, wait," she said, straightening up. "We could pretend we're from a Lincoln dealership and there's been a recall."

The idea was starting to sound less crazy, but even so. "All right, so we establish that one of these men has a Lincoln like the one Floyd saw at the tunnel. Then what? What does it prove?"

Angie leaned in close, whispered. "We *follow* them."

"You've been watching too many cop shows."

"Well, it was just an idea."

Decker moved his chair a quarter turn to the left, for a better view of Katie and the band. They were starting to catch stride now, with the saxophonist wailing some wild licks that caught even Katie by surprise and made her laugh from the pure spontaneity of it. Decker was laughing, too, when Angie tapped him on the shoulder.

"Don't look now, but we've got, like, big-time company."

Filling the doorway to the courtyard was Derek Jameson, the Bengals star quarterback, and clinging to his waist, some young, chic thing in Raybans. Her hair was cut exactly like Angie's.

Decker leaned over to Angie. "Derek at Arnold's instead of a disco? He must have pulled a groin muscle."

Angie smiled. "Yes, but look who's with him."

Decker watched the couple as they settled into a corner table by the entry, all cozy and alone in the shadows. The girl was dressed chic-casual and all in black—black blouse, black trousers, black slippers. Derek couldn't have been more attentive. He cradled the table candle in his hands while she lit a cigarette.

"So who is she? A karate expert or something?"

"No, you dummy. It's Cody Blair."

The words hit Decker like a one-two punch. "Come on. You're kidding. Cody has long hair."

"It's her 'new' look. Don't you read *People* magazine?"

Decker was gawking now. He recognized the doll baby face, the bee-stung lips. "My God, she really does exist. I honest to

God don't believe it. There really is a Cody Blair—right here in River City."

Decker took another look at Angie's hair and grinned.

"Don't say it. It was my hairdresser's idea."

Decker turned his attention back to Derek and Cody. Surely it was a match made in image heaven. The tall, dark, handsome quarterback, featured in national TV ads for a popular breath mint, and the rising Hollywood starlet, whose pouty face had become a magazine cover cliché.

"What the hell do they talk about?" Decker said.

Angie smiled. "Who needs talk?"

"But, my God, she's only seventeen. He's old enough . . ."

"To be her older brother," Angie finished. "You're just jealous, Rick, admit it."

"Bull."

Decker continued watching from the corner of his eye as Derek got up from the table. The two were looking soulfully into each other's eyes as Derek let Cody's hand slip out of his.

"He's leaving," Decker whispered. "This is my chance." He sprang to his feet and wobbled a moment on jelly-filled knees. In the distance Cody's face appeared and disappeared like an apparition, glowing softly in the penumbra of candlelight.

"Rick, where are you going?" Angie whispered fiercely.

"I'm getting an exclusive with the young Miss Blair. Just sit back and watch a pro do his stuff."

"Rick, come back. You're in no condition . . ."

But he couldn't hear her for the pounding in his ears. Destiny called. He was going to do it. By God, come hell or high water, he was going to land an interview with the elusive, glamorous, *People*-magazine-cover-person Cody Blair.

Cody's eyes were fixed on Katie as Decker rolled her way. She looked smaller, frailer than he remembered her in movies. Her neck and cleavage were ghostly white against the open blouse. Her lips were shiny red as vinyl. He wondered for a second if she was real at all.

Suddenly he found himself standing by her table, his lips

moving but not all the words coming out straight. "Excuse, Ms. Cody, but, uh, could we talk?"

She slid the Raybans down her button nose and looked up for just a second. Long enough to communicate a glare that said who-the-hell-are-you. She turned her attention back to Katie.

Decker was trapped. He was too afraid to sit at the table, but too determined to leave. He continued to hover, hands in his pockets, grinning like a fool.

"You see, I'm a reporter here in town, and I've been trying for some time now . . ."

She gave him a withering smile. "Look, geek, I really don't care who you are. I just want you to mind your own business."

"But that's just it," Decker said, lisping some in his overexcitement. "You celebrity-type persons want it both ways. You want your face blown-up in big lights all over the place. In the magazines, movies, the papers, TV. The Big Lie, you know. But then when reporters like me try to break through all that image crap, you start screaming about your privacy. Well, I'm sorry, it just doesn't work—"

Decker didn't get out his next word because an arm wrapped around his neck like a steel coil. His feet were suddenly about two inches off the ground and he was gasping for air.

"No, I'll tell *you* how it's going to work, buddy." The down-home voice was just beside his ear, the breath hot and smelling of Listermint. "You got that?"

Decker nodded, struggling to touch his toes to the ground.

"Good," the voice said. "Now disappear."

The grip loosened, his feet landed, and Decker filled his lungs to bursting. Two big breaths, that's all he needed. One, two—he was ready. He pivoted and took his best roundhouse at Derek's lantern jaw, but was stopped halfway by an explosion in his stomach. He was reeling backward, cut in half, his wind knocked out, his insides collapsing ever inward like a black hole. Just when he was convinced he would never draw breath again, air came roaring back into his lungs.

Decker was down on his hands and knees on the hard cement when a pair of hands cupped his face and lifted. He was staring into the bright green of Angie's midriff. He heard himself panting, croaking.

"That's it," she said, still holding his face. "Just take tiny breaths for a while, okay?"

He was wretched with embarrassment, but too helpless to do anything about it. She helped him to his feet, and the small crowd around them dispersed. As he stood, the muscles in his stomach knotted like rubber bands.

"Come on, baby," she cooed. She took him by the hand. "Enough excitement for one night, huh?"

"One more flight of stairs," she said.

"You're kidding?"

"No, I'm not. Just one more. You can make it."

It was amazing to Decker how a punch in the stomach could leave your legs feeling so weak and useless. His thigh and groin muscles were quivering as he forced himself up the last set of steps to Angie's fifth-floor apartment. She was several steps ahead, not at all self-conscious about the view her miniskirt offered from his lower vantage on the stairwell. They were both sweating from the climb. The air seemed to grow hotter and more stagnant with each ascending floor.

Angie's place was on upper Main Street in Over-the-Rhine, the top floor of a tired gray brick building, tucked between a discount furniture store and a bar with rotting plywood nailed over the windows. It was one of the first, and last, buildings in the neighborhood targeted for renovation—an outpost in a yuppie invasion that never followed. Strider had seen to that: If the poor couldn't have the neighborhood, then no one would.

The owner had brought the plumbing and electrical up to

code, slapped some paint on the inside walls, and left it at that. But the rent was just right for a young reporter fresh out of college—$200 a month, plus utilities.

"Promise you won't look at the mess," Angie said. She turned the dead bolt and applied a shoulder to the door. It unstuck with a reverberating twang.

Decker looked inside. "A loft," he said, mildly surprised. You didn't find many in River City.

"Cozy, huh?"

It was wide open with bare wood floors. A futon with un-made sheets lay in a corner by a front window, clothes and books piled all around. Hanging from the ceiling, a metal pipe served as closet and clothes hanger. The bathroom was at the back of the room to the left, behind a burlap-covered screen. The "kitchen" was opposite on the right—a rusting refrigerator flanked by a low sink and a TV cart for holding a toaster oven and a hot plate. In the very middle of the room was a tiny CD player and two small speakers—the only concessions to the consumer electronics age.

He looked around, struck by the lonely sparseness of the room; it brought back his own first apartment—just a place to crash at night.

A row of stand-up mirrors was propped against the left wall.

"You dance," Decker said matter-of-factly.

"Gee, how'd you guess?" she said. She opened the one small window in the back, then hurried across the room and threw open the three larger windows in the front. Warm night air rushed into the room, bringing with it the city sounds of distant sirens, muffled traffic.

"Would you like something to drink?" She was bustling toward the refrigerator. The high heels worked like hammers on the loose wood.

"Just a soda."

"Soda? Are you sure?" Her head was down in the refrigerator, her well-formed behind in prominent display. He looked away.

"Sure I'm sure." What he wasn't sure of was why he was there, alone with Angie in her apartment—except that he was too potted to drive, and he didn't feel up to being by himself.

"Tell you what," she said, kicking off one, then the other shoe in the direction of the futon. "Why don't you go on up to the roof and check out the view. It's a lot cooler there. I'll be right up." She pointed to a straight ladder next to the door.

"There's a hatch right above the ladder. Just snap the hook and push it open." She reached for the zipper behind her dress, and Decker decided he'd better get going.

The ladder was loose and wobbly. He took one slow step at a time and felt safer once he'd popped open the hatch and could lay his hands flat on the roof. He lifted one knee up, then the other, until he was on all fours on the hot, scratchy tarpaper.

When he stood, it was like breaking through to another world. There was an enormous black dome of sky above, complete with half-crescent moon, and canyons of dimly lit streets in every direction below. A warm, husky breeze blew up from the shadows of the back yards and alley behind. It nuzzled against his trouser legs like a cat.

The roof was pitched downward toward the alley, and with careful half steps, Decker made his way to a wide strip of foam rubber Angie had apparently laid down for sunbathing. By the time he reached it and sat down, Angie was climbing up through the hatch. She had changed into an oversized T-shirt that stopped short of her knees, and a pair of flipflops. She was carrying a bottle of champagne by the neck and two plastic champagne glasses.

"I distinctly remember asking for soda," Decker said.

"Same thing." She smiled. "They both have bubbles." She handed Decker the unopened bottle. "You do the honors. Just don't hit any low-flying aircraft."

Decker coaxed the plastic cork with his two thumbs and sent it sailing over the back fence as Angie shouted, "Watch out be-e-e-l-o-o-o-oow!"

"You're the one that should be drinking soda," he said, pouring her the first glass. She sat next to him on the foam rubber, her legs in the lotus position and her hand in her lap to hold the T-shirt in place.

They tapped glasses, plastic to plastic. "To us," Angie said. "The best damn reporting team in town."

Decker assented. "A pair of aces."

At night Over-the-Rhine reclaimed some of its charm. The jagged silhouettes of brick chimneys and uneven rooftops stretched as far as the eye could see. It was grand as long as you didn't look too closely, didn't count the number of abandoned and burned-out buildings, their windows black and empty as skull sockets.

A hundred years ago, on a warm summer night, the streets would have been throbbing with the sounds of beer halls, oompah bands, the rowdy good times of the city's hard-working, hard-playing German immigrants. Now all you heard was the empty hum of vapor lamps, the swoosh of downtown traffic.

Angie took a deep, measured breath, let it out. "You know," she sighed, "I get so much energy when I'm up here. It's like . . . it's like I'm getting this clear-channel reception from the cosmos. Nothing out there to block the vibrations."

"Nothing but polluted air," Decker said.

"Pessimist," she said.

"Pollyana," he replied.

She laughed and raised her glass. "Truce?"

"For now."

They touched glasses again and drank. Far to the west, lit bright as day, Music Hall loomed above the rooftops, its rose window keeping watch over the city like the eye of God.

Angie threw her head back and purred, "Don't you just love it up here?" She uncoiled and lay back on the foam, hands behind her head, feet crossed. She found Decker's hand and gave it a small squeeze. "Why don't you relax? I'm not going to attack you."

"Promise?"

"Maiden's honor."

"Hoo boy."

She let go of his hand, and he settled on his back by her side. Their elbows touched; no matter. The warm breeze played across his body, and the moon, directly above them, was a half-opened lid in a starless sky. Decker stared into its pale, translucent glow. It was eerie. For a moment he imagined he could see through the moon and into some cold, bright dimension beyond. Suddenly the alcohol took hold, and he was seized by a sense of falling—falling upward toward that hole in the sky. He snapped his head up and found the safety of the horizon again. He felt woozy.

"What's the matter?" Angie asked.

"Nothing. I just drank too much."

"Well, feel free to throw up on the roof. Everybody in the neighborhood does."

"Thanks."

Decker settled back again, closed his eyes. Angie took his hand again and began to smooth her fingers over it.

"Angie," he said, annoyed.

"What are you afraid of?" she said.

"I've got someone."

"You do?" she said, still stroking his hand. "Where?"

"Angie, you know what I mean."

"No, I don't know what you mean." There wasn't a trace of irony in her voice.

She leaned over and kissed him, lightly at first, her tongue prying playfully at his closed lips. He opened his eyes and saw the half-moon appear above her head and felt himself falling again. He closed his eyes. She pressed her mouth against his, determined; he kissed back, hard, almost in retaliation, and found himself thinking how different she tasted—hot, sharply spiced, quick to clear the palate. So unlike Janet's slow perfume. He was thinking he would stop and tell Angie that. Tell her how you could taste the essence of someone in a kiss. But in the next instant she was on top of him, her knees gripping his waist, her heat against his, and his heart started beating so fast he lost the words.

14

It was pouring at 6:30 A.M. when Decker pulled up in front of his house on Butler Street. He walked from the car, letting himself get soaked, and stood for a moment dripping on the porch. He didn't shiver. It was a warm, enveloping rain, a miracle after the weeks of drought. It came down in sheets, rattling the dry leaves in the treetops, stroking and swirling the surface of the river, prodding it to move again. Decker watched and felt something like absolution seep into his aching skull. He reached for the cigarettes inside his jacket. Soaked, limp. He crushed the pack in his hand and stuffed the soft, damp wad into his pocket.

He listened again. Something in the rhythm of the rain. A hissing. A chant.

He started crying for no apparent reason, and that's when he told himself he'd start all over again. There had to be a way out of this mess. He was certain of it. Certain until his tongue tasted the perfumed drops pooled above his lip, and the pain stabbed through his head again.

The night with Angie had been all heat and friction, like two pieces of flint striking and sparking at each other. He remembered her body leveraged above his, the imploding intensity of her face, the cinnamon heat of her breath, the muscled light-

163

ness of her movements, as quick and determined as a machine. He had responded in kind, surprising himself with his aggressiveness. The release for both of them was simple, inevitable, and when it was done, they started again, not a word spoken between them, unthinking, uncomplicated. No past. No future. No shame.

But now all three were closing in on him.

He opened the door and stepped inside. The clean, plant-soaked smell of the place was Janet's smell, as real as if she were there. He left his wet shoes by the door, found a hanger in the closet underneath the stairs, and hung his jacket to dry on a corner of the mantelpiece. He went to the kitchen to start a pot of coffee. On the counter, the message light was flashing on the answering machine—ominously, it seemed. He pushed the "play" button, thought better of it, and quickly hit "rewind." He'd wait until he'd cleared the cobwebs first.

When the coffee was finished, he took a clay mug out to the porch and watched the rain again. The morning light was gray and muted in the heavy downpour, and easy on the eyes. He studied the river. It seemed higher already, on the verge, it seemed, of collecting its strength again for the long trek downstream to the Mississippi. A couple of mallards paddled near the shore, their quacks piercing the muffled hiss of rain. Birds everywhere seemed to come to life. Bands of them raced from treetop to treetop, caroming through the downpour, wild, excited.

He went inside and checked on Janet's plant collection in the bay window. The soil was still plenty damp. Then, wondering why he'd killed every plant he ever owned, he went back to the kitchen, poured himself another cup, and sat in the gray light and drank. His sour stomach began to talk. He thought about going upstairs for some Tylenol and Maalox, and to brush his coated teeth, but he couldn't prod himself. He'd had worse hangovers, he told himself. When the time seemed right, he got up and hit the "play" button on the answering machine and sat again.

First, a long ad for a carpet cleaner, followed by an urgent message from Farlidge—a meeting in his office, first thing 8 A.M. ("Try to be on time for a change, okay?") And then what he'd been waiting for with half dread, half anticipation: Janet's voice. She sounded tired, a little hoarse, but trying to be spirited.

"Hello, Rick? Are you there? I know you'd pick up if you were. Oh, well, it's about eleven thirty or so . . . P.M., that is. I'm at my father's. I'm sorry I didn't have a chance to return your calls today. I flew to Denver this afternoon with Dr. Klingshirn and the transplant team. It's been a long day, I guess. We went to Denver to harvest a heart from some poor dumb kid—brain dead from a motorcycle accident—"

The message beep suddenly cut her off; she called again. "Rick, I'm sorry about the way I acted at lunch today. I didn't give you a chance. To be honest, I was surprised to discover how jealous I was. I guess I always thought I was above that, but you never know until . . . Well, anyway, I'm sorry I missed you. I'll try again later." She ended with a whispered, " 'Bye."

He stopped the machine and listened to the blood pounding in his skull. He pressed the play button again. There was a pause, another beep, and then—nothing. Only the pulsing of blank tape. A phantom call.

A thought struck him with the force of a blow—Janet had made the call. Maybe at two or three in the morning, just wanting to talk, and getting no answer. She could put two and two together. Christ. He punched the number for Janet's father. It was one of the emergency numbers listed on a sticker by the phone. Her father answered on the first ring, with a gravelly but pleasant hello. Decker considered hanging up, but stayed on. He asked if Janet was up.

"No, I'm letting her sleep in this morning. Is this Rick?" He sounded downright cheery.

"Yes."

"Well, how the hell are you?" Somehow it seemed a strange question to pose at seven in the morning during a pouring rain.

"Fine, Doctor. I was just hoping I could catch Janet before she went in to work."

"I'll go get her . . ."

"No, no, no. . . . That's fine, Dr. Shoemaker."

"I'm sure she wants to talk to you. . . ."

"No, no, forget it. Let her sleep. I'll try to reach her later in the day."

"You'll have a hard time catching her."

"I know. But don't wake her. Tell her she can try me at work, too."

"You know, if you don't mind an old fool sayin' so, I think you two need to do some talking."

Decker laughed a little, enough to make his head ache. "I know. We will. I just don't want to drag her out of bed."

"Well, okay. Why don't you drop by sometime? I've been brewin' my own beer in the bathtub. Did Janet tell you?"

"No, sir, I . . ."

"My new hobby. Great stuff, too. Has some real body to it. None of this namby-pamby pisswater passes for beer these days."

"I'll take you up on that."

Decker hung up and sat at the kitchen table a little longer, waiting without hope for the throbbing in his head to go away.

He arrived on time for the eight o'clock meeting in Farlidge's office. Stein had called in to say he'd be late that morning, but Angie was already there, looking rested, alert, full of energy. She was dressed in a tie-dyed T-shirt and jeans, sitting slouched in a chair and wobbling her knees back and forth a little. She gave Decker a wink and a smile as he sat down next to her. He smiled back, although it made his scalp hurt.

Farlidge dispatched his orders with unusual alacrity and assertiveness—almost as if they'd been his own ideas. Angie was being sent to Flagstaff that morning to track down the identity of the Indian. Decker was to remain behind and cover

166

whatever developments might emerge. He bristled under the second-string status, but kept his mouth shut. This was Angie's big chance.

Farlidge turned to Decker. Farlidge looked aggressively yuppieish that morning in a freshly starched white shirt and a bright pink tie. "I need you to check on a very interesting report a friend of mine called in last night." He smiled coyly, building the suspense. "It seems there's a budding romance between our own Derek Jameson and the visiting Cody Blair."

Farlidge's gray eyes were lit up as though a Pulitzer hung in the balance. "And that's not all," he said. "My friend informs me the two were spotted at Arnold's last night, and—get this—Derek had to defend her against a crazed, psychopathic fan."

Decker and Angie looked at each other at precisely the same moment. Angie burst into shrill laughter. Decker winced.

"Well?" Farlidge's eyes were darting back and forth between the two.

"Ron," Decker sighed, "the crazed psychopath was me."

"What! You mixed it up with Jameson?"

Decker winced again. There was no need to shout. Angie compressed her lips to keep from laughing again.

Farlidge picked up his Cross pen and tossed it down hard on the desk blotter. "Dammit, Decker, you could have been arrested. Then what? The paper would have been the laughingstock of the town. . . ."

"I was only trying to get an interview, Ron. Per your orders."

"And, dammit, there goes our page one story." Farlidge was really disgusted now. "Sally Beth was all excited."

"I'd hate to see that," Decker said. Angie giggled.

Farlidge sat back and adjusted his tie, in charge again. "All right then, let's get on with things. Angie, you have a plane to catch. Check with Louise on your reservations. Decker, you'll be helping with the rain coverage this morning. I'll see you at your desk."

Angie was still stifling a good laugh when they left Farlidge's office. Decker headed straight for Vendville. "I'm in need of large quantities of coffee. Can I get you something?"

"No, thanks." Angie smiled. "My every little need has been taken care of."

Decker clutched his aching forehead as Angie followed him down the hallway. "Poor baby," she said. "Too much whoopee last night, huh?"

"We need to talk." He tried to sound ominous.

"Of course we do," Angie said playfully.

Fortunately, Vendville was empty. Decker bought two cups of machine coffee—both for himself—and sat across from Angie at one of the folding tables. He was squinting in the glare from the overhead lights, trying to collect his thoughts, when Angie reached across the table and took his hand.

"Well?" she prodded.

Decker put her hand back and closed his eyes for a second. Every word he rehearsed in his head sounded trite, but there was nothing else he could say.

"Angie, you and I both know we make a great reporting team."

Angie grinned.

"*Now*, dammit, stop that. We do. But what happened last night."

"Was just groovy," she finished. "All that nervous tension we released. Don't you feel so much better? I know I do."

He looked at the shining green eyes and the fresh young face and realized what some men, using their best barroom logic, would tell him: "You lucky shit. Just sit back and enjoy it."

"It shouldn't have happened, Angie. Not when I'm trying to make things work with Janet. Do you hear me? It won't happen again."

For a long time, she just stared at him, on the verge, it seemed, of either tears or laughter. But then she got up from her chair, leaned over the table, and kissed him lightly on the forehead. She caressed his cheek a moment and walked away.

*   *   *

When Decker returned to his desk, Farlidge was waiting with a grocery list of ideas for the rain coverage. Decker was to contact the Cincinnati Water Works and find out if the rainfall would improve the taste of the drinking water, then phone surrounding suburbs to see which areas were lifting their bans on lawn sprinkling. Last but not least, he was to contact the Health Department to see what effect, if any, the rain would have on what was now being called "the city's plague threat."

When Farlidge left, the first thing Decker did was to call Janet's pager and leave his number. This time, he told himself, he would not panic if he didn't get an instant response. Besides, there was a good chance she was on her way to work.

By habit, he looked into his desk drawer for his cigarettes, then remembered he'd officially quit. Finis. Cold turkey. He took a deep breath and plunged into the morning's work.

The answer from Water Works was yes, they expected the river level to rise enough by tomorrow afternoon to remove "the organic taste" from the city drinking water. Sales of bottled water, soda, and beer would no doubt plummet. However, most of the suburbs said they planned to continue bans on lawn sprinkling and car washing, since they drew their water from underground aquifers that took longer to recharge.

Still, everyone agreed that the change in the weather was the beginning of the end for the drought.

Decker phoned the Health Department. Murdock was handing off his calls that morning to his assistant, Dr. Wells Lawson. That was fine by Decker. Lawson was Murdock's antithesis—folksy, direct, and devoid of pretension. The rain, he said, was a mixed blessing. While the downpour would recharge the sewers and keep the rats from scurrying down to the riverbank, it would also hamper the extermination efforts at the shelter. The rats were likely now to disperse throughout the sewer system.

Decker was banging in the last of his notes when Stein

showed at his desk. Stein apologized for missing the meeting with Farlidge, then explained he had been helping his wife pack for the movers.

Decker felt something close to panic. "But I thought you weren't leaving for another month?"

"I'm not. Barb and the boys are. They want to get settled in before school starts."

Decker could hardly conceive of life at the *Eagle* after Stein. He saw himself alone, embattled, bitter. He pushed the thought out of his mind and gave Stein a rundown on the meeting. Stein got a chuckle from Decker's increasingly wry account of his one-round bout with Derek Jameson.

"Have you heard yet from Wolters, about the syringe?" Stein asked.

"God, I completely forgot." Decker gave in to another twinge of despair. "Barry, if you go to Florida, I'll be a wreck."

"You'll do just fine. Shut up and call."

Wolters was in his office, but took his sweet time coming to the phone. Decker was put on hold four separate times by three different assistants, each of them answering the phone in a panic.

Finally: "Yes, Wolters here." He was harried, too. The whole city was harried. Maybe the sky was falling. Decker got to his question.

"The syringe?" Wolters asked faintly.

"Yes, the one we found in the subway tunnel."

"Oh, that," he said, as if it were a forgotten nuisance. "Yes, the report came in, I believe, yesterday afternoon."

"And?" Decker was losing patience.

"Let's see. Here it is. Test results were negative for plague bacilli. Negative for narcotics and . . . yes, negative for sedatives as well. Are you quite satisfied, Mr. Decker?"

"Not as easily as you are, Dr. Wolters."

There was a pause at the other end. Wolters was his cool and condescending self when he spoke again. "I'll ignore that nonquestion, Mr. Decker, and bid you good day."

"Wait just a minute. You say the tests on the syringe were negative for plague. But that doesn't rule out the possibility it once contained live bacteria, does it?"

"I'm not interested in possibilities, Mr. Decker, only proof."

"What about theories? Any interest in those?"

"Mr. Decker, I'm very busy at the moment . . ."

"One last question. Do you think Dr. Murdock is downplaying the plague threat?"

"What do you mean by downplaying?"

"I mean we've had two, maybe three deaths in just four days. How many more can we expect?"

"Mr. Decker, let me explain. There hasn't been a serious outbreak of plague in this country since the late 1800s, and that was in San Francisco under squalid, boomtown conditions. Since then we've developed a panoply of antibiotics effective against the disease, not to mention vastly superior methods of rodent control. So far, there's no evidence that this strain of bacillus is any more virulent than others we've encountered. I doubt we'll see more than a handful of infections."

"But what about the people who are too poor or too crazy to get medical care? What happens to them?"

Wolters' voice went flat. "It's up to the social agencies and charitable institutions that deal with these people to screen for the disease and take the appropriate action. Now, may I return to my duties, Mr. Decker?"

"Thank you, Doctor, for that scintillating quote."

"You're welcome, Mr. Decker. Any time."

Decker made a note to quiz Murdock about whether social agencies were screening for plague, then looked at his watch: 10:15, and still no call from Janet. He tried the pager again, thinking he might have entered the wrong number the first time.

He went back to typing his rain notes, but ten minutes later, when the phone still hadn't rung, he sat back and stared at it as though it were a living thing gone dead. Maybe this was it. Maybe he'd blown things completely with Janet.

He sat numbed in front of his screen until a sharp beep and a message brought him to: "Where's notes? We've got package to pull together—R.F."

He switched into automatic pilot. Fifteen minutes later, just before 11 A.M., he filed his notes and messaged Farlidge. It was time for more coffee.

But when he got up from his chair, he felt lightheaded and a little dizzy, as though he'd emptied everything in his brain into the computer. He decided to grab a bite to eat, something his stomach could handle, like maybe a bagel from the deli across the street.

He'd grabbed his open umbrella from the floor when the phone rang. He ignored it. He needed to escape outside—away from the phones, the humming fluorescent lights, away from Farlidge.

He was in the hallway when Stein called out.

"Rick, there's a call for you on line one."

"Who is it?"

"Your beloved, I do believe."

"You're kidding?"

He ran back to his desk. It was Janet, sounding harried but pleased. "Rick, at last! It's really you. I'm sorry it's taken me this long, but they paged me straight into surgery this morning. The heart transplant patient had to be cut open again. One of his sutures was leaking."

"Ooh, poor guy." Decker's voice was higher than he wanted it to be. "I bet it's a killer of a plumbing bill."

"Listen, Rick. Dad would like to have you over for dinner tomorrow night. Then he promises to disappear so we can talk. Would you like that?"

He would. They agreed to meet at seven, and then she was gone, just like that, her excited voice leaving a kind of pleasant ringing in his ear.

Instantly, it seemed, his hangover was gone. He was ravenous, ready to test his stomach with solid food. He headed off to an early lunch, amazed at how quickly things had turned around that morning. Now if only Floyd's story would begin to fall in place . . .

On his way to the elevator, he stopped at the reception desk, thinking he might tease Becky out of one of her bad moods. She was twenty-four or twenty-five, thin, pretty, but seldom happy. She sat clacking away at her computer keyboard, her jawline set as hard as the bow of a battleship.

"What's the matter, Becky? Boy trouble again?"

"No," she snapped, holding up a stack of wedding announcements from her desk. "Wendy trouble. Look at the mess she left me this morning." Wendy was the night receptionist, and she and Becky shared responsibility for typing wedding announcements into the computer system.

"I'm telling you, that girl is a pig. A real oinker."

Decker was determined to stay neutral in the long-running feud between Becky and Wendy. "Can I bring you back a Coke or something?"

"No, but wait a minute," she said. Her thin, nervous hands riffled over piles of announcement forms and glossy photos of ecstatic young couples. "I think there's a message for you somewhere in this mess. From that smelly guy with the hat."

"You mean Floyd?"

"Yeah. Wendy left a note this morning. Why she just didn't put it in your mailbox, I'll never know."

Decker started sifting, too.

"Hold it," Becky said. "Here it is." She handed Decker a pink telephone slip: "Be sure and give this to Rick Decker. It's from a Floyd somebody—Wendy." Clipped to the back was another memo, folded in half. Decker opened it and discovered Floyd's wriggly, childish scrawl. "Mr Decker. Gess what? Fond the Lincan. Will back later."

Decker picked up Becky's desk phone. "What's Wendy's number? You got it here?"

"Hold your horses." She moved some forms from the bottom left-hand corner of the desk. The number was taped there.

Decker punched the number. His teasing mood had suddenly turned manic. "He found the Lincoln, Becky! Can you believe it? Floyd found the goddamn Lincoln!"

"Well, whoopee-shitty-doo."

15

Wendy didn't have much to add to Floyd's note, except that he was exhaling wine fumes when he dropped by the *Eagle*. Decker thanked her and headed out to lunch, his good mood still intact.

Outside, the night's downpour had dissipated to a steady drizzle. Weeks of unflushed litter had backed up the sewers, and most of the downtown gutters were flooded.

Decker decided he could handle some real food. He crossed the street to Fausto's and downed most of a three-way—chili, cheese, and spaghetti—before walking, and burping, the three blocks to his car in an open cheap lot near Central Parkway. He suffered through the wet-weather ritual demanded by the Dart's internal demons: starting the engine, stalling it, starting it again, stalling it, then finally flooding the carburetor and holding the gas pedal to the floor before all six pistons could be coaxed into a fast-idling arrhythmia. He crept through the monster puddles on Broadway and feared for the Dart's aging electrical system.

There were only so many places Floyd could be at 11:30 in the morning. Decker guessed he would be finishing his daily can collection rounds—a four-mile trek that took him along Second Street, across the Central Bridge into Kentucky, then back across the river again to Central Parkway, where he was paid twenty-two cents a pound at the Ameri-Can recycling center.

When Decker reached the center, a toothless old man in a Reds ball cap was operating the conveyer belt that dropped the cans into a giant compactor. He shouted over the din of rattling, crunching, popping. "He's arunnin' mighty late this mornin'! Usually in here by eleven!"

Decker took the Clay Wade Bailey Bridge into Covington and drove around the parking lots of three or four of the larger riverfront nightclubs, where he knew Floyd often scrounged through dumpsters. Outside The River Palace, near the gangway to the kitchen, he saw a younger man with long greasy hair digging through a trash bag. When Decker pulled up, the man froze, startled—like a rat transfixed by headlights—and ran away.

He went back to his car and sat in the drizzle, annoyed by a leak he'd just discovered under his dashboard. It was dripping onto his vinyl floormat with the regularity of a metronome—*plunk, plunk . . . plunk, plunk . . .*

Floyd could have canceled his rounds because of the weather, Decker thought. In which case he would have shown early at the St. Frances Seraph soup kitchen. He was probably there now, slurping a hot bowl of overstocked beef stew and chewing the fat with the regulars.

Decker drove to 13th Street in Over-the-Rhine and checked out the crowd, a dichotomous mix of young blacks and old whites—a brotherhood of lost hope—both wearing the same outdated, shabby clothes passed out at the church missions. Decker found the director, Father Tom, a thin, bearded man in his forties who looked infinitely gentle and infinitely tired. No, he hadn't seen Floyd that day. "But I think Friday is one of his donor days. You might check at the plasma center over on Vine Street."

Like most of the homeless in Over-the-Rhine, Floyd had two ways of picking up honest cash—can collection and plasma donation. By law, you were limited to giving plasma twice a week, and always at the same location. It paid fifteen bucks a pint. The giving itself was painless and took about twenty minutes. The hassle was the paperwork and the waiting, which could run into hours on a busy day. Then again, Floyd wasn't a slave to an appointment calendar.

The Dyna-Tech plasma center was located in a converted supermarket at Vine and Green streets, right next to a state liquor store. Decker noted the convenient juxtaposition of input and output. With the weekend nigh, the center was hopping. The waiting room was SRO, stuffed with about thirty or forty clients, mostly young black men who kept up a lively chatter. To Decker's surprise, the place was spanking clean and brightly lit.

There was a long white Formica counter, where clients filled out questionnaires, gave blood samples, and had their blood pressure taken. Behind the counter, a picture window showcased the donor room, where forty people were lying head-to-head on rows of rubber mattresses. Each person was hooked to an IV and two blood bags. The room was a strange mix of high-tech and ghoulishness, like a vampire's assembly line. But again to Decker's surprise, the atmosphere seemed cheery. Donors flipped through newspapers and magazines, or joked and laughed with the nurses, as they waited for their blood bags to fill.

It wasn't long before a young black nurse came up to the counter and, smiling pleasantly, asked Decker if she could help.

"I was wondering, has an older man by the name of Floyd Deekins been in today?"

"You mean Floojie—the little old man with the knit cap and the beard?" She had a lovely high-sounding voice.

"That's him. I didn't know they called him Floojie."

"Oh, that's just me. I'm the only one 'round here calls him that. Floojie's my sweetheart—with the floy, floy. Get it? It's an old song my daddy used to sing."

Decker nodded. He liked this woman.

"But no, honey, I haven't seen him come 'round yet today, although I expect he'll be here. Sometimes on Fridays he doesn't show till close to closin' time."

"Which is when?"

"Four P.M.," the nurse said. "Although we've been runnin' late the last few days. With all this plague business, our screenings are taking longer."

Decker thanked her and left.

He hadn't thought to bring an umbrella, but he didn't mind getting wet as he walked outdoors. Not many people did that day, smiling as they made their way through the warm drizzle. After the weeks of drought, it felt like a baptism. Water was pouring down the hill from Clifton Heights, turning lower Vine Street into a swollen river. Traffic was slowed to a crawl, and garbage was floating everywhere. Kids in underwear splashed and played in the gutters while their mutts pranced around the water's edge and barked their heads off. It was Norman Rockwell come to the ghetto.

Decker was inspired to take a break. He left his car on Green Street and headed on foot to the Neon Café, a block over on Race, where he planned to sit down with a cup of coffee and watch the yuppies and the locals rub shoulders across the street at Findlay Market.

He took a shortcut through the Dyna-Tech parking lot, where he found some boys taking turns jumping from the top of a dumpster onto a pile of old mattresses. They were executing belly floppers and back floppers, heedless of the rain or the possibility of missing their target. One of them tumbled off the mattress, somersaulted, and almost smashed his head on the door of a nearby car. The boy stood up, laughing, and raced to the dumpster for more—and that's when Decker saw the Lincoln.

It was a big blue town car—an '83 or '84—one of the last of the Great American Road Hogs. No streamlining. No fancy halogen headlights. Just a solid chunk of steel. The dark blue paint job was polished to a sapphire consistency. It sported a creamy white landau roof and little oval-shaped opera windows for the backseats—the feature that so impressed Floyd.

There was a sign on the center's cinder block wall, just above the car hood: DYNA-TECH EMPLOYEE PARKING ONLY. ALL OTHERS TOWED AT OWNER'S EXPENSE. Decker went back into the plasma center and looked for the nurse who'd been so congenial. He checked the waiting room, peered into the donor area, but she was gone. He scanned the nurses and technicians for another approachable face, but all of them were occupied now, taking blood pressures and temperatures, performing lab tests, filling out charts.

He stood at the end of the counter, puzzled over what to do. The Lincoln no doubt belonged to somebody important—an owner or the manager—but the trick was to find out without seeming too curious.

Something Angie had suggested popped into his head: He could be a car dealer announcing a recall. No, too weird. But maybe he could be a buyer. Somebody smitten with the last of the butcher-block Lincolns. He waited until one of the clerks—a washed-out, obese young woman in a white polyester pantsuit—came shuffling out of the office at the back of the waiting room. She was carrying a stack of charts.

"The blue what?" she responded. She was about thirty, apple-shaped and bloated in the face. Her brown hair was a drooping mass of split ends.

"The blue Lincoln town car in your parking lot. Do you know who it belongs to?"

"Why—is it blocking something?" She moved behind the counter, where she began filing charts on the open shelves. Her movements were slow and deliberate. In the midst of so much bloodletting, she looked anemic.

"No, I'm interested in buying it."

"Buying?" She kept filing without looking back. "Does this place look like a used-car lot?"

"Can you tell me who the owner is?"

179

"You mean the big job with the white top and all?"

"Yeah, that's it."

"I don't think Dr. Cousins is interested. He's mighty attached to that car. Treats it like a baby."

"Who's Dr. Cousins?"

"He's the boss—and to tell you the truth, I don't think he wants to be bothered just now."

Decker looked into the donor room again. The IV poles at each bed were numbered 1 through 40, the patients like so many cows lined up at milking stations.

"What if I called him later?" Decker had his notebook and pen out. Few people could resist an open notebook; there was an unspoken obligation to set the record straight. "What was that name again—Dr. Cousins?"

The woman filed away the last of the charts and came over and pressed her soft, bulging tummy against the counter. She sighed and said, "Okay, it's Dr. Darren Cousins," and began to spell out the name.

Suddenly the office door opened, and a short, thick-bodied man in a double-breasted blazer came walking out with a curious air. Decker said a hurried thanks to the clerk, but it was too late.

"What seems to be the problem, Michelle?" He spoke with a faint foreign accent. Indian? Filipino? He had a round face, a flat nose, and a balding forehead that gleamed in the fluorescent light. His copper-colored cheeks were pockmarked, like a stone Buddha badly eroded by the elements.

"No problem, Dr. C. This man here just wants to buy your car is all."

Cousins turned and broke into a smile. His dark brown eyes were heavy-lidded and expressionless. Like a scanning machine, he looked Decker up and down, up and down.

"Pleased to meet you. The name's Decker. Rick Decker."

Cousins' handshake was firm, but the skin was delicate and slightly moist, like fine leather worked too long with oil.

"Excuse me, Mr. Decker, but I don't recall having a 'For Sale' sign posted on my car."

Decker could feel the sweat breaking from his scalp. Any second it might start running down his face and give him away. He grinned and tried to play redneck. "I was just telling Michelle here what a cherry that Lincoln of yours is. Hell, they just plain don't make cars like that no more. They all look like Mercedes now, like they're afraid to use chrome or something. I tell you what, Dr. Cousins. I'd like to make you a generous offer. I'm talking hard cash. No checks. No funny business . . ."

"The car is *not* for sale, Mr. Decker," he said with finality. "Now if you'll excuse me . . ."

"You know, I'm one that believes in the old American cars. Big engines, big comfort. None of that front-wheel drive stuff. Now I own something of a classic myself . . ."

Cousins' eyes sparked a little, caught between impatience and suspicion. "Mr. Decker, I'm extremely busy at the moment. But if you'd like to leave your name and number, I may perhaps change my mind. Do you have a card?"

"No," Decker said, "but I can write it down." He toyed with the idea of giving out a phony number, but decided that would arouse even more suspicion. He wrote his work number on a notebook page, tore it off, and handed it to Cousins. "Call any time."

Cousins folded the page in half and stuffed it neatly into his handkerchief pocket. He broke into his little smile, eyes impenetrable again, taking their measure.

"I might just do that, Mr. Decker."

At 1:30, while Decker watched, Stein polished off a final edition rewrite of the day's front-page rain story, then followed Decker back to his desk. Decker had brought White Castle coffee for both of them, heavy on the cream, and they sat drinking while Decker talked about his discovery of the Lincoln and the encounter with Dr. Cousins.

"You're sure it's the same Lincoln?" Stein asked.

Decker threw up his hands. "I don't know. And I won't know for sure until I find Floyd. But it certainly sounds like it. How many dark-colored Lincolns with opera windows could there be in this town?"

Stein sipped his coffee and rolled his eyes.

"Okay," Decker said. "Maybe a couple dozen—at most."

Stein left Decker with a couple of obvious follow-up suggestions. One, see if Cousins was among the principals in the Crown Pointe development project. And, two, check with the state medical board to see if there were any complaints on file against either Cousins or the plasma center.

Both were easy enough to check. Cousins wasn't listed among the Crown Pointe partners, unless there was a "straw party" fronting for him. And, according to the state medical board in Columbus, no one had ever complained about Dyna-Tech. Cousins, for now at least, appeared clean.

Still, Decker was eager to tell Angie what he'd stumbled onto. He called her hotel in Flagstaff, was told she hadn't checked in yet, and left a message to return his call.

Decker looked at his watch. He hadn't had a cigarette since he'd thrown out his pack early that morning. That was more than six hours ago. He opened his middle desk drawer and rooted among the forgotten papers and chewed-up ballpoint pens. Underneath his Delta benefits manual he found what he was looking for: three pieces of nicotine gum in a twelve-piece bubble pack. The leftovers from the last time he'd quit.

He peeled off the plastic backing on one of the bubbles and popped the small square into his mouth, careful to bite it only once before tucking it between his cheek and gum. The burn of nicotine spread slowly through his mouth. The flavoring was a bad joke, like the rancid taste of Juicy Fruit after ten hours of chewing. He tossed the pack into his drawer, bit again into the soggy gum, and felt the burn. *The things we do for love.*

At two Farlidge came around, distributing the day's home edition. He tossed one to Decker and quickly disappeared—always a bad sign.

The local rain package took up most of the front page, putting the rest of the world on hold. Anchoring the page was a big color photo of a couple of white suburban kids in yellow macks and red boots, kicking puddles at each other. Cute, but the ghetto kids had more imagination. There were boxes and charts aplenty, including one comparing the area's rainfall that summer to the dust bowl days of the Great Depression. The main story, at least, was a good read, a seamless piece Stein had woven from the notes of five different reporters.

Decker zipped through the rest of the paper. There was no mention of plague. The rain angle dominated nearly everything, even the Lifestyle page, where the staff had thrown together a quickie feature on 101 things to enjoy in Cincinnati on a rainy day. Hey, why not pack up the kids and visit the insectarium?

A banner headline on the business page caught his eye: Crown Pointe Developers Ready Mammoth Project.

Decker recognized the story's byline and cringed. Alfred D. Zahn. A burn-out who should have retired years ago. Decker devoured the first few graphs, then got up to find Stein. By telepathy, it seemed, Stein arrived at Decker's cubicle just as he was leaving.

"You saw it?" Decker said, holding up the page.

"Yep."

"So, scooped again by our own paper."

"More like 'fluffed.' Did you read it?"

Decker sat again and raced through the rest of the story. The rumors had all been true, and then some—a coalition of developers was planning a thirty-story, twin-tower complex of residential, office, shopping, and entertainment space, on nearly the same scale as Boston's Back Bay. It would cover a two-block area bounded by Central Parkway, Ninth Street, Race, and Elm. It was being touted as "a city within a city," the largest and most ambitious commercial real estate venture in Cincinnati history.

Price tag: $660 million.

"No mention of the shelter," Decker said. "And nothing, of course, about Eric Strider."

"But it does mention the old brewery. Did you see where Andersen said they're counting on the city to condemn it?"

"No. Where does it say that?"

"The fifth 'graph or so—the part about the 'strategic undeveloped block' on Central Parkway."

Decker saw it. "Jesus, Alf must have taken straight dictation from Teddy."

"Does lean a bit toward the boosterish side, doesn't it? I suspect every *i* was dotted by Maloney himself before it ran." Frank Maloney was the *Eagle* publisher.

"So you don't think it was Sally Beth's doing?"

"Could have been. On Maloney's behalf. Frank and Teddy are golf buddies, did you know that?"

Decker shook his head. Nothing surprised him anymore, not so far as the *Eagle* management was concerned. "Where did you hear that?"

"From Farlidge, of course." Stein grinned. "He makes a point of finding out whose toes he shouldn't step on."

Decker took another careful bite into his gum. His mouth was almost numb now with the tingle of nicotine. "So where do we go from here, Barry? Suppose we do find out that Cousins killed the Indian. How do we link him to Crown Pointe, or to Murdock, for that matter?"

"I don't think we worry about it for now. Let's concentrate on what we've got: growing evidence of foul play, at least in the Indian's death. If we can show that, I think people will start asking the right questions."

Decker smiled and shook his head. "Always the optimist."

* * *

At 3:15 Decker drove back to the Dyna-Tech plasma center. He decided not to go inside, since Cousins' suspicions were already piqued. He found an open metered space on Vine, just in front of the entrance, parked the Dart, and waited. The center closed at four. If Floyd had arrived late that afternoon, chances were he wouldn't get his cash until quitting time.

Decker rolled down his window. Although the rain had stopped, the streets were suffused with an eerie yellow light, a kind of mute afterglow, and the air was moist and cleansed and somehow palpable, like the smell of wet skin after a shower. The street flooding had receded into gutter lagoons, leaving behind bits of trash in fan clusters along the sidewalk. The kids in underwear had long since gone, in search, no doubt, of other cheap adventures.

Decker had seen enough cop films to know what you did on stakeouts. You drank coffee and ate sandwiches. On the way, he had stopped at the White Castle on Liberty Street and picked up a dozen "sliders"—the bite-size, grease-soaked burgers for which the place was famous—and two more cups of coffee to wash them down. He knew he was putting his usually iron-cast stomach to a test after the three-way chili at lunch, but there was something in a man that craved grease during moments of stress. He wondered if the cholesterol researchers had bothered to check that out. He paced himself for the long run, eating one burger approximately every four minutes, hoping to make his supply last the full forty-five minutes until closing time.

The men came out of the center in sporadic groups of twos and threes, with gauze patches taped to the crooks of their arms. Most headed straight next door to the state liquor store. And why not? The long hot summer had finally snapped, the air was cool and clean, the weekend on its way. Time to pack up those blues.

The minutes and the burgers ticked away, but Floyd failed to appear. At five minutes of four Decker considered peeking through the front window to see if Floyd was among the stragglers. But by the time he stirred himself from his burger-induced inertia and opened his car door, the lights went out in the waiting room. A janitor stepped outside and started sweeping away the day's debris.

Decker pulled his door shut. There was only one thing left to do: head down to the river and see if Floyd had gone back to his campsite.

Decker fired up the Dart four times before the moisture-clogged carburetor allowed enough air to seep in. He let the engine idle for a while, certain it would stall if he tried to drive away. The car was still idling when Cousins came walking out of the center, followed closely by a much bigger man. Decker scootched down in his seat. He was close enough to hear Cousins remind the janitor to turn off the Xerox machine in his office and wish him a pleasant weekend. The janitor replied with "Mmmm-mmm," already relishing the prospect, then said, "G'night, Dr. C. G'night, J.T."

Decker looked again just as Cousins rounded the building into the parking lot. The man behind him, "J.T.," was tall, maybe six feet five, blond, and built like a cartoon action figure. A redneck flag of ratty hair spilled over the back of his collar. He could have been a studio wrestler—the handsome hero type. Gorgeous Johnny T.

Then it clicked for Decker: J.T. matched Kevin's description of the blueprint thief. Blond. Handsome. Homogenous.

The chase was on.

Decker tapped the gas pedal to stop the fast idle. The engine died. In a panic he mashed the accelerator to the floor, snapped the ignition and felt the whole car shimmy and rock as the engine came roaring back to life. So did the burgers and chili in his stomach. He gulped and held his breath.

With one foot on the gas pedal, he stood on the brake and threw the transmission into drive. The car lurched forward, straining against the brake linings like an unruly dog on a leash. A second later the big Lincoln glided out of the lot and turned left onto Vine. It seemed to float on its own cushion of air. At the next intersection it signaled left, and for no reason except to satisfy his curiosity, Decker followed.

He knew enough about tailing to know he couldn't keep it up for long, not alone. But there were a couple of things in his favor: rush-hour traffic would help hide his car, and, secondly, the Lincoln was cruising at an ocean liner's majestic pace. Decker couldn't see through the Lincoln's tinted glass who was driving, but he assumed it was Cousins and not J.T. It would have ruined the latter's macho credentials.

Within a few blocks it was clear the town car was headed for Kentucky. It lumbered down Race to Third, hung a right, and three blocks later, at the entrance to the Clay Wade Bailey Bridge, took a quick left on a last-second yellow light. Decker had to let them go. When the light cycled again, he started across the bridge, on the outside chance the Lincoln had been tied up in traffic. No such luck.

Decker loved the way TV detectives could follow somebody for miles and never lose them. And on top of it, they were usually driving a Corvette or a Ferrari. Nothing, of course, that would attract attention. He reached the end of the bridge in Covington and took a right on Fourth Street, thinking he'd pick up I-75 North back to town. But at the next light there it was—like a dark blue ship on the horizon—turning right on Bakewell toward the riverfront.

Decker laughed to himself. He could guess now where the two were headed: Friday happy hour at The River Palace. He let them cruise a safe distance ahead.

The River Palace was a favorite meat market for the gold chain and polyester set. It was the closest thing in town to L.A. glitz, complete with overpriced restaurant, outdoor and indoor discos, and six separate bars. It was famous, too, for the shirtless hunks who served drinks in the women's lounge.

When Decker arrived, the Lincoln was two cars ahead in the valet parking line, just behind a red 300-Z. He watched as the Lincoln pulled up to the valet booth and the two wild and crazy guys got out. He was right, Cousins had been driving. The little man stepped out and rose to his full height of maybe five feet four. He buttoned up his blazer with the air of a visiting dignitary. J.T. crossed in front of the car and, like a mismatched circus attraction, the duo headed down the gangplank to the Palace.

Decker squeaked to a stop at the valet booth. The Dart's slant six chuffed and wheezed in the moist air along the river. The valet, a tough-looking teenager, was close to snickering.

"Take good care of her," Decker told the boy, winking, "and there's an extra buck in it for ya."

The kid burst out laughing. He hopped in the car and tried his best to lay rubber as he pulled away, but the engine only stalled. The Dart always had the last laugh.

Decker took his time walking down the loose metal gangplank, hoping to give Cousins and J.T. a chance to settle in. He still had no idea why he was trailing the two, or what he expected to find. He only knew that he was too caught up in the chase to quit now.

Happy hour was upstairs in the main disco, at the top of a winding brass staircase with footlights that flashed in sequence as you climbed the stairs. At the Palace, everybody was a celebrity.

At 4:45 the place was already jammed with young secretaries and middle managers on the make, all getting an early start on the weekend. Drinks were half price until seven, and trays of greasy hors d'oeuvres were laid out on tables across the dance floor. The music was low enough for the men to try out their latest pickup lines.

Decker waded into the crowd and took up a position behind a palm tree overlooking the dance floor. The decorative theme was tropical glitz, with lots of frondy plants and piles of lava rock coexisting in bad taste with chrome and mirrors.

It wasn't long before Decker spotted J.T. He was standing at the far end of the dance-floor bar, blond helmet shining, towering over some young thing who seemed to be more hair than anything else. Frizzed and curled, it sprayed from the top of her head like a fountain, then tumbled in cascades over her bare shoulders. She was about Angie's age, with the same tight build. So tight you could hold her close and twang her like a string.

The hulkster was standing crotch-close to the big-haired girl's bar stool and leaning down at times to whisper something in her ear. He hit her giggle reflex every time. He was full of himself, but was he clever enough to snatch a blueprint in plain sight? Maybe. With enough coaching.

Decker looked around for Cousins and couldn't spot him. He wondered now if he might be downstairs in the restaurant mixing it up with an older crowd. He decided to stay a little while longer and see what developed between J.T. and Big Hair. He walked down the two or three steps to the dance floor and over to the near end of the bar, where he ordered a Christian Moerlein for the duration. Three sips later the girl next to J.T. got out of her chair, grabbed her tiny silver handbag, and left. J.T. grinned as she strutted away. He was either used to being shot down or too dumb to let it matter.

J.T. stayed put, and a few minutes later the same girl returned with a blond variation by her side. J.T. broke into his best Tom Selleck grin, boyish but aggressive, and during the introduction, took the blonde's hand in both of his. He must have seen it in a movie or something. After a bit of chitchat, he escorted Big Hair One and Big Hair Two across the dance floor and up the steps on the other side of the disco.

Decker lost them in the crowd. He picked up his Moerlein and started for higher ground, moving so quickly he bumped into the ample behind of a woman in a red power suit. She was mid-thirtyish, with brown hair in a precision page boy cut, oily skin under heavy makeup. She smiled at Decker as though the bump had been no accident.

"Excuse me," Decker said, trying to slip on through.

"Anytime," she said, flashing a cigarette in her hand. Her fingernails were the color of red hots. "Too bad," she said, glancing down at his Dockers, "can't afford an iron, huh?"

Decker smiled back and kept on moving. Another of life's missed opportunities.

By the time he reached his palm tree again, J.T. and the girls were nowhere to be found. Decker swore under his breath, then realized they couldn't have left without passing him, since there was only one way downstairs—the brass staircase. He sipped his beer and bided his time. Ten minutes later, his beer gone and his patience running out, he moved down the steps again to the dance floor, and there, passing through the crowd in the opposite direction, were the hulk and Cousins, trailing after the two bimbettes.

They were leaving.

Decker backpedaled a step or two into the crowd, and nearly jumped out of his Rockports when somebody grabbed his behind.

"Back again?"

It was the woman with the red-hot nails. She was running her tongue along the rim of a martini glass.

"Nope. Just leaving. Have a nice day."

He started up the steps, wondering what his next move should be. If he left now, he might bump into Cousins, and the jig would be up. But if he waited, he'd lose them for sure. He pushed through the crowd, hoping now to beat the foursome downstairs. He had almost reached the staircase when he spotted J.T.—this time outside the door to the ladies' room, apparently waiting while the two young things freshened up. But where was Cousins?

It didn't matter, as long as Decker reached his car before the others reached the Lincoln. He made quick steps down the stairs and out the door to the end of the gangplank, where he handed his parking ticket and a dollar bill to the valet.

"Listen, if you don't mind," Decker said, "I'd just as soon get the car myself. I'm in kind of a hurry."

It was a different kid from the one who had parked the car. Still, he looked at the ticket number and smirked. The Dart was famous now. "No problem. I'll get the keys."

Decker kept his eye on the door to the Palace, quietly snapping his fingers. *C'mon, c'mon, c'mon.* The kid returned from the booth and handed him the keys. "Third row, second space from the left. Just climb the steps there and you'll see it."

Decker walked fast without looking back. The parking lot was on a terrace overlooking the access road to the restaurant. When he reached the car, he surprised himself by starting it on the first try, then moved to an empty space in the front row of the terrace. He arrived in time to see J.T. holding the back door of the Lincoln for the two bimbettes. Cousins apparently was already inside. Front or back, Decker didn't know. J.T. slipped into the driver's seat.

Decker's heart raced—the thrill of spying and not being spied.

It was clear they'd switched drivers. J.T. roared the big Lincoln up the one-way access road and around to the parking lot. Decker slid down in his seat as the Lincoln flew behind him toward the exit. He waited until they reached the cut in the levee, then backed out.

Decker followed in time to spot the Lincoln taking a left on Third Street. He floored the gas pedal to shorten the two-block deficit, rolled the stop sign at Third, and floored it again. He didn't catch up until a red light stopped the Lincoln at Fifth and Madison in downtown Covington. It was two cars ahead in the left lane. Decker eased into the right.

The tinted windows gave the Lincoln a sinister look. Secret. Impenetrable. Decker would have given anything at that moment for a peek inside. He imagined it was party time, with Cousins entertaining his two young guests with an impressive quantity of coke.

When the light changed, J.T. snapped a quick left onto Madison. No signal. Decker couldn't switch lanes in time. He followed the traffic across Madison as the Lincoln sped away. His luck, it seemed, had begun to turn.

Decker calmed himself and followed a hunch. He turned left

on Court Street and, rather than doubling back to I-75, drove north toward the old Suspension Bridge. There was a good chance Cousins and his party girls were headed for downtown Cincinnati. But when he reached the bridge, the Lincoln was nowhere in sight.

To hell with it then. The whole chase had been a crazy idea anyway. Pure impulse.

He looked at his watch: almost six. He'd stop by the office, see if Angie had left any messages, and then go looking for Floyd down on the riverfront. When he entered the bridge, he scanned the Ohio riverbank and spotted a thin column of smoke rising through the trees, not more than a hundred yards upstream. It might be Floyd and his buddies down there, passing around a bottle of MD 20/20 and drying their clothes and blankets by the fire. A cozy thought.

He rolled his window all the way down, stuck his elbow into the cool, moist slipstream of air. Time to wind down. He turned on the radio and found NPR news—he loved the phony British accents. There was a telephone report from Beijing: more trouble in Tiananmen Square.

By the time he reached the end of the bridge, Decker was relaxed and settled in, his mind fixed on the international scene, and that's when the Lincoln zoomed by at about sixty. It bounced and swerved on the uneven metal grate like a cruiser in heavy seas. Decker punched the accelerator, and, surprisingly, the Dart responded.

The Lincoln took a hard right from the middle lane, taking the Main Street exit to downtown. Decker fought his steering wheel around the curve, trying to keep up. At Third Street J.T. rolled the stoplight, snapped right, and zoomed ahead three blocks to the dead end at Broadway, where he turned right against a yellow. Decker was left behind, faced with a "No Turn on Red" sign and a cop station across the street. The Lincoln disappeared.

Decker laughed at himself this time. Why in God's name

was he trying to play detective in a '73 Dart? He couldn't keep pace with a tractor on a country road.

He turned left on Broadway, back toward the *Eagle*, and turned up the volume on the radio. A correspondent for *All Things Considered* was reporting on a government study that showed nearsightedness had tripled among the Eskimos in Alaska since mandatory schooling started there in the 1950s. No kidding. And here Decker had always been taught it was self-abuse.

He yawned as he drove the familiar stretch up Broadway to Eighth, past the Southern-Western Life building, as bland as its name would imply, and the neo-imperialist pavilion of P&G headquarters.

He was nearing the end of his second or third wind that day after the long night with Angie. Clarity of thought had given way to an empty restless hum inside his head, as though his brain waves were out of sync. Into the void popped memories of Angie, parts of Angie, strutting naked from the closet of his subconscious. The silky warmth of an inner thigh (pliant, too, his hand discovered, on such a hard, tight body). The soft weight of a cupped breast, pendulous, palm-filling.

The Dart splashed and skidded through a puddle, and he was jarred from his daydreaming. He remembered Janet and felt ashamed.

When the headlights appeared in his rearview mirror, his first reaction was half-formed curiosity. Who would have their brights on this time of day? The lights flashed once, twice. It was a Type A jerk in one hell of a hurry. Decker slowed and pulled into the far right lane. He waved his hand out the window. *Go on. Get around me, asshole.* But when he turned his head, he saw the blue Lincoln tight beside the Dart. The car's back window powered down smoothly, and there was Cousins, his Buddha face staring with impenetrable eyes.

"Giving up so soon, Mr. Decker?"

16

Decker drove to the west end
of the public landing, just below the stadium floodwall, and
made a quick U-turn before parking. In the event of trouble,
he wanted the car facing upstream toward the exit.

His heart was still pounding from the encounter with Cousins. The Lincoln had zoomed up Broadway and around Eighth
Street, disappearing as quickly as it had appeared. Cousins'
sneer had not only frightened him; it had made him feel like
a first-class fool. He'd been caught trying to play private eye,
and not playing it very well. He remembered what his father
told him once when he came home crying from a football game
with some older kids: "If you play with the big dogs, you can't
piss like a pup." He'd been whipped like a pup, all right.

He was determined more than ever to find Floyd and confirm the identity of the Lincoln. He was parked now a hundred
yards or so from the Suspension Bridge, just below the stadium garage where the second plague victim had been found
the day before.

He knew Floyd's favorite spot was near the base of the
bridge, where there was plenty of cover and yet easy access to
downtown. He could see the smoke from a campfire hovering
just above the treetops, white against the evening's slate-gray

sky. He passed the sewer pipe where Plaxton had pointed out the rat prints leading down to the river. The prints were gone now, washed clean by the day's rain. The river, too, was higher, lapping in small waves against the cobblestone apron.

Decker traced the smoke to the top of a small hill, just beyond some heavy brush and weeds. He waded in, his sports coat snagging on small branches and his feet sticking in the mud. He could smell the campfire, hear the sound of low, muffled voices, jovial, comradely, at peace. But the moment he broke through, the three men huddled there sprang to their feet.

"Get back, motherfucker!"

It was an old black man, thin and stooped, clenching a rusty meat cleaver in his hand. The other men, one white, the other black, were wrapped in blankets.

"No trouble, gentlemen. I'm just looking for someone."

"Well, there ain't nobody here lookin' for you, so git the hell out." The cleaver trembled in the man's hand. He was more frightened than Decker.

Decker looked again and realized the men were draped in green trash bags, not blankets. The white man, the shortest of the three, was wet and shivering. His face was ghostly pale, and there were dark circles under his eyes.

"You should have your buddy there checked out," Decker said. "He doesn't look so well."

"Ain't none of your concern," said the man with the cleaver. "Just leave us be."

"Then I'll send somebody down here," Decker said. "You could all be in danger if this man is seriously ill."

"We don't need no favors."

But the other black man began to soften. "Who you lookin' for?"

"A man named Floyd Deekins. About yay high." Decker held his hand out at chest level. "Has a gray beard and long hair, wears a blue cap."

The white man tried to speak up, but was stopped short by

the man with the cleaver. "Shut up! It ain't none of our business." And then he turned back to Decker. "We don't want no trouble with nobody. Now go on and git."

The men had built a makeshift duplex by placing a couple of refrigerator boxes side by side. Decker saw a sleeping bag poking out of one box, and beer and wine bottles scattered around the campsite. An old bucket seat from a sports car made a nifty easy chair.

"Listen," Decker said. "I'm a friend of Floyd's, and I need his help. Now if you can . . ."

The second black man spoke up again. His voice was hoarse and raspy. "We seen him yesterday. He got his home down there by the riverbank."

The cleaver man dropped his guard, but he wasn't happy. "Leon, shut your mouth. This is white man's shit."

But Leon pointed downriver to some willow trees not far from the waterline. "He shared a bottle with us 'bout two, three nights ago. Said he got plenty more where that come from."

"Is he there now?"

"No, sir. Ain't seen him since day before yesterday."

The man with the cleaver glared at Leon.

"Is Floyd in trouble?" Decker asked.

The white man coughed and finally spoke up, slurring something in a deep, angry voice.

"Shut up, dammit!" The cleaver man lunged toward him as though he meant to cave in his skull. Decker doubted he had the strength. The cleaver man turned back to Decker, his weapon quivering in his bony hand.

"Now, mister, this ain't none of our affair. Go on and leave us alone. We ain't bothered nobody. We just tryin' to live, man. We just tryin' to live."

Decker backpedaled a little. "All right. Just one quick look around Floyd's place, and I'm outta here. Okay?"

"Just don't be comin' 'round *here*."

Decker started down the slippery bank toward the willow

trees, taking tiny steps on the balls of his feet. Once he made level ground, he quickened his pace through the muck and glop.

There were no signs of a struggle at Floyd's campsite, just the usual evidence of his ingenuity and his drinking. Floyd had made a tent by tying a rope between two trees and draping it with a heavy plastic sheet. The four corners of the tent were anchored by large rocks. His "stove" was a battered metal desk drawer, placed upside down over some stacked bricks. He had been using an old coffee can for a cookpot. It was filled now to the brim with rain water and bits of rotting vegetables.

Decker stuck his head inside the tent. There was a tangle of musty woolen blankets and a tattered sleeping bag. Bottles were everywhere. It reeked of stale wine and urine.

He wondered why the three men had seemed so frightened. "White man's shit." Well, that's for sure. The nastiest kind. Brutal and premeditated. He could see Cousins' face again—sneering from the dark recesses of his Lincoln like a mummer's mask.

"Giving up so soon, Mr. Decker?"

He kicked a loose bottle into the weeds and heard it crash against something. Then he took out his notebook and scribbled a note. "Floyd. Come see me at the office as soon as possible. Rick." He left it at the head of the sleeping bag and walked away.

Decker was greeted with some grim news on his return to the *Eagle* newsroom: another plague victim. And this time it wasn't a vagrant, but an old woman who lived by herself in a basement apartment on Race Street in Over-the-Rhine, just a few blocks from the men's shelter. Police found the body around 5:30 that evening after neighbors began complaining of the smell. Bart Petkamp, the *Eagle*'s police reporter, was tipped by a source and gave Decker a call. It looked like an *Eagle* scoop.

Decker reached Murdock at his office just after seven. Murdock sounded tired, wrung out, but to Decker's surprise, was willing to talk. The woman, he said, was almost certainly a victim of plague, although laboratory tests would be needed to make it official.

"What about the man who collapsed at the cathedral?"

"Yes, it's now been confirmed."

"So that makes four plague deaths in all?"

"Technically, only three." He explained that, although the body on the river had been infected with plague, the more immediate cause of death was shock.

"From being attacked by rats, you mean."

"Yes, if you care to put it that way."

Decker saved his knockout punch for last. "Would you agree, Doctor, that this latest case marks a significant turn in the plague threat?"

"How so?"

"Well, you've been saying all along that the general public isn't at risk, and now one of the victims is a woman who was supposedly safe in her own home."

Murdock sighed audibly. "This has been a long day, Mr. Decker, and you're not making it any shorter."

"You're not answering the question, Doctor."

"Then the answer is this: The old woman represents a special case. She was living under incredibly unhygienic conditions."

"Such as?"

"To put it bluntly, there was trash and garbage piled everywhere in her apartment. This woman evidently had a long history of obsessive-compulsive behavior."

"So you're talking about a playground for rats."

"Correct. We don't believe the average resident has anything to worry about."

Decker asked Murdock if he knew anything about Dr. Darren Cousins.

"Who?" Murdock's puzzlement sounded genuine.

"Darren Cousins. He runs a plasma center in Over-the-Rhine."

"You'll have to check with our blood products division."

Decker switched gears again. "Tell me, Dr. Murdock, how many more victims can we expect?"

"I don't have a crystal ball, Mr. Decker, but I believe the worst is already over. Dr. Wolters and I concur that all six victims were most likely infected before our extermination efforts began."

"You lost me there. Six victims?"

"Yes, six, Mr. Decker. We've treated two victims successfully with streptomycin. We were waiting until both patients were completely recovered before making an announcement to the press. They'll be released from Cincinnati General tomorrow."

"Are there any other surprises in store, Doctor?"

"I assure you every effort is being made to contain the problem, and we *will* contain it."

Echoes of the *Titanic*, Decker thought. He decided to use the quote in his story anyway. Who knew, it might look great in a history book someday.

Around 8:15, Angie called from her hotel room in Cameron, Arizona, and Decker took a break from his writing. Angie was in typically high spirits, eager to talk about her contact that afternoon with the Navaho tribal council and the local sheriff's office. The latter appeared close to confirming the identity of the dead Indian.

"They're pretty sure it's this old medicine dude named Gray Deer. He's a widower. No kids. Has a place by himself out in the Painted Desert, miles from the nearest town. Somebody saw him standing at a reservation bus stop on Route 89 about a week ago. No one's seen him since."

"So what's the holdup? Why can't they just check dental records?"

Angie snorted. "Dental records? Most of the Indians out here don't have electricity or running water. You can't imagine the poverty, Rick. It makes Over-the-Rhine look like Club Med."

"Does anybody out there know why this 'medicine dude,' as you put it, would bother coming to Cincinnati?"

"I've been asking around. The cops say it's hard to under-stand because the Navahos think of their land as the center of the universe. I mean, literally. They worship just about every-thing out here. The mountains, the rivers. Even the prairie dogs."

"What about our damsel in distress—Little Bear?"

"The name doesn't seem to ring any bells out here. The council office is working on that for me. To tell you the truth, I didn't find the Indians on the reservation very cooperative. They don't much trust white folks."

"Can you blame them?"

"No, but it doesn't make my job any easier."

Then it was Decker's turn to bring Angie up-to-date, and she listened with little oohs and ahs as he told her about finding the Lincoln, tailing Cousins and J.T., then being out-witted by the two.

"Ouch! Poor baby," Angie said. "Maybe you should take some lessons from Tom Selleck."

"Tom Selleck drives a Ferrari, not a Dart."

"Whatever fits your karma, sweetie."

Angie ended the conversation with a plaintive, "Gee, wish you were here, pal." The "pal" was heavy on the irony.

"Same here, chum. I could use the moral support."

He thought for sure she'd come back with a crack about Janet. Instead, she sounded concerned. "Be careful, Rick. This Cousins guy sounds pretty kinky."

"Hey, nobody's more careful than me. You know that."

"Don't I."

* * *

Decker checked his rearview mirror every block or so on the drive home that night, half-expecting, but not finding, the big blue Lincoln. To be on the safe side, he parked his car one street over on Euclid and walked around the corner to their house on Butler Street. The night air was crisp and cool after the day of rain, and he felt his fatigue begin to lift a little as he walked. Still, he had only one thought for his arrival home—a quick beer in front of the fridge and then downstairs to his sofa in the den, where he planned to crash till morning.

Their house was at the bottom of the street, lost in the gloom along the riverbank, far from any street lamp. Decker arrived to find the front porch completely dark; he'd forgotten to leave the light on. Muttering to himself, he stepped carefully around the porch furniture and found his way to the front door.

He was poking his key around in vain, trying to find the slot to the dead bolt, when he caught a whiff of something rancid lying just at his feet. He held his breath until his key at last slipped in. Then he threw open the door, jumped into the hallway and snapped on the porch light. There on the doorsill lay an enormous dead rat, its paws sticking in the air.

He slammed the door shut and caught his breath. He was more angry than frightened. He'd love to find Cousins, rub his oily nose in it. But he couldn't just leave the thing there.

He went to the kitchen cabinets and pulled out a trash bag and found a pair of rubber gloves in a bucket under the sink. Thus armed, he went back to the front door. He picked up the rat by its tail and dropped it into the bag. He'd forgotten to bring a twist lock, so he tied the top of the bag in a double knot. The rat was heavy. It weighed down the bottom of the bag like an overripe melon. Decker left it on the porch and returned with two more garbage bags. He triple-bagged it, then took it around to the back of the house, where he dumped it deep inside a trash can.

Back inside, he soaked the rubber gloves in a bucket of water and bleach, then went around the house, checking the locks on every door and window. That finished, he called Stein.

"Are you sure it wasn't some kids playing a prank?"

"Barry, what kids in their right minds would pick up a dead rat? Especially now?"

"Would you feel safer spending the night over here?"

"I don't think it's a question of safety. It's a matter of intimidation. Cousins wants me to know he knows where I live. He's messing with me, and it pisses me off. I'd like to throw the thing back in his face."

"I'd be careful how I disposed of it. There could still be fleas on it, you know."

Decker shivered a little. Maybe there were fleas in the house now. "I'll get somebody from the Health Department out here tomorrow."

"You sure you don't want to come over?"

"I'm dead tired, Barry. Besides, if Cousins were really serious, he'd do more than leave a dead rat on my doorstep."

"Keep a phone by your bed."

"You bet."

From the phone, he went straight to the cabinet under the kitchen sink, grabbed the can of Raid and returned to the front door. He fogged the whole entryway and retreated to his den.

Decker's den was in the basement, a room the landlady had proudly displayed when he and Janet first looked at the house. "Just perfect for you young people to throw your little parties, don't you agree?" There was a wet bar in the corner, pine board on the walls, and thick red carpeting bleeding over the floor. The room had a damp, clayish smell, a reminder that the river bottom was not far beyond the walls.

Decker had his computer there, where it gathered dust on a worktable he'd thrown together from an old wooden door and a double set of file cabinets. His stereo was there, too—a Yamaha with fat, squatty speakers the size of hotel refrigerators, a system he'd bought on credit after landing his first newspaper job ten years ago. All this had been spared when some teenagers had broken in the year before and taken off with their TV set. They'd never thought to look in the basement.

The rest of the room was crammed with items too old or too tacky to display upstairs, yet too sentimental for Decker to throw away. Framed and hanging above the computer were his swimming and tennis letters from high school. An HO-scale model train set—the last Christmas gift from his father—was laid out on plywood and set above the wet bar. Over the bar was a great-uncle's pencil drawing of a German street scene, said to be the family's ancestral village.

For comfort, he had installed his green velour sofa, an ancient discard from an aunt in Pittsburgh, with pillows big and mushy enough to drown in.

Decker slept on the sofa most nights when he was alone. He was there now, snuggled under the afghan his mother had knitted for him when he first left for college. After the long, stressful day, his body ached for sleep, but his mind was still working overtime, playing back bits and pieces of the day, back and forth, back and forth, like a broken VCR. He could see the blue Lincoln, always a block or two ahead, disappearing behind a truck, around a corner, across a bridge. Cut to Cousins, toothy smile, sneering. Those flat shark's eyes, empty, soulless. Cut to the old black man, meat cleaver in hand, like an Indian tomahawk. The other men draped in plastic bags. Wet, cold, shivering. *"We just tryin' to live, man. We just tryin' to live."* Cut to Angie, all heat and leveraged slickness. Her body taut, quivering. Her moist breath in his ear. "Rick, Rick . . . Rick."

The phone rang and his whole body sprang in a single reflex action from the cushions, grappling for the switch on the floor lamp. He turned it on, hurried to the worktable, eyes half-closed, moving through a white fog.

"Hello?"

A second of silence. Click. A dial tone.

He slammed the receiver and threw himself back on the

sofa. He lay there a few minutes until the light from the floor lamp became intolerable, then jumped up, turned it off, and buried himself in the cushions again.

Angie? Embarrassed, perhaps, that she'd awakened him. Or Cousins? Doing what? Seeing if he was home, or trying one more way to scare him?

His mind went over every door and window in the house. Yes, he'd checked them all, some twice, before retreating to the basement. He told himself to go back to sleep and forget it, but the pounding in his chest wouldn't let him.

He picked up his wristwatch from the floor and held it close to his face: 10:25. He got up, snapped on the light again, loaded a tape into his stereo deck, then turned out the light and curled back on the sofa, determined to sleep.

It was one of the Bach organ tapes he'd inherited from Turk. A toccata and fugue that began with a deceptively simple melody, rhythmic and urgent—*dotta-deeta, deeta-dotta, dotta-dotta* . . . trailed quickly by a bass voice resonating with the same urgency—*tumpa-teepa, teepa-tumpa, tumpa-tumpa* . . . Suddenly a third voice, an overlay of high notes, loose and ethereal, rising above and mocking the simplicity of the earlier melody, only to be chased and finally swallowed by the reverberating bass, so that the whole cycle could be repeated anew.

Decker tried to separate the lines of the fugue and hear just one voice at a time—a task that never failed to make him sleepy. It was impossible. No single note existed in isolation, but only in relation to the other voices, a pattern that wove in and out and through itself like the tangled fabric of a tapestry.

He woke in a panic, hard on his back, gasping for air. The darkness pressed down on his chest like a weight. He felt around him and realized he was on the basement floor. Christ. He'd fallen out of bed. Something he hadn't done since he was a kid.

He waited for his eyes to adjust to the dark, then rolled to his side and stood up. His left hip and shoulder were sore, probably where he'd hit the carpet. He sat down on the sofa, ran his fingers through sweat-soaked hair. The stereo speakers were hissing.

He looked at his wristwatch: 11:35. He stretched and yawned. Maybe he should read a book. Go for a walk. He'd have a hell of a time getting back to sleep again.

Just then the old gas furnace kicked in with a shudder— *kerplunk, kachunk.* Had the temperature fallen that low? Wait—the furnace wasn't even lit. When he heard the noise a second time, he realized it was coming from upstairs, in the kitchen, just above his head. Drawers were being opened and closed. *Kerchunk,* slam! *Kerchunk,* slam! Footsteps raced across the floor.

Decker rushed to his phone, bumping his groin against a corner of the worktable. He cried out and dropped to his knees.

Dumb. Dumb. But it was too late now. The door to the basement opened. Light was streaming from the kitchen down the stairs. Decker scrambled on his hands and knees over to the bar, scooted behind it and hid there, hands and knees on the cold, hard linoleum. The overhead light flicked on. Footsteps started down the stairs, light and quick. Somebody small. Cousins? A punk from the neighborhood?

The intruder began searching through drawers again. Decker could hear him rooting in the old dresser near the laundry room—*kerchunk,* slam, *kerchunk,* slam. What the hell was he looking for? Money? Jewelry? Why not take the stereo?

Decker glanced around for a suitable weapon. On the floor next to him was a case of empty Moerlein bottles. He could smash one against the bar top and give the kid the scare of his life.

But what if it was a real burglar, with a gun?

Decker froze as the footsteps started across the room, headed, it seemed, straight for the bar. No, wait—the old wardrobe next to the bar. Decker got up on his knuckles and the balls of his feet, poised like a lineman for a quarterback blitz. He locked his sights on the wardrobe. Come on, kid. Just a few more steps. He'd blindside the little sonuvabitch. Knock him to the floor and tie his hands with his belt and keep him there until the cops came.

One . . . two . . . three steps . . . And suddenly a pair of blue-jeaned legs broke into his field of vision. Decker sprang. He hit the kid right on target, just below the waist, and dropped him cleanly to the floor. He was still gripping the kid's legs when a shower of blows rained down on his head, neck, shoulders, anywhere the small hands could reach.

"Dammit, Rick, what the hell are you doing!"

He twisted his head around and saw the shocked, angry face of Janet glaring back at him. She was pinned to the floor, her neck muscles straining to hold her head up.

"Jesus, Janet, I'm sorry. I can't believe . . ."

He crawled up from her waist and wrapped his arms around her shoulders and buried his face in her hair. They were both breathing heavily, chest heaving against chest.

"I thought you were a burglar. Honest to God, Janet. I went crazy."

They both started laughing, partly from relief, partly from the absurdity of the situation.

"*You're* surprised? What about me?" she said. "I come home looking for a hot-water bottle, and I nearly get killed."

She pushed his shoulders away from hers and held him aloft and looked at him, a little angrily at first, but then her eyes went moist and wide as though she were seeing him for the first time. He cupped his hands around her face and brought his head down and placed his mouth gently on hers. She melted into a kiss and then pulled him down hard, mouth open, and he went spinning deeper, ever deeper, into that familiar warmth and softness.

17

He woke the next morning spooned to Janet, his face buried in the crook of her neck, breathing in the warmth of her skin. It surprised him to find her there with him on the sofa, where he had always awakened alone. It surprised him even more that he had slept so well, like a college kid sharing a sleeping bag.

He gently retrieved his arm from under her neck and slid from the sofa onto the floor. Parted, he felt a brief sensation of loss, a sudden chill in the loins, as though he had just separated from his twin.

He rearranged the afghan to cover her, then found his pants in the scattered piles of clothing on the floor. He could tell by the light through the small curtain above the sofa that it was late morning and a nice sunny day.

Upstairs the kitchen looked buttery in the morning sun, and the sparrows in the bushes just outside the back window were enjoying a game of air tag, or whatever it was birds played. For the first time in weeks, the wind was gusting, swaying the treetops along the riverbank. The river was rippled like a lake, the sun glinting gold off its uneven surface. Everything—the trees, the grass, the weeds—looked greener than before, but things were still far from their normal late-summer lushness. It might have been early March rather than late August.

He went upstairs to the bathroom, came down again and started coffee. It was almost ten—late rising for both of them, but not too late to start making plans for the day. Janet had a well-deserved weekend off, and Decker wanted to make sure that she—both of them—got the most from it. Floyd, Cousins, Crown Pointe, the whole tangled mess could wait a day or even two.

And then he remembered the rat in his trash can.

He called the Cincinnati Health Department emergency line, got a busy signal, and tried two more times before he got through.

"You live in Ludlow, Kentucky, sir?" The woman spoke in the nasal monotone of every dispatcher.

"Yes, 429 Butler Street."

"Then you'll have to call the Kenton County Health Department, sir. That's outside our jurisdiction."

"But this could be an infected rat."

"You'll have to ask them, sir."

Decker decided the rat would keep until he could talk to Murdock or Wolters about it, and turned his attention to the rest of the day.

He had it all worked out. They'd start with a huge breakfast at Pete's Corner, spreading *The New York Times* all over their booth. And then they'd take a long drive east along the river to Augusta, where they could picnic together on the grassy banks and make out like a couple of teenagers. Even cornier, they could drive up to Devou Park and fly a kite together. And when they were tired and flushed and drowsy from the outdoors, their skin salty-sweet from the sun, they'd come back to the house for "a nap," and maybe even a real nap, before heading over to her father's for dinner.

It would be a day of renewal and lasting redemption. He could feel it.

Contrary to what he had expected, the night with Janet had made him feel less, not more, guilty about the previous night with Angie. It was as if he'd been washed clean in Janet's arms, in the recesses of her body, and made whole again. Still, he knew his redemption was built, in part, on a deception—that he still hadn't told Janet about Angie, and that he probably never would. But now that it meant so little, he reasoned, why should he risk spoiling what they'd found together again? That was plain common sense. He didn't need Ann Landers to tell him that one.

He filled two heavy mugs with coffee and plenty of skim milk and was about to take them down to the den when the basement door popped open and Janet stepped squinting into the kitchen light. She was clad only in panties and his Oxford shirt, with most of the buttons open and the bottom snug around her hips. She smiled a little crookedly, as though apologizing for being a sleepy mess.

He kissed her and handed her a cup of coffee and they went out to sit together at the dining room table. He gave her a chance to take a sip or two and adjust to the morning brightness before spilling out his plans. She listened and made "hmmmmmm" noises in agreement and rubbed her bare foot against his ankle underneath the table.

"Or we could stay inside all day," she said.

"True," he said, testing her seriousness. "I don't know why I'm always in such a rush to get out and do things."

"Because you want it all," she teased.

"Yes, I want it all. Every bit of it." He grabbed her foot between his and squeezed.

"But," he said, "we mustn't forget the hot-water bottle for your father."

"No, we mustn't."

"After all, that's what led to our rapprochement."

"Yes. That and Dad's bad back."

Decker succumbed to a twinge of guilt. "Why don't I run it over now while you take a shower?"

"He's all right. I talked to him last night. He wants us to be together."

"You know, your father's an okay dude." He was surprised to hear himself talking like Angie.

"Yes," Janet said, "but he's not my number-one dude."

She stared at him over her coffee cup, her blue eyes unfocused and dreamy-looking without her glasses. He nestled his foot between her legs. She smiled. Maybe they *would* stay inside all day.

The phone rang.

They looked at each other to see who would make the first move.

"I don't really care if it's for me," Decker said.

The phone kept ringing.

"Sorry," Janet said, rousting Decker's foot from its warm nest. "It could be Dad."

She answered the phone with a bright hello, followed by a long silence, and then, "Yes, he's here. Just a second."

Decker threw his head back in mock anguish. It was either Stein or Farlidge. He didn't know which he wanted to talk to less.

"You should have said I was dead."

"That's for you to say," Janet said, returning to the dining room. "It's someone from work. Bart Petkamp."

Decker brightened a little. "Bart Petkamp? That's not work. Petkamp never worked a day in his life."

"I heard that," Petkamp said when Decker picked up the phone. "And after all the things I've done for you. Who told you about the body on the riverfront, big guy?"

"You did, Bart. You're always giving me stories, Bart. Why don't you keep a few for yourself?"

"Because I can't do near as good a job as you do, big guy. You know that."

Rick turned and caught Janet's worried glance from the dining room table. "All right, so what's up, Bart?"

"I've got another body for you."

"Dammit, Bart, why today?"

"Bodies don't plan to show up, you know."

"All right, all right." He reached for the phone pad. "Where?"

Janet turned away and looked out the window to the river. "110 Central Parkway."

"That's the shelter, isn't it?"

"All they gave me was an address. You know how the frigging cops are. I wouldn't waste any time getting down there, though. I understand the CDC team is poking around right now."

"Thanks, Bart. Thanks for ruining my day."

"Think nothin' of it, big guy."

When he went back to the table, Janet was still looking out to the river. When she turned, he expected to find her angry. She wasn't, but the tight smile couldn't quite mask her disappointment.

"They found another body," he said, not looking at her.

Janet got up and fetched the coffeepot.

"So," she said, warming up his cup, "I guess I'll see you later then—for dinner?" She sounded very understanding. They were both trying hard to keep their new direction on course.

"It shouldn't take long. I'll check it out, bang in a story, meet you at your father's. What's one more body?"

He was downplaying for her sake, and she knew it. She shook her head. "No. The question is, how many more?"

It was a day in which death seemed improbable if not impossible. After the long rain the temperature had settled into the low 70s, and the dense cloud cover had broken into a bunch of fat, lazy stragglers, drifting now in a bright blue sky. The air was cleaner, clearer than Decker had seen it in months. Crossing the bridge into downtown, he could see every art deco flourish, every microwave dish on Carew Tower.

The Dart's slant six hummed along, rediscovering its well-tuned youth. Even the unpredictable turn signals were cooperating. In fact, the only glitch in the smooth-functioning machine were the brakes, still a little wet and grabby after plowing through yesterday's puddles.

Decker creaked to a stop in a metered space on Central Parkway, just west of Elm. The shelter was in the next block, its dark turrets surreal-looking and slightly comic—like a phony set in a horror flick—against the blue intensity of the sky.

Four cruisers, an ambulance, and a Health Department van were lined up in front of the Elm Street entrance. Decker spotted Wolters' rental car—a red Taurus with an Avis bumper sticker—at the head of the line near Court Street.

A handful of onlookers had gathered on the sidewalk across from the entrance. Decker joined them, scoping out the scene. It looked good. No TV crews, no reporters—Petkamp had landed another scoop. Better yet, the cops looked approachable. They were milling around their cars, shooting the breeze, grooving on the mild weather.

The ambulance was backed up to the shelter's open double doors, blocking out the view inside.

Decker recognized a cop he'd worked with before, a young black patrolman named Cooper, perched on his cruiser hood with one foot on the bumper. He was staring into the cavernous gloom of the shelter.

"Officer Cooper. Rick Decker, from the *Eagle*. Remember?"

Cooper smiled a big open smile, extended a hand. "Yeaaaaaaah. I remember you. The Dorfman case. You even spelled my name right."

"Aim to please," Decker said. "Can you tell me what we've got here?"

Cooper shook his head. He had a round face and smooth perfect skin. "You probably know as much as I do. We got a call at district this morning from somebody in the Health Department. They apparently had a crew checking out the building early this morning, seeing what the rain had done, I guess, and they come across this body in the basement. The medics have been in there, oh, I'd say half an hour at least."

"But I thought the building was sealed." The instant Decker said the words, he had the answer—the tunnel.

"Well, the way I figure it, he musta been in there when they shut the place down. Drunk or passed out most likely. Then when they pumped in the gas, he was a goner."

"The gas?"

"Oh, yeah. To kill the rats. Cyanide gas. Deadliest stuff around."

Decker thanked Cooper and walked over to the shelter door. The other cops didn't hassle him. They were like thieves and drug dealers. In with one, in with 'em all.

Decker saw roaming lights through one of the basement windows—the same barred windows that, as a kid, he'd seen glowing orange-red from the kettle fires. For an instant he saw himself walking with his mother past that same window, holding her hand tight and thinking only she could save him from the devils that lurked there.

He stood next to the open door. He couldn't see much, but he could hear voices in the back of the shelter, echoing, it seemed, up the basement stairs.

"Watch it now! The weight's shifting! The weight's shifting! Take it easy!"

Decker recognized the sonorous tones of Dr. Murdock. Soon his big frame appeared in a patch of window light just inside the shelter, ahead of two medics pushing a stretcher. The body was draped in sheets and buckled down. Wolters and a young female assistant trailed behind.

The parade reached the ambulance doors with Murdock still barking orders. Decker retreated toward Wolters' Taurus, hoping to catch him for a quick quote. But after the body was loaded and the ambulance gone, Murdock and Wolters withdrew again into the shelter. Meanwhile, the young assistant headed for Wolters' car, clutching a clear plastic bag in both gloved hands. The bag was taped and bulging with clothes.

Decker caught up with her and identified himself as a reporter from the *Eagle*.

"From the what?" she asked, squinting through big red-framed glasses. She kept walking toward the car. She was tiny, blond, precise—a female clone of Wolters, only a lot cuter. She had bright blue eyes and creamy skin and pale eyebrows that disappeared as they curved around her forehead. She spoke with a slight German accent.

"The Cincinnati *Eagle*—it's the afternoon paper."

She laughed a little. It made her even cuter. "It's really called the *Eagle?* I like that. The *Eagle*. Like this big bird swooping down." Her *th*'s were hard and Teutonic, almost like *d*'s. So was her attitude.

"Can you tell me what you found in there?" Decker asked.

She smiled coyly, but kept walking. "Perhaps you should talk to Dr. Wolters. He is the head of the investigative team, you know."

"I will. But some background would help. We can keep it off the record if you'd like."

"Off the record? Ooh, I like that." She laughed again. "Just like Watergate."

Decker wouldn't let up. He followed her to the car, where she fished some keys out of her lab coat and opened the boxy trunk to the Taurus. She carefully set the bag in a corner, wedged next to a box of plastic gloves.

"Is that what the victim was wearing?" Decker asked.

She stood on tiptoe to reach the trunk lid, then slammed it shut. "Yes, most of it. He was dressed very peculiarly."

"In what way?"

"He was wearing a woolen cap when we found him."

"Like a ski cap?"

"Yes. A navy-blue one."

"Oh, Jesus." It hit Decker with a force that weakened his knees.

"Was he a little man with a beard and long hair?"

214

"Yes, quite small. Maybe a hundred twenty, a hundred twenty-five pounds. A Caucasian. Did you know this man?"

It took Decker a moment to answer. He was almost trembling with rage. "His name was Floyd Deekins. About the most defenseless man I ever knew."

Decker closed his eyes, saw red through his sunstruck eyelids. Why Floyd? It didn't make sense. Unless Cousins had recognized him from that night in the tunnel.

When Decker opened his eyes again, the assistant was staring at him with a look of puzzled concern. She pointed up the street. "Why don't you talk to Dr. Wolters now?"

Murdock and Wolters were outside the entrance to the shelter, talking to each other at a professional distance, ego to ego. Both were wearing lab coats and rubber gloves.

If Cousins had been there, Decker might have taken a swing at the little bastard. But questioning Murdock would do for now. Decker headed straight for the big man.

It was Wolters who noticed Decker first, his bored look giving way to an apprehensive stare. Murdock was still facing away, pontificating on some point about cyanotic tissue.

"Excuse me, gentlemen," Decker interrupted. "But I need to ask a few quick questions."

Murdock wheeled around. He was not used to being interrupted, and you could tell he didn't much like it. "I have no statement for the press at this time."

"When will that be?" Decker shot back. "When they tear this place down and build Crown Pointe?"

Murdock was shorter than Decker, but he did his best to peer down his nose. "Pardon me, but which paper did you say you worked for?"

"The *Eagle*. The name's Rick Decker." Decker didn't offer his hand.

There was a flash of recognition in Murdock's eyes, and then a sudden calm, as though he were above petty disputes. "All right then, Mr. Decker. I repeat, there will be no statement at this time. There has been no determination of cause of death."

"How about murder?"

Murdock snapped off one of his rubber gloves and stuffed it in his coat pocket. "Mr. Decker, I seem to remember from our previous conversations that you have quite an attitude about this story. Now I don't know, or care, what your problem is, but I won't have you badgering me when I'm trying to conduct official business. Now if you'll excuse us, please." He squared his shoulders and turned away.

Decker went for broke. "Isn't it true, Dr. Murdock, that you own a number of properties in Over-the-Rhine? And isn't it true, Dr. Murdock, that once this shelter is torn down and Crown Pointe goes up, you stand to make a great deal of money?"

Murdock turned on him with haughty contempt. He took off his other rubber glove and stuffed it in his pocket, a heavyweight refusing an unworthy opponent.

"You know, Mr. Decker, I grew up in Over-the-Rhine, on Walnut Street, not more than four or five blocks from where we stand now. I lived there at a time when there were black doctors, black merchants, a whole black middle-class residing there. Those men—honest, hard-working men—were my role models at the time. By emulating them, I pulled myself out of the mire of poverty and into a position today of some authority.

"And then you know what happened, Mr. Decker? Not long after I left for medical school, the city decided our neighborhood didn't have enough poor people in it. So they bought up properties all up and down the streets, fixed them up so they looked quite charming, then invited all the people we never wanted there in the first place to come live in our neighborhood for practically nothing."

Decker was taking it all down in his notebook as fast as he could, thinking he might hang Murdock by his own words.

"And now you know what, Mr. Decker? Today you won't find any black role models for the youth of Over-the-Rhine. You won't find any black doctors there, or black merchants, or anything that constitutes a black middle-class. And do you know who's to blame, Mr. Decker? It's white liberal do-gooders like yourself who think they know what's best for everybody, especially the black people whom you profess to love, but actually fear and loathe."

Decker put his notebook down. "I'm just a reporter, sir, working on a story."

Murdock harumphed and turned back to Wolters. "I'll have to call you later, Doctor. It seems we'll have no peace here."

Murdock headed for the Health Department van, leaving Decker and Wolters together in the silence after the storm. Wolters spoke first.

"Well, at least you saved me from a very long-winded sermon on the post-mortem indications of cyanide poisoning."

Decker lifted his notebook. "Was that the cause of death?"

Wolters shrugged. "The body was very cyanotic, or blue, shall I say—a possible indication of having inhaled cyanide gas. Dr. Murdock thinks the man was somehow trapped in the basement and gassed during the fumigation."

"But they fumigated the building on Monday, didn't they?"

"Monday or Tuesday. You'd have to ask Dr. Murdock."

"What if I told you I'd seen the victim as late as Thursday morning?"

Wolters stared at Decker, then pulled some Polaroids from his shirt pocket and showed them. The face was discolored but recognizable.

"You knew this man?"

"Yes, he was working with me on a story." It hurt to keep looking. "I didn't see him Thursday, but he left a message at the office."

Wolters twirled the corner of his mustache. He looked almost pained as he stuffed the photos in his pocket. Something wasn't computing in his linear brain.

"But the building was chained and padlocked. There was no way in."

"I know," Decker said. "But he didn't break in. He was

taken there, or dragged there, through the old subway tunnels. The same way the Indian got there. Why can't you believe that?"

Wolters started abruptly for his car, almost as if he had been frightened. "Call me later in the day. I'll be late for the post-mortem."

Decker trailed after him. "I can show you," he said.

"Show me what?" Wolters walked around to the passenger side of the Taurus, Decker following.

"I can show you the connection between the tunnel and the basement of the shelter."

"And what will that prove?"

"Nothing. But do you have a better explanation?"

Wolters stood by the open car door, mulling things over. The young assistant was in the driver's seat, checking her makeup in the mirror. There was a glossy travel brochure on the seat next to her. Decker saw blue water and palm trees.

Wolters looked at his assistant; she smiled back. Then he looked back toward the shelter, ruefully, as though it were something that had come to haunt him. He turned to Decker and said without enthusiasm: "How do we get access to this tunnel?"

"Easy. There's an entrance off I-75. I'll make you a map. Can you meet me there at four?"

Wolters stared at the ground, twisting a corner of his mustache. "Let's make it five."

18

As luck would have it, Stein was heading the city desk that Saturday, and Decker was able to write the story he wanted, complete with the unanswered question on how Floyd got into the sealed shelter, and the possibility of foul play in his death. For background, he worked in the brewery's long and controversial history, leading up to the massive Crown Pointe project now proposed for the site. He almost threw in Teddy Andersen's quote about Crown Pointe being the "dawning of a new day" for downtown, but decided against it. There'd no doubt be plenty of chances to write about Teddy in the weeks to come.

Decker was finished by two o'clock and zipped his final version of the story into the metro-edit computer basket, along with a note for Stein: "OK to write Floyd obit—even though no official ID on body?"

Stein's response was immediate: "With my blessing."

Decker toyed around with a number of leads, but settled on the most direct. "Floyd Deekins, whose body was found Saturday in the men's shelter, last lived in a makeshift tent of rope and plastic sheeting underneath the Suspension Bridge. His exact age was unknown."

Decker wrote matter-of-factly of how Floyd had spent his

days—walking for miles collecting cans and picking through trash, doing odd jobs at produce loading docks, eating at church missions, selling plasma, drinking wine.

"He refused, always, to panhandle. It was just a matter of time, he always said, 'until my ship comes in.'"

Floyd's age was "about 60," the story said. His survivors were "also unknown, but possibly living in the Spartanburg, S.C., area."

He let go of the piece around four and sent it to the obits basket with a message for Stein "to read it through and check it for the hankie factor."

Stein messaged back: "At least a three-hankie job, but wouldn't change a word. Go home."

Decker sat for a moment in his chair, feeling depleted but at peace with himself again. Who could tell about Floyd? Maybe his drinking had been part of a death wish, the same buried impulse that may have led him to confront Cousins, or do whatever he did to put himself in danger. In that sense, at least, his ship *had* come in.

Decker phoned Janet again, leaving a message that he still planned to meet at her father's for dinner around seven. "But go ahead and eat if I run late. I'm playing explorer in the subway tunnels again."

There was one last thing to do before meeting Wolters: call Angie with the bad news about Floyd. She wasn't in her hotel room, however, so he asked to leave a message.

"Is this Mr. Ricardo Decker?" the hotel operator asked. Her voice was mirthless.

"No. I mean, yes. It is. It's Rick Decker." Angie was up to her tricks again.

"I have a message for you from Miss Lola Lapola. You may reach her at the following number until five P.M., our time."

He tried the number, and a cop barked into the phone as if the call were one more hassle in a long bitch of a day: "Sheriff's office."

"Excuse me, but is there an Angie Lapola there?"

220

The voice brightened. "You mean Big Red?"

"I guess I do."

"Comin' right up."

He could hear the man shouting across the room. "Hey, Red. I think it's your lover boy. You want me to transfer?"

After a moment Angie was on the line. "Well, hello there, darling. How are things in S'natty?" Decker could hear macho laughter in the background.

"Probably not as good as they are out there. It sounds like you've seduced the entire sheriff's department."

"Shame on you, Rick. I'm just developing sources. And I've landed some juicy bits of information. Wanna hear?"

"You go first."

"All right, there was a case out here about two years ago, a seventeen-year-old Navaho girl who disappeared and was never seen again. Her Anglicized name was Peggy Evans. Her Navaho name was Little Birch. Sound familiar?"

"Little Birch?"

"Remember the letter, the one Clem told us about? He thought it said something about 'Little Bear' being in trouble."

"Of course."

"Now get this. When this Little Birch disappeared, the police suspected this older man she was seeing in Tuba City at the time. It was quite a scandal; she got preggers and her parents like officially disowned her."

"But who . . ."

"Let me finish. There's more. This older guy who knocked her up was a doctor working for the Public Health Service at the time. Well, not working, really. They say he was serving out a sentence for a federal narcotics conviction, and part of that was working with the Navahos."

"Cousins," Decker said matter-of-factly. Everything was falling into place now, and his mind went racing ahead, trying to fit together the other pieces.

"You got it, sweets. The doctor pretty much matches the

221

description of Cousins. Only his name back then was Julio Carvajal. Costa Rican or something. They say he was short, balding, slightly built. A careful dresser—whatever that means. I mean, I'm a careful dresser, but I wouldn't *dream* of like killing anybody, even if . . ."

"Angie, tell me about Carvajal."

"All right. All right. So this Carvajal jerk finished out his time and left the area about a month or so after the girl disappeared. The cops say they wanted to keep him in town, but they couldn't make anything stick."

"So you think Cousins—or Carvajal—sent the letter to Gray Deer knowing he would come here to rescue Little Birch?"

"Exactly. The cops say Gray Deer never refused a request for help from anybody in the tribe. He saw it as his sacred duty."

"And all Cousins had to do was meet him at the bus station, then haul him off somewhere and inject him with plague so it would look like he'd brought it here."

"You got it."

Decker marveled at the planning, the calculated viciousness, that went into the scheme. He flashed back to the dead Indian's face—the eyes rotated back into their sockets, the clenched teeth biting through the lower lip.

With Floyd, at least, it had been quick.

He told her the news on his end.

Angie drew in a sharp breath, and then they were both quiet for a moment.

"My first big story," Angie said, "and it's all become so totally radical. I mean, it's like I keep expecting to wake up and find myself working as a copy clerk again, and this whole thing just never happened. I hope you're being careful, Rick."

"Me. What about you? They may have people working on your end, too, you know."

"Who's 'they,' Rick?"

"Cousins and Teddy Andersen, for sure. And maybe Murdock. Who knows? Like Barry says, we have to stick to what we know, and just keep pushing. But I've got some good news, too. I've finally convinced Wolters something's rotten in Denmark. We're going down into the tunnels."

"Oooh. To find the missing link?"

"Just like Rogers and Clark. We're meeting in a couple hours."

"Rick, can I tell you again?"

"Tell me what?"

"Please, please, *please* be careful."

At a few minutes before five, Decker pulled off I-75 North, just south of the Hopple Street exit, and walked up the gently rising hill toward the tunnel wall. The grass was yellow-green, the ground springy beneath his feet after yesterday's downpour. He saw a rabbit—a big cottontail—standing still as a lawn ornament in front of a line of forsythia bushes.

Decker found Wolters waiting at the top of the hill.

"Where'd you park?" Decker asked.

"I didn't. I had my assistant drop me off."

"Any trouble finding the place?"

"Your directions were explicit."

"Good. Well, I'm glad to see you're prepared."

Decker suppressed a chuckle. Wolters looked like a Boy Scout outfitted for a week of Everglades camping. He was wearing a bright red mack over baggy shorts and yellow wading boots, an ensemble straight out of L.L. Bean. His accessories included a heavy-duty flashlight, a crowbar, and a backpack. He seemed nervous.

"You know," Decker told him, leading the way north along the wall to the rabbit hole, "this isn't *Journey to the Center of the Earth* or anything. It's really very safe in there. In fact, it's dry as a bone."

"Well, yes," Wolters said, "but you never know what you might encounter in a sewer. Especially a sanitation sewer."

Decker hadn't thought of that. He looked ruefully at his Rockports. They were only a few weeks old.

Wolters had trouble squeezing under the concrete, until he took off his mack and boots and tried a second time. With Wolters inside, Decker pushed their gear through, then slid under on his back. The hole seemed bigger and less scary this time.

Decker stopped to show Wolters where Floyd had found the syringe. The fist-sized hole they'd dug up on the last excursion was still there. Wolters dropped his backpack, pulled out a garden trowel, and started breaking up the dirt around the hole.

"You *are* prepared," Decker said.

"I assumed there'd be digging. I brought the proper tools."

Wolters dug up a shallow circle about a foot in width around the deeper hole, but failed to uncover anything except a couple of smooth rocks. They moved on.

The two-mile trek down the tunnel seemed to go much more quickly this time for Decker, perhaps because his mind was fixed on reaching the Race Street station and beginning the search for a sewer connection. Everything that had happened in the last week pointed to such a link, and now, like a physicist posing a radical new theory of the universe, Decker was eager to put it to the test.

Wolters was quiet during the hike, checking his wristwatch with his flashlight every five minutes or so, as though he were running late for another appointment—no doubt with the lovely Ulrike, or whatever name his blond assistant went by, Decker thought. Wolters had also brought a small canteen of water for washing down the tunnel dust, but didn't offer to share. Decker didn't blame him. If you worked for the CDC, bottle sharing was probably akin to Russian roulette.

They reached the Race Street station at 5:25. It was just as Decker had remembered it—the long, empty platform and double staircase, as dry and intact as the day they were built. Decker was struck again by the enveloping silence of the place, as if time had never existed here. He felt certain everything would be exactly the same if he returned in another hundred years.

"You're sure this is the spot?" Wolters asked.

"Positive," Decker said. "Above those stairs is the intersection of Central Parkway and Race. The shelter basement is directly across the street, behind this south wall."

"So what exactly are we looking for?" Wolters asked. He dropped his backpack in the dust and began to gawk.

"Anything that looks like a sewer entrance. A manhole cover. A metal plate. Anything."

"Anything," Wolters repeated distractedly. He began examining the tunnel wall while Decker climbed onto the platform. Decker started at the staircase and moved west, swirling his flashlight beam over every inch of the platform surface.

Nothing.

His heart was beating fast now, stirred by a strange frenetic mix of frustration and anticipation.

He walked to the top of the staircase, decided it was silly to think a sewer entrance would be positioned that high, then walked down the staircase to the eastern half of the station. There, at the foot of the stairs, was the dull gleam of a manhole cover.

"Bingo, Dr. Wolters! It's over here!"

Wolters was a good twenty yards down the tunnel, inspecting new territory along the wall. "Are you sure?"

"See for yourself."

Decker helped Wolters, and his gear, onto the platform. Wasting no time, he asked for Wolters' crowbar and stuck the pointed end into the cover's center hole. He pushed down hard on the crowbar with both hands, putting the whole weight of his body into it, but the cover wouldn't budge.

"No, no, no," Wolters cried out. "Use the curved end of the crowbar. It's a fulcrum."

"A what?"

Wolters snatched it away. "Haven't you heard the tale of

225

Archimedes? He bragged that if he had a fulcrum large enough, and a place to stand, he could move the moon."

"Be my guest," Decker said, stepping aside.

The curved end flattened into two sharp teeth with a notch in the middle. Wolters inserted the teeth into the hole and, from a crouching position, pulled back on the crowbar. With a small grunt, Wolters popped the heavy lid from its hole and rolled it carefully off to the side before letting it drop. The clatter was almost deafening.

"My regards to Archimedes," Decker said.

He shone his flashlight into the hole. It was about seven or eight feet down to a gravel bottom.

"It looks dry," Decker said, feeling better now about his Rockports.

"Of course," Wolters said. "It's only a crawl space. Not the sewer itself."

"I'm going in," Decker said. He tossed the crowbar down into the gravel, stuffed his flashlight into his back pocket, and started down a metal ladder secured to the underside of the platform. He jumped before reaching the last rung, and hit the gravel harder then he'd expected, tumbling to his hands and knees.

"You all right?" Wolters was shining his flashlight into the hole. His face was invisible behind the bright circle of light.

"Just dandy." There were bits of gravel imbedded in his palms, but that was all.

Decker recovered his flashlight. The glass fronting was shattered, but the bulb was working. He picked up his crowbar and started looking around.

The space was tighter than he'd imagined—about four feet across and six feet high, almost like a crypt, although its length ran fifty or sixty feet underneath the platform.

"You coming down?" Decker shouted.

"Yes. Just give me a second to organize my things."

Decker crouched as he worked his way down the gravel path. He had never been claustrophobic, but he wasn't thrilled about cramped underground spaces, either. He had read some-where about the dangers of sewer gas. He sniffed the air. It was cool, with a touch of dampness in it. Water was somewhere near.

Within ten steps he found a second manhole cover. It was set low and at an angle in the south platform wall.

"Yeeehaaaa! We've got door number two!"

Wolters was on the last rung of the ladder. "You found it?"

"I think so. I'll give it some fulcrum."

Bracing his left foot against the wall, Decker inserted the proper end of the crowbar and popped the manhole cover with ease. It dropped with a dull, heavy thud into the gravel by his feet. Instantly the smell of dense raw sewage—acrid in its strength—wafted through the exposed hole.

"I believe it's a sanitary sewer," Wolters said.

"No shit, Charlie."

Decker knelt and pointed his flashlight into the hole. There was about six feet of terra-cotta pipe, just wide enough for a man to crawl into, slanting downward at a 45-degree angle and ending in darkness.

Decker took a deep breath, held it, and poked his head inside for a closer look. A few feet below the pipe was a brown, swift-moving river, dotted with clumps of white.

Decker pulled his head out and sat against the wall. "You know, this may not be worth it."

"Come, come now, Mr. Decker," Wolters said. "This was your idea. Besides, I'm very curious now to see where all this leads."

Decker spotted his light at Wolters' feet. "Yes, but some of us have boots."

"Would you care to trade?"

Decker stirred himself from the wall. "Let's get it over with."

Decker handed his crowbar and flashlight to Wolters and rolled up his pants to the knees. "How deep do you think it is down there?"

227

Wolters took a quick look. "I'd say not more than a foot or two. Sanitary sewers are usually shallow, unless there's a tremendous amount of storm runoff."

"What about the rain we had yesterday?"

"I'd say it's pretty much subsided. Would you like me to go in first?"

"No, dammit, I'm going," Decker said. "I just hope I've had all my shots."

"Yes, well, I'm sure you have. The chances of contracting anything are really very slim, you know. Hepatitis is probably the biggest concern."

"Gee, thanks, Doc. Just what I needed to hear."

Decker sat and inserted his feet and most of his legs into the pipe. Wolters handed him the flashlight and crowbar, which Decker placed in his lap, and then he started slowly down the slanting pipe, crab-style, on his hands, feet, and buttocks. When he reached the end of the pipe, he dangled his feet over the water and clutched the crowbar and flashlight in either hand. Before he could think too long about it, he let himself drop.

"Sh-e-e-e-i-i-i-t!"

His feet hit the curved bottom of the sewer, and he slipped and fell backward, slamming his coccyx against the wall, but, by some miracle, regaining his balance and avoiding immersion in the smelly mess. The water came about halfway to his knees. It was cold, swift-flowing, viscous. He tried not to look too carefully. The smell almost made him faint.

There was no danger, at least, of claustrophobia. The sewer was enormous, maybe twelve feet across, and very old. Moldy brick showed through where the plaster had given way.

Wolters slid his backpack down to Decker, who nabbed it just before it hit water.

"What have you got in this thing? Lead bars?" The pack must have weighed fifty or sixty pounds.

"Investigative tools. Leave it alone."

Wolters crawled down the pipe in the same crablike fashion,

but instead of jumping at the end, he slipped his boots into the water until they touched bottom.

"All right," Decker said. "Let's get moving. I'm not spending one more second in this shit than I have to."

They both began an inspection of the south side of the sewer, Decker working his way downstream, Wolters upstream. Their beams reflected eerily off the water, throwing ripples of light along the sewer's curved walls.

It was Wolters, a minute later, who called out first.

Decker slogged upstream. Wolters' light was shining on a large pipe that jutted through the sewer wall.

"That's it," Decker said. "That's got to be it."

The pipe was cast iron, three to four feet in diameter. It was stuck through a hammered-out section of the wall, about waist high. Fallen bricks were piled underneath.

"It doesn't look legal, does it?" Decker said. "I'll bet the brewery was dumping waste into the sewers."

"Could be. Perhaps when they cleaned out their vats."

Wolters beamed his flashlight inside. "Uh-oh. I don't think you're going to like this."

Decker moved Wolters aside and had a look. "Oh, no. Christ, not that!"

The length of the pipe, maybe twenty feet in all—Decker couldn't see to the end—was littered with dead rats.

Wolters sighed. "Well, I guess it was to be expected."

Decker glared at him.

"I mean, with the extermination and all."

"Hell, I always expect the worst," Decker said. "But not this bad."

Wolters grinned. "They could be alive, you know."

"What about the cyanide? Am I safe going in there?"

"I would think," Wolters said. "It's been several days now since they fumigated. But if you start feeling dizzy or headache-y, I'd pull back."

"Thanks. I will."

Decker shone his light into the pipe again. The bodies

started piling up about ten feet down the pipe. He turned to Wolters. "Let me borrow your mack."

Wolters slipped off his pack and handed him the mack.

Decker spread the mack over the inside bottom of the pipe, laid his crowbar and flashlight on top, and clambered in head first on hands and knees. With his flashlight in one hand, he gripped the mack by the collar, sliding it forward a few inches at a time as he crawled.

After a minute or so, he came to the first bodies and stopped. They were big rats—possum-sized—dark brown and fat, with blood oozing from their mouths. Surprisingly, there was little smell, only a sweet almondlike odor, very faint, which Decker recognized as cyanide.

He lifted the mack over the bodies and moved on, but couldn't help shuddering a little when his knees squished into the plump mounds underneath.

A disturbing thought struck him—if Floyd's body had been dragged in this way, why weren't the rats already crushed? He considered a moment.

It was easy. A key. Somebody, probably Murdock, had a key to the shelter, and a way to sneak in at night. There had been no need to use the tunnel a second time—not after the Indian had been dumped and the shelter closed.

The bodies began piling up as he worked his way up the pipe. After a while the mack was riding a solid cushion. Surely he was coming to the other end. He stopped and aimed his light, only to find a dead end about ten feet ahead.

"I can't believe this." He shouted: "Dr. Wolters!"

Wolters's voice was distant and echoey. "What's the problem?"

"It's a dead end!"

There was a long pause. "Well, look above you! Maybe it's an elbow pipe!"

Decker pointed the flashlight upward, craned his neck. No opening. But then it might be closer to the end of the pipe. He continued squishing ahead—at least it was easy on his knees. A foot or so from the end, the bodies were stacked three deep and, just as Wolters had predicted, they lay directly below an overhead opening in the pipe.

"You were right!" Decker shouted.

He poked his light into the hole and twisted his head sideways for a look. The elbow extension was about two feet high and wide enough for a man's body. Beyond it was darkness.

Wolters' voice rattled down the pipe. "Does it open into the brewery?"

"I can't tell," Decker said.

"Well, take a look."

"All right, dammit. Give me a second."

Decker used the mack to push some of the bodies ahead, then stood up one foot at a time on the soft, uneven base. When he was fully upright, his head and shoulders stood above a funnel that fed into the pipe—a basin, no doubt, for dumping illegal waste.

He flashed his beam around, eager to discover his surroundings. The pipe opened into the brewery all right; it was cavernous. There was a row of four or five copper brewing vats—enormous—with only their flask-shaped bottoms showing below a network of catwalks and I-beams. Pipes ran everywhere—overhead, along the floor, across walls. The place smelled faintly of cyanide, but also of dampness and yeast, as though decades of fermented hops were sweating out of the brick walls.

Decker yelled down into the hole. "I'm in the basement, Dr. Wolters! Are you coming in?"

Wolters' muffled reply was barely audible.

Decker shouted again. "I said, ARE YOU COMING IN!"

Decker crouched into the funnel and cupped his ear for the answer. None came.

"Well, dammit then, I'll check the place out myself."

A cough echoed in the basement and Decker jolted. He turned this way and that, sweeping his flashlight through the darkness. "Who's out there?"

His answer was a blinding beam of light, directly in his eyes. Then to his right, a voice: "I'm sorry, but Dr. Wolters won't be joining us."

Decker snapped his head around—there was Cousins, his bald head gleaming just above the basin. Decker ducked into the hole again, ready to scramble down the pipe.

"Excuse me, Mr. Decker." Cousins was peering into the basin, grinning. J.T. was standing beside him now, holding the flashlight in one hand and what looked like a small cannon in the other.

"I hate to tell you this, Mr. Decker, but I think you'll find the other end blocked now."

Decker yelled into the pipe. "Dr. Wolters, get the police!"

"You're wasting your breath, Mr. Decker."

"Bullshit." Decker yelled into the pipe again. "Wolters!?"

He listened; it didn't seem possible—far down the pipe he heard the thunk and scrape of bricks being positioned.

"But the man works for the CDC," Decker protested.

"True," Cousins said, his voice a grin in the dark. "And at one time both of us worked for the Public Health Service."

"You were both in Arizona?"

"Among the gentle Navaho."

"Then both of you . . . from the beginning." The cold-blooded nature of it was hard to imagine. "But you could have started an epidemic. Hundreds of people—"

"Nonsense. At most, Mr. Decker, we have sacrificed a speck of human detritus: parasites on the body politic. The shelter is closed, and now the city gets its spanking new downtown. Everyone is happy, am I right?"

"Especially you and your Chippendale buddy here. How much was Teddy Andersen paying? A hundred thousand? Two hundred?"

"Why don't you come out, Mr. Decker. I'll be happy to tell you the whole story."

J.T. jerked the flashlight impatiently. The gun barrel glinted in the beam.

"Just get that damn light out of my eyes." Decker had a trembling grip on his crowbar, but he knew it was useless. He was a fish in a barrel.

Cousins put out his hand, and Decker slapped the crowbar into his palm.

"The flashlight, too."

Decker tossed it; it clattered on the floor. J.T. flinched from the noise and shoved the gun barrel hard into Decker's chest.

"Forget it," Cousins said. J.T. eased off.

Cousins retrieved the flashlight and snapped it on and off. "Still working," he said. "You buy quality products, Mr. Decker."

"It's yours—a token of my low esteem."

J.T. shoved the gun barrel in his chest again. "Shut up, asshole, and get down here. Now!"

Decker swung his legs over the lip of the basin and dropped three or four feet to the floor. Cousins began immediately to tie his hands behind his back. Like a true doctor, he worked quickly, efficiently, but with no unnecessary roughness.

Decker pled his case. "What you're doing is really very stupid, Dr. Cousins. At least three people—including my editor—know exactly where I am right now. And they know you're a prime suspect in the deaths of Floyd and the Indian. Killing me won't gain you a thing."

"Yes, I know," Cousins said, giving a sharp tug to the knot behind Decker's back. "Only we don't intend to kill you," he said.

J.T. shoved him toward a corner of the basement. His flashlight was spotted on an old freight elevator there. He kept the barrel of his gun just behind Decker's left ear, the cold, hard feel of it making his neck hair stand on end.

Cousins went ahead and raised the elevator's wooden gate. J.T. held Decker back by the collar, gripping it so tightly the shirt pinched under his arms.

"There's something very interesting about this building, Mr. Decker," Cousins said. "I want you to have a look."

233

Cousins got down on his knees and pulled up two loose planks from the elevator floor and set them aside. He then reached between the exposed planks and twisted something. There was a sudden springing noise and a reverberating thud. The sound of a trap door opening.

J.T. shoved Decker by the neck onto the elevator, and Cousins closed the gate and pulled back the drive lever. The elevator clanked and whirred on its slow, unsteady descent. The air turned cold and dry.

"You may wonder, Mr. Decker, as I often had, how the poor Doppelman family managed to survive the Prohibition days," Cousins said. "Well, the answer, Mr. Decker, lies just ahead of us."

The elevator jolted to a stop, and Cousins flashed his light ahead into what looked like a makeshift mining tunnel. Thick timbers, some of them bowed and rotting, supported a dirt tunnel wide enough for a single man.

"After you, Mr. Decker," Cousins said, pointing with the crowbar. J.T. gripped him by the back of the hair and shoved him forward, head down.

The tunnel went on for about fifty feet before it bore through a concrete wall into a darkened room. J.T. yanked Decker to a stop short of the wall, and Cousins stepped ahead with his flashlight.

The room was enormous in its cold black depths, like the insides of a sunken oil tanker. Cousins' beam lit up snatches of the barrel-vaulted ceiling, the graffiti-covered walls, and rows of giant boilers. He spotted his light on the nearest boiler, encrusted in layers of dust. Tubing coiled from the top of it and reached halfway to the ground.

"Bootleg," Decker said.

"Very good, Mr. Decker. Gustav Doppelman found this transformer room ready-built for him. Sturdy, ventilated, totally hidden. All he had to do was bribe a few people in the city engineering office, and his whole enterprise could operate from underground. Very hush-hush. Now you know why the Doppelmans have never wanted to sell their dear old brewery."

"Why show me all this?"

"Because I like to satisfy a man's curiosity. Mr. Decker, and you have been a most curious man." Cousins shone his light at Decker's feet. "J.T.?"

J.T. let go of his hair, and Decker—playing out some TV-inspired fantasy—whirled and tried a karate kick on J.T.'s groin. J.T. snared his foot in midair and flipped him backward onto the tunnel floor. Decker recovered in time to land on his behind, but then J.T. grabbed his feet and flipped him over onto his stomach like a slab of bacon. With his face hard on the concrete floor, Decker could feel J.T.'s weight pressing on his lower back, while Cousins fiddled with one of his pants legs.

Decker couldn't see Cousins, but he knew instinctively what he was up to. He kicked, hoping to catch Cousins on the chin.

"Stop him!"

J.T. dug his gun barrel into the base of Decker's skull, and the pain shot through his head clear to the backs of his eyeballs. Every thought of being a hero scattered from his brain. In a second or two, J.T. let up and the blinding pressure was gone, but there was a ringing now in his ears and, more ominously, a sharp burning sensation just above his ankle.

"You can take the rope off in a minute, J.T. Mr. Decker will soon feel very sleepy."

With J.T. off his back, Decker rolled to his side and shouted, "It won't work, Cousins. Somebody's bound to find me."

"I'm sure they'll find you, Mr. Decker. Eventually. But by then, you'll be dead. One more tragic victim of the city's plague outbreak."

"They'll know it was you, Cousins. What would I be doing down here?"

"Curiosity, Mr. Decker. And an unfortunate accident. But you won't be conscious long enough to see."

Decker formed the word "bullshit" in his head, but it vanished into some nether region of his brain before it could reach his mouth.

He saw J.T. put down the gun and Cousins hand him the crowbar. It was all happening now as if he were watching from a distance—Cousins spotting the beam across his upper legs, and J.T. stepping up beside him, feet splayed like a batter at the plate. When the crowbar came down, he felt no pain, only a cartoon sense of his body being cut in half—a cheap magician's trick—and that was all.

19

He opened his eyes into a darkness so heavy it seemed to crush him with its weight. He was flat on his stomach, pinned hard to the ground, an awful gravity bearing down on his shoulders, his back, his legs. He gasped for breath; pain shot through his ribs. He took another breath, shallower this time, held it, and felt his heart flutter, squeezed between his chest and back as if clamped inside a vise.

He raised his head, blinked, and tried to see. There was nothing around him but liquid blackness, silence.

Was he buried alive?

His heart pounded against his ribs like an animal throwing itself against cage bars.

Calm. Stay calm. Or die.

Where could he be?

He clawed the ground, felt clods of dirt, stones, dry splinters sift through his fingers. He took another breath. Dust and the sharp mustiness of rotted timber filled his nostrils. He was beginning to remember now. The corridor. A secret room.

He tried to move his legs, couldn't, then felt the pain. A deep throbbing in his upper left leg. J.T.'s work.

He forced himself to think—one thing at a time.

The load on his back had to be displaced; he could hardly breathe. He positioned both hands flat to the ground and began to push upward. His arms and shoulders trembled from the strain, but soon his chest was off the ground, and he could feel the timber across his shoulders begin to shift and move by inches down his spine, scraping the skin along the way. He cried out from the pressure and the pain, but kept pushing until his arms were upright and his elbows locked, and at last his chest and shoulders were free. He lay down then and filled his lungs as far as they could fill.

His mind began to focus. He could guess now what had happened. Cousins and J.T. had knocked out the wood supports, left him for dead.

How long had he been out? Hours? Days? There was a dull aching pressure inside his skull, hot and feverish, as though his head were ripe and about to burst. His parched throat rasped with every breath. He had no trouble recalling the burning sensation in his ankle. The injection from Cousins. He knew he didn't have much time.

He got up on his elbows, dug them into the dirt and rubble and, using his arms and shoulders again, tried pulling his body forward from the debris. The weight seemed to shift again, but only a little, and his legs wouldn't budge. He lay flat again, panting, thinking, trying to suppress his panic.

His thoughts went back to what Wolters had said about Archimedes. Leverage. Lifting the moon. A lever—that's what he needed.

He groped in every direction at once, feeling for a loose piece of timber, and soon found one to his left, just within his reach. It was a length of 4 by 4—he could feel its squared thickness—and he was able to get a good, tight grip on it with his left hand. He tugged, felt the wood give an inch or two, but his one arm was no match for the weight of the debris.

When he rested again, the face of the dead Indian came back to him—teeth severing lower lip, neck tendons like guide wires about to snap. He had to break free.

He tried again for the broken piece of wood, this time twisting his whole torso to the left, as far as the pain in his back would allow, until he got both hands on it. He pulled. His cries echoed in the dark, came back to him like the wailing in hell. He heard the scrape and *thunk* of timber, the skitter of loose dirt as the debris shifted and resettled. The beam sprang loose.

He brought it closer and spread his arms to measure. It was three feet, maybe more. Enough, he hoped, for leverage.

He dragged the wood around to his right side, then slid it lengthwise along his torso, easing it below the pile of timber on his back until he could feel the end of it go just beyond his hip. That was as far as it would go.

The beam had enough give that he could squeeze his right hand underneath it. He forced his arm under until the beam was pinned against the back of his bicep. Placing his hands flat, he took a deep breath and tried a push-up. The beam dug into the bunched muscles of his arm, and his whole torso trembled from the strain, but it was working. The crushing weight on his back eased just a little, enough so that he could lunge forward an inch or two and collapse onto his chest.

He repeated the maneuver again and again until he had freed the length of his legs. Then, exhausted and panting, he lay curled amid the rubble. Slowly the flow of blood returned to his legs, and he felt the muscles begin to throb and twitch from groin to ankle. The broken leg came to life as well—the throbbing became a ballooning. For several minutes the pain was almost unbearable, but it was reassuring proof that his spinal cord was still intact.

What now? He could try to claw his way through the rubble back to the elevator. But which way was that?

He tried getting up on his hands and knees, but the moment he lifted his behind, his lower back went into spasms and gave out. He lay down again, literally a broken man.

He would have to slither his way through the rubble, like some cave-dwelling salamander, and feel his way out. It seemed hopeless, but he had no choice. They'd never find him here.

The instant he set out, his shirt snagged on debris; he unbuttoned it and left it behind. His belly took the abuse now over splintered wood and stone, but it turned out to be a smart move. He'd crawled only a few feet when his chest rolled over something cold and smooth—metallic. He reached under with his hand. It didn't seem possible: a flashlight. His? Of course. Cousins would have had to plant it there to authenticate the "accident."

He pushed the toggle switch, and there was an explosion of light. He could see nothing at first but the shadowy web of vessels at the backs of his eyes. After a moment he saw the bright cone of light spreading from his hand. In its path, form and shadow began to take shape. He shone the light behind him. There was a hill of fallen timber and dirt rising all the way to the ceiling. He was at the bottom of that hill, where the last of the debris had pinned him. Out front, the rubble began to thin out and ended ten yards ahead, just inside the distillery. Decker took heart. There might be a way out.

He checked his watch. It was shattered, the hands stuck at 6:24—no doubt the precise time when J.T. and Cousins had sent the roof crashing down. He had no idea how much time had passed since then.

He checked personal damage next. His left leg was either crushed or broken just above the knee; the swelling bulged like a melon through his jeans. He found a splintered length of wood, pressed it against the jeans and strapped his belt around it, careful not to restrict the movement of his knee. For a splint, it was a joke, but it would at least keep the leg from flopping around.

He crawled into the open room on his forearms and elbows, his leg trailing uselessly behind, and flashed his light around. There were two rows of copper stills, three deep, each set above a pair of cobweb-entangled I-beams. The floor was scattered with dark green bottles, some upright, some toppled, all of them empty and coated thickly with dust. In the corner to his right were stacks of old shipping crates and, next to them, an antique corking machine sitting on a workbench. Definitely a low-tech operation.

He turned his attention to the walls. There *had* to be a door. Either out to the subway or up to the street. He checked the wall behind him first—the reinforced concrete was dry and intact, just like the tunnels—then shone his light as far as he could see on either side of the room.

No sign of a door, but just below the ceiling on his right, he saw something that gave him hope—a series of small grated vents, six in all, each with a built-in fan. That could mean only one thing: freedom was just beyond that wall.

He started to his right, around a corner still and past the crates and workbench. The crawling was easier on concrete. Near the far right corner, he spotted a recess in the wall, tall and wide enough for a man. He continued crawling, past the second and third stills, moving quickly now with anticipation, but his hopes were soon dashed.

He had found a door, all right—a thick metal one—bolted shut and padlocked.

He pounded the heel of his flashlight against the metal and screamed for help. He stopped when he was out of breath, then turned off the light and lay panting on his side. After a while his breathing slowed, and in the silence, he thought he'd heard someone tapping on the other side of the door. It was only his teeth chattering. He touched the back of his hand against his ear, his forehead. The skin was hot and tender.

So this is how it begins, he thought. The first signals from the tiny beasts within. He could see them propagating like so many microscopic worms, spewing their poison into his bloodstream, and the vision set his heart pounding.

They'd find him, he told himself. Wolters would lie about their meeting, but Stein would put two and two together, and he and Janet and Rebo would come looking.

But then he laughed. How many people knew about this

room? Old Man Doppelman, for sure. And maybe half a dozen old-timers who used to work in it—assuming any of them were still alive. They'd find him all right. When the digging began for Crown Pointe, they'd find his black, desiccated corpse clutching a burned-out flashlight.

Without warning, he suddenly vomited, leaving the meager contents of his stomach on the floor by his cheek. The smell was so vile he turned to his other side. He lay there, teeth chattering, stomach muscles knotting, thinking about what he would do when his blood began to curdle and the pain got to be more than he could stand. There were bottles in the room. He could smash one, slit his wrist, get it over and done with. In the Middle Ages, didn't they dance in a circle until they dropped? Too bad he couldn't dance.

He would try to sleep. There was nothing more he could do now. He laid his cheek on folded hands and shut his eyes. But soon sweat broke from his scalp, and ran down his face in icy rivulets. When it reached the back of his neck, he shivered and drew into a ball.

How much longer?

He hugged himself and tried to think of nothing now, to merge his mind with the black void pressing all around. He remembered reading Jack London's *The Star Rover*—about a prisoner in solitary confinement, all his senses deprived, who could travel in time and space. Astral projection, they called it. He was wondering if it might be true when he heard a soft thud nearby, followed by a skittering sound. It stopped, started again, coming closer.

He turned on his flashlight. Frozen in its beam, two small eyes glinted like a pair of rubies. The rat was so near that Decker could see its nose twitching, picking up his clammy scent. Slowly, he reached for a bottle by his hand and, without sitting up, sent it flying. The bottle crashed against a still and the rat bounded away in little leaps, back to the corner where the crates were stacked. Its long naked tail was the last thing to disappear.

There was more skittering. Decker turned his beam just in time to catch another rat, smaller and less brazen, scurrying underneath a still. Decker crawled back to the door, where half a dozen bottles were lined up along the jamb. He picked one up and waited, heart pounding, eyes glued to the rat's hideout. He felt strangely lifted, almost ebullient. Here was something visible he could fight.

A few seconds later a shadow darted between the stills. He let loose. The bottle missed everything, but the rat went tearing away—into the same corner where the first had disappeared.

Decker laughed out loud. This was fun. This was what he needed. He lined up his bottles within easy reach and sat against the wall. By God, if he was going to die, he'd take a few of the little furballs with him.

Again he heard a soft thudding noise to his left. Followed by three more. *Plop, plop, plop.* There were four rats on the floor beside him, and more, it seemed, dropping from the ceiling. A shower of rats. He raised his flashlight. No, not the ceiling. The rats were squeezing through the ventilator grates. Dozens of them now, raining down to the floor.

He threw bottle after bottle at the writhing mass, most of them short of the target, until he realized the rats weren't interested in him at all. They were stampeding back to the corner where the crates were. In the dead silence of the room, the skittering of their feet sounded like wind through the trees.

He put down the bottle in his hand and watched. Why torment the poor bastards? Let them run. They were just trying to live. Like him. Like the men camped out on the river.

In a few minutes it was over. Dozens, maybe hundreds of rats in all, had dropped from the vent and disappeared into the corner. Maybe they were running from the cyanide in the shelter. Or maybe they just liked to run. Down to the river for a nightcap and then . . .

Suddenly it struck him that why didn't matter so much as where. He had a hunch now that stirred his hopes.

243

He crawled to the corner and began pulling away the empty crates, one by one. They were stacked as high as a man could reach, three or four deep, and, as Decker removed the bottom layer, the ones on top came tumbling down on him. He pulled and flung until he found a winch attached to the wall, well above his reach. It was an old-fashioned hand-crank job, with thick rope wrapped around it, and he followed the rope down to the floor where it threaded through a pulley. He pulled away some more crates and found exactly what he had expected to find—a tunnel.

The opening was hobbit-sized, about three feet high, four feet wide, crudely hammered through the cement. Like the corridor leading into the bootleg room, it was a makeshift piece of work, carved from dirt and supported by wood beams and pillars. Only one thing was different—a pair of wood rails had been laid down on the tunnel floor. The rope from the winch lay between the rails, disappearing into the distance.

Decker smiled. The Doppelman delivery system. A dumb-waiter on tracks. He started tugging on the rope, bringing it upward through the pulley, and felt the pull and give of something deep within the tunnel.

In a minute or two, a wooden cart came clattering up the rails. He could hardly believe his luck. It was a flatbed whiskey cart, big enough to lie on. His free ride from hell.

He found an empty bottle underneath the work bench, smashed it against the floor, and used the broken end to hack the winch line from the cart. The rope was dry, almost powdery, and frayed easily. Then he crawled on top of the cart and faced into the gloom of the tunnel.

He found another line attached to the front of the cart, and fearing it might tangle in the wheels, cut that as well. Then, with the broken bottle in one hand, his flashlight in the other, he propelled the cart by digging and pulling along the dirt floor like a cross-country skier poling through the snow. One, two . . . One, two . . . It was working. The cart moved in small spurts down the rails, creaking mightily under Decker's weight.

For the first time, Decker felt he might actually return to the living. The tunnel had to emerge somewhere within civilization, some place where Mad Gustav could have safely distributed his bootleg. From the position of the tunnel, he guessed he was headed north under Central Parkway, into Over-the-Rhine. But there was no way of knowing for sure.

He stopped every few yards or so and rested, pointing his flashlight down the tunnel and looking for the end but never finding it. It was a straight shot, mostly on the level, although at times the pulling became so strenuous he was certain he was going uphill.

The tunnel dragged on and on, with no sign of rats at least, but after a while—minutes, maybe hours later—he began to wonder if he was hallucinating. The tunnel, the cart, the wood rails might all be products of his fevered imagination. Perhaps he was already dead and this was the slow way to hell.

He was stopped by another wave of nausea. With his stomach in knots, he lost control of his bladder, and a warm, viscous liquid spread beneath him on the cart. He pitied his rescuers. He was a vile, stinking mess.

He started down the tunnel again and, after several more yards, found reason for hope. The skin on his face was tingling. His eyes began to water. There was a draft from somewhere down the tunnel.

He had his answer very soon. In the lower left wall of the tunnel, between two pillars, a hole just big enough for a man's head had been punched in the dirt and down through a single layer of bricks. He poked his flashlight inside. It was an old brick sewer line, flooded with fast-moving runoff and crawling with rats. Decker shivered and pushed on.

He had no way of knowing how far he had traveled. There was blackness ahead of him, blackness behind.

In the human mind, distance, like time, could be stretched only so far, and then it snapped and something else took its place—a kind of dull despair. Decker remembered a nightmare as a kid: descending a set of stairs to a dark landing and finding the door locked, and continuing on down the next set of stairs, and on and on, always finding the same locked door. His panic grew and grew until something gave way inside and the loss of hope was eased by the joy of motion itself, and he began to jump two and three and four steps at a time.

There had to be an end to the tunnel soon. His arms and shoulders were beginning to stiffen; the muscles quivered along his flanks. Every yard of movement along the rails became a triumph.

He remembered what Janet had said about the Indian, about how plague could clog the blood vessels and choke a man from the inside out. He was cycling every few minutes now between hot flashes and cold chills. He couldn't be far off from the worst of it.

A few yards later, while taking a rest, it happened. His whole body convulsed as though a current had surged through it. His head snapped back, neck bulging, and his tongue, like a swallowed rat, began pushing and burrowing its way down his throat.

He happened upon a small cave where Floyd was sitting on a washtub. The cave walls were slick and shiny with moisture, and the air rang with the sharp, echoey sound of water dripping into pools. Decker stopped his cart.

"Would you kindly turn that off? Cain't stand that much light no more."

Decker snapped off his flashlight.

Floyd struck a match and lit the mashed end of a cigarette butt, and for a moment his face became a bright circle of orange against the darkness. He blew out the match and his face disappeared into darkness again, with only the orange tip of his cigarette to show where his mouth was. After a moment the tip moved in an arc and steadied itself near the washtub.

"Am I dead?" Decker asked. He heard himself as if he were another person. It wasn't his voice at all. Too calm. Too soft and sad. Like a lonely child at play.

"Oh, my, no," Floyd answered. The orange tip went back to the mouth again, glowed brighter for an instant and waned. "Broke leg is all. Chance of a percussion, too."

Decker felt his mouth lift into a smile. "You mean a concussion, Floyd?"

"That, too."

"And I've got plague, right?"

"A touch of it."

"What if they don't find me in time, Floyd?"

"Oh, they'll find you, all right. When people love you, they always find you."

"Who loves me, Floyd?"

"Oh, lots of folks. I love you."

"But you're dead, Floyd. Aren't you?"

Floyd made a gravelly noise way down in his throat, waved his cigarette again. "Ain't nothin' ever dies. I thought you knew that."

"Who else loves me, Floyd?"

"A girl name o' Janet."

"I know that. I love her, too, Floyd."

"And another girl. Name o' Angie."

"Angie loves me?"

"Come on now . . ."

"But I don't love *her.*"

"You sure 'bout that?"

Decker thought for a while. "I have to make a choice, Floyd, don't I?"

Floyd laughed a little. "That you do, by cracky. That you do." The orange tip burned bright again.

"Floyd?"

"Mmmm?"

"I wish there was a way out, Floyd."

Floyd's voice was whispery soft. "Shhhhhhhh. Quiet now. Whyn't you just relax and git yourself a little nap?"

Decker remained silent for a while. He took deep breaths. He tried to concentrate on the glowing orange tip.

"Floyd?"

"Yes, sir."

"Is it true nothing ever dies?"

"Not where love's concerned."

"Good," he said, and then suddenly it seemed it was his own voice speaking again. "I guess I'll take a nap then."

"You just do that."

He came to, lying belly down on his cart in a slick ooze of sweat and urine. His throat was on fire, his head was pounding, and every muscle and joint in his body seemed to have stiffened and fused. He had to keep moving.

He barely had strength to pick up his flashlight and bottle. More slowly now, he started down the tunnel again, right hand reaching out, then left hand, like a swimmer without water.

The good news happened so gradually he hardly detected it at first: The cart was picking up speed. He lifted his flashlight and bottle from the dirt, and the cart began rolling forward on its own, moving ahead faster and faster as gravity pulled it downhill. Soon the wheels were chattering along the rails like a runaway train's.

At one point, the cart nearly jumped the track, and his elation gave way to fear of being capsized and stranded in the tunnel. It wasn't long, though, before the cart began to slow and he could feel the tunnel leveling off again.

When the rolling cart came to a stop, he saw a light in the distance. It was the most beautiful light he'd ever seen. Cylinders of pale gold slashing down through the darkness, beckoning with the promise of another world.

With renewed vigor, he propelled himself along the rails again and soon reached the place where the gold rays were sifting through. He turned around slowly onto his back and looked upward into a brightness so dazzling it seemed to burn into the backs of his eyes. He blinked, squinted. Above him was a square metal grate, big enough to crawl through, and blazing through it, points of light arranged in circles, one within the other, like the angelic orders of heaven.

He pressed his palms flat against the grate and was surprised at how easily it gave way. He pushed it free, the weight of it balancing a moment on his trembling hands, then slid it aside.

Suddenly, he was staring upward into an orange sun against a black sky. It seemed miles above his head, so far it took his breath away, and for an instant, he felt the whole world had turned upside down and he was looking down instead of up. The feeling set off another wave of nausea, and this time his entire insides seemed to collapse inward and convulse, until his eyes rolled upward into the blackness inside him, and he lost consciousness.

He heard the sharp ringing of church bells, very near, and he smiled, dreaming of Sunday mornings in spring. But when he opened his eyes, the sky was still black and the vapor lamp still burning above the open grate. He reached out to shield his eyes and saw his hand trembling.

He stirred himself to action. The opening was only a foot or so above his head. Carefully, he moved his broken leg to one side, then planted his good foot on the tunnel floor. He pushed. Pain shot down both legs from the pressure on his spine, but he managed to slide his back along the cart and, with a second push, brace his shoulders against the tunnel wall.

The top of his head was just above the open grate now. He lay both hands flat on the asphalt and drew his foot up onto the cart. Then, pushing up with his leg, he clawed at the asphalt, tearing at his fingertips, and dragged himself by force of will from the grave.

After a moment's rest, he looked around, disappointed by

what he saw. An empty courtyard in an old building he didn't recognize. He saw a foundation of massive stone. Above it, gray brick walls and story after story of pane-glass windows. The windows were black, the courtyard an eerie pink-gold from the vapor lamps. There were vans parked in a row—official-looking—with black lettering that said MAINTENANCE SERVICES.

Behind him, struck through the massive stonework, he found a driveway leading out to the street. But there was no one there. No sound either. Only the hum of the vapor lamps filling the courtyard's empty space.

He tried calling out, but his tongue was so swollen he could only groan. He started crawling; the street seemed his only hope. It was just twenty or thirty yards away, but the driveway was slanted uphill.

He clambered forward on his elbows, six inches at a time, dragging his belly over the asphalt like something half human, half snake. He feared he would black out for the last time.

He'd progressed several yards when the next convulsion came; it arched his back and bounced his stomach against the asphalt. This was it. It was over and he didn't care; all he wanted now was to stop the writhing and the pain. But when it passed, he was still conscious.

He lay on his back with his eyes closed against a starless sky, amazed that he was still breathing, amazed that there was still a beating in his chest. He thought of Janet, of the times he lay beside her after lovemaking, his body wrenched and drained, yet glowing in the wonder that he was still alive.

When he heard footsteps coming toward him, he only smiled. A mirage of sound.

And then: "Hey, are you all right?"

He saw a black face just above his own. The eyes were soft brown, opaque, like melted caramel.

The man tugged at his gray cap and pulled out a two-way radio. He pressed his mouth against it; the lips moved. Then he turned to Decker.

"How the hell did you get here looking like that?"

Decker tried to force words past his swollen tongue. "Where am I?"

"Where are you? Mmmmm, boy. I'd say you had a rough night, all right. This is City Hall."

20

He remembered semi-lucid moments even during the worst of it. The jolt and sway of his body against the straps, the piercing bleep of the siren en route to the hospital. And, later, a big-bosomed nurse at his feet, scissors in hand, cutting through his jeans and smiling, he thought, mischievously. He remembered laughing, too, and shouting: "Mad Gustav owns City Hall!" At one point, as the doctors deliberated off in a corner, Decker had sat up, pulled the IV from his arm and asked permission to go to the bathroom. White uniforms pounced on him from every direction, and things went black again, and he didn't remember anything more after that except the horrible violated feeling of something long and thin being forced down his throat and, later still, Janet by his side, wiping his forehead and telling him everything would be fine.

That all seemed long ago and even enviable considering his current aggravations. He tried to ignore it as long as he could, but, dammit, there was only so much a man could take. He grabbed the pica ruler tucked between his armrest and cushion, plunked his right foot on the ottoman, and leaning forward as far as his body brace would allow, snaked the metal ruler between cast and thigh. He had a long way to reach.

When he finally hit the spot about halfway down the back of his calf, he worked the ruler back and forth like a bow across a fiddle, scratching and scratching with a vigor that was almost sexual.

The itch subdued to a painful tingle; he sighed and sat back, savoring the moment. He knew it was only a matter of minutes before another itch tormented some part of his body.

A week after his Pilgrimage to City Hall, as Janet now called it, Decker's biggest problems were boredom and dried-out skin. There was an oversized cast on his left leg from mid-thigh to big toe, and a sling on his left arm to protect his damaged shoulder. But he would have gladly suffered both compared to the torture of his spinal brace—a thick plastic shell molded to his torso like Roman armor. He couldn't bend. He couldn't twist. He could only sit there and itch like a fool.

Decker wobbled the pica ruler before his eyes and smiled at it. His hospital bed was engulfed by flowers and cards and boxes of candy—yes, thoughtful, each and every one—but only Mullins, the *Eagle*'s slot man, had had the good sense to give him this, his magic scratching wand.

A boy's voice shot through the open door. "Paper today?"

"Yes!" Decker shouted, reaching for his bedstand. "Come on in!"

But the boy was already gone.

"Hey! Come back here!"

Decker swore the kid did it on purpose. He slammed the bedstand shut and picked up his crutches from the bed. He felt like the Tin Man, hinged at the hips, as he struggled to rise from his chair. It took him half a minute.

As he hobbled and klunked toward the door, the metal pin in his femur vibrated painfully each time his foot hit the floor.

Out in the hall, Decker hissed to keep his voice down. "Jason, come back here, dammit."

The kid was already three rooms away and about to stop at his fourth. He turned and grinned and shuffled back. He was a red-haired, freckle-faced terror with braces on his teeth—the kind of precocious, wisecracking smart ass you found on TV sitcoms. The problem was, it was just about impossible not to like the kid.

"*Alllllllll right,*" Jason said, his voice full of a thirteen-year-old's buoyant sarcasm. "It's the Teenage Mutant Ninja Turtle. So how ya' doin' today, Ninja?"

The reference to Decker's spinal brace had been funny the first time, but, frankly, had worn thin over the last few days.

"Listen, here, Mr. Smart Mouth." He tried his best to sound angry. "If you make me come out on my crutches one more time like this, I'm reporting you to the head nurse."

"Oooooh, is she the one with the dirty knees?"

Decker lifted his right crutch and tried to whack the kid across the meat of his arm. Jason blocked it easily with his newspaper bag, then pulled out a copy of the *Eagle.* "Extra! Extra! Read all about it! *Eagle* Ninja reporter exposes downtown crooks!"

Decker shooshed him. "You want the nurses down here?"

"Hey, they don't own the place." The kid rolled the paper and slapped it in Decker's hand.

"Go get the money out of my drawer," Decker said.

The kid shook his head. "Nope. Can't take money from Ninja turtles. Besides, you're paid up for the next month."

"When did I pay?"

"You didn't. It was some bitchin' babe with red hair. She said to make sure you got out of your chair every day."

"I'll be sure to thank her," Decker said, and started hobbling back toward his room. Honestly, Angie was more of a kid than the kid was.

He settled into his chair again and unrolled the paper. There was a screaming 60-point headline across the front page: COUSINS NABBED IN MIAMI AIRPORT.

Decker read Angie's story greedily.

> Dr. Darren Cousins, a suspect in the deaths of three homeless men and the attempted murder

of an *Eagle* reporter, was arrested by police at
Miami International Airport last night while trying to board a plane to Costa Rica.

Cousins, 42, was carrying a Nike gym bag
stuffed with more than $400,000 in small bills,
police said.

Cincinnati police say Cousins, owner and medical director of a plasma collection center in
Over-the-Rhine, allegedly induced plague in two
of the homeless victims, as well as the *Eagle*
reporter, by injecting them with the bacteria. A
third man was murdered by cyanide gas poisoning. Two of the bodies were found inside the
men's shelter, formerly Doppelman's brewery,
on Central Parkway at Elm Street.

The shelter was closed August 22 by order of
the Health Commissioner, soon after the discovery of the first plague victim there. On Wednesday City Council will consider whether to
condemn the building and open the site for development.

You mean hand it over to Teddy Andersen, Decker thought.
He scanned the rest of the story, and just as he'd expected,
there wasn't a word about Andersen or Crown Pointe. Maloney
had seen to that. But it didn't matter, not to the final outcome,
anyway. In time, Cousins would begin to sing—if he wasn't
already singing to the Miami police—and then Andersen
would need more than a good whitewashing in the newspaper
to keep his hands clean.

Decker tended to a fresh hot spot just above his knee and
started reading again.

Miami police disclosed today that Cousins, a
Costa Rican native, migrated to this country in
1979, when he married an American woman liv-

255

ing in Phoenix and divorced her six months later. Cousins' name prior to his migration had been Ricardo Carvajal. He used his native name in trying to board last night's flight, airport officials said.

Monday, Covington, Ky., police arrested Cousin's personal secretary and bodyguard, James Terence Smith, 29, in a Covington tanning salon. Smith has been charged with complicity in the case.

Cincinnati police and the FBI are still seeking a third suspect in the murders—Dr. Bradford Wolters of the U.S. Centers for Disease Control in Atlanta. Wolters headed a CDC team sent here two weeks ago to investigate the plague death of an 82-year-old Navaho medicine man, identified as Cletus "Gray Deer" Nanchez. Nanchez's body was found inside the men's shelter August 22.

The *Eagle* has learned that Nanchez may have been lured here by an anonymous letter for help sent by either Cousins or Wolters, both of whom had worked as public health physicians at the Navaho Resource Center near Flagstaff, Ariz., from 1981 to 1983.

Beautiful, Decker thought. Angie had pieced together a very complicated story and yet made it simple and readable, just like a pro—no doubt with some help from Stein. The rest was mostly background, which Decker skimmed, until he saw his own name toward the end of the story.

Eagle reporter Richard P. Decker [Decker groaned. He'd begged her not to use his full name.] was injected with plague and left for dead after Cousins and Smith toppled rubble on his body in an underground passageway below the

256

brewery. He is listed in good condition at University Hospital . . .

Although he could go crazy any minute from itching, Decker thought. He grabbed his trusty ruler again and slid it down between his back and brace. There was an itch just below his right scapula—like a swarm of ants crawling there—but he couldn't reach it. The brace was too tight.

He looked out his window and tried to concentrate on the view. It was a warm, blustery September day, the sky above Burnet Woods a shifting pastiche of broken clouds. Below, the trees were flush and dark green again, having recovered from the drought just in time to be zapped by fall.

Decker would have given anything to fly out his window and cruise just above the swaying treetops. He hovered there in his imagination—that sacred sphere between ground and sky—looking down on sun-warmed leaves, until the itching below his scapula brought him back to earth.

There was only one thing to do. He grabbed the remote from his tray table and snapped on the TV. In the last few days Decker had become addicted to the afternoon soaps. He found himself entranced by their unrelenting air of crisis.

He knew now why so many women had unrealistic expectations of men. The ones they watched on soap operas were not only uniformly handsome, but willing at any moment, and under any conditions, to bare their innermost feelings. These were men who seemed never to experience the smallest emotion without verbalizing it—and what's worse, they actually enjoyed doing so.

Hell, they could probably dance, too.

Decker had watched ten minutes of "Guiding Light" when Janet walked smiling into the room. She had her hair cut now into a smooth page boy that wrapped behind her ears. She looked crisp, professional, and—to use a New Age term—self-actualized.

She glanced up at the screen. "So this is how you spend your time now."

Decker snapped it off. "Dammit, it's the only thing that keeps my mind off the itching."

Janet kissed him on the forehead. "I can think of some other things that might help."

Decker pulled her face down and kissed her on the lips. She tasted sharp, familiar—of everything he wanted right now.

"Bar the door," he said.

"You know what Dr. Stamford said."

"Screw Dr. Stamford. Even prisoners get conjugal visits."

She smiled and sat on the edge of his bed and crossed her legs. Her dark skirt stopped just short of her knee. "Has Harry been in yet today?" Harry Stamford was Decker's orthopedic surgeon. It was Stamford who had discovered Decker's crushed lower vertebrae and ordered the brace.

"Yes, and he pinched, hammered, and twisted every inch of me he could get his hands on. It was like getting a massage from a plumber."

"Good," she said. "It means your peripheral nerves are coming back. What about your PT? How did that go today?"

"I think I set some kind of speed record on crutches," he said proudly. "The therapists started applauding."

Janet broke into a gleeful laugh. "Wonderful. You know, you're really doing much better than anyone could have predicted. Dr. Stamford thought it might take weeks to get you up on crutches."

Decker grinned. "Must be my positive attitude."

"That reminds me. Dr. Murdock stopped by again this morning. While you were sleeping."

"Very nice. I'll send him a thank-you note."

Decker fought off a twinge of guilt. He'd heard the story several times now, about how Wolters had lied and said Decker had failed to show up for their meeting at the tunnel, then refused to let Janet and Stein search the shelter, arguing that there was still too much danger from cyanide gas. Stein had tracked down Murdock at home, demanding that someone check the shelter.

Murdock, too, had refused them at first—on liability grounds—but then agreed to conduct the search himself. He was the first to discover the collapsed tunnel underneath the brewery. Decker, of course, was long gone by the time rescue crews broke through the rubble.

With a little digging, Angie had found that Murdock was in no way associated with Crown Pointe development. In fact, he had declined an early offer to be a partner in the venture.

In retrospect, Decker's long-held suspicion of Murdock had led to some recent soul-searching. "Do you think I'm a racist?" he had asked Rebo during a visit the day before.

Rebo had been standing by the window, his big chest and shoulders blocking out most of the afternoon sun. He had folded his arms, considered it awhile, then said: "No more racist than any other honkie sonuvabitch."

Janet now glanced at her watch and hopped off the bed. "Well, I've got to be at grand rounds in about two minutes." She gave him a quick kiss. "Can you live without me a few more hours?"

Decker waved his pica ruler. "As long as I have this."

She sat sideways on his armrest and kissed him again, slowly this time, stirring old memories, promising new ones. They were still kissing when Decker sensed that someone had entered the room. He opened his eyes, and Angie was standing just inside the door, all arms and legs poking out of a blue sun dress.

"I'll come back another time," she said in a low voice, and started backpedaling.

Janet smiled and gave Decker's hand a squeeze before letting go and slipping off the armrest. "No, I was just leaving," she said in her most reasonable voice. "I'm sure he'll appreciate the company."

The two women stood at the end of his bed for a moment, each looking at the other, and Decker, seeing them together for the first time, saw both in a new light. The younger trying to look poised—hands folded at her waist, knees locked at attention; the other poised and trying not to seem stuffy—hands in her coat pockets, a generous smile on her face. And as Janet strode toward Angie, and past her, Decker found himself wishing for a second that the two might walk into each other and meld into a third person who shared both their qualities. A totally selfish thought, he knew.

"Come on in, Ace," Decker said. "Give me the latest."

With Janet out of the picture, Angie became the same old Angie. She stepped out of her shoes and stretched out on his bed, one hand caressing her hip, the other propping her head. The sun dress showed off her cool white shoulders.

"Did you get your paper today?"

"Yes, dammit. And the forced therapy, too, thank you."

She was pure pixie again, green eyes sparkling.

"So what did you think?"

"I think it was another brilliant Lapola scoop." Decker packed all the enthusiasm he could into the compliment, but Angie detected the strain. Her eyes lost some of their sparkle.

"Barry and I fought all morning with Farlidge, you know. They won't let us use Andersen's name in anything."

Decker nodded. "All you can do is fight."

Angie looked pleased with herself again. She tucked up her legs, tugged on her dress. She looked as lovely and delicate as a porcelain doll.

"Oooh, guess what I did? I'm sure the *Times* is ready to kill us for this one." She smacked her hand against her hip a couple of times. "After I called Miami and got my interview yesterday afternoon, I talked the police chief into holding off his press conference until this morning. And, *voilà, le* scoop."

"You're learning fast, kiddo."

"I've had some good teachers."

"Teachers?"

"Well, mostly you. But Barry has been a real sweetheart this last week. You know, I think he's part android or something. How can anybody be that calm?"

"I know," Decker said, looking down at the swollen toes sticking out of his cast. He suddenly felt alone. "When's his last day?"

"He promised Sally Beth he'd stay on an extra week, although things are beginning to settle down. You were the city's last officially recorded case of plague, you know."

"How many in all?"

"Seven, if you count the guy on the river. There haven't been any others for a week now."

Decker reached for his ruler. His left forearm needed urgent attention. "I just hope somebody nails Andersen's butt," he said.

"The word from the cops is that Wolters and Cousins each got a cool half-mil from Crown Pointe. They're still trying to trace the money."

Decker probed under the sling and scratched quickly, stopping short of ecstasy lest Angie get ideas.

"Yeah, but think about it," he said. "One million isn't much when you compare it to six-sixty million. More like a nuisance fee. Andersen and his partners could have divvied it out from petty cash."

"I suppose you're right," Angie said, subdued now. She sat up straight and hugged her knees. "You know, I made it to Floyd's funeral last week."

"Good. Anybody else there?"

"A couple dozen people, actually."

"Any of his family there?"

"I doubt it. Murdock said no one claimed the body. I talked to three or four people at the funeral. They all said they came because of your obit. You pulled their heartstrings, big guy."

"Good."

"Oh, and Eric Strider was there, too."

"Of course."

"The money's really rolling in for a new shelter."

"I know. I saw your story yesterday. Ain't this a funny town?" Decker shook his head.

"A riot. You think Council will approve Crown Pointe now?"

Decker shrugged. "Andersen still carries a lot of clout. And he's got the Downtown Business Council behind him. My guess is, Strider will have to build a new shelter somewhere else."

Angie was staring out of Decker's window now. She looked glum.

"What's the matter?" he asked.

"I might be leaving," she said. She was looking straight at him now, her eyes forming a question.

Decker stared at his toes again. They were so pink now they hardly seemed his own. "Good for you," he said. But he felt the aloneness again like a chilled draft. He would miss her, but not for the reasons she wanted. "Where?"

"Well, it's not a sure thing yet, but Barry said he thinks he can get me on with the St. Pete *Times.* He says I can go to any paper in the country from there."

Decker forced a smile. "It's a damned good paper."

"But then I think about leaving here, and then—well—I don't know. I thought there was no way I could miss this place."

"You probably won't. Not after you get down there."

"Maybe." She looked at him from the corner of her eye.

Decker tried to sound cheery. "If it makes you feel any better, I may not be around much longer, either."

"Really?"

"Janet and I are thinking we'd like to start fresh, when her residency's done. Maybe somewhere out in Oregon." But Decker knew it wasn't true. That was just Janet and he talking.

Angie nodded. "Beautiful state."

"Yeah," Decker said, lip curling. "Probably has clean rivers and air you can breathe."

Angie laughed and hopped off the bed, scrunching her feet

back into her shoes. "Well, I've got to get back to the ranch. Barry thinks something may break on the Andersen front. If nothing else, he wants me to do a profile on the Tedster."

"You should. He's been hiding under a rock too long."

Angie stood in front of his chair, head bowed, hands folded at her tummy, looking like a kid waiting for her first kiss.

"When are they sending you home?" she asked.

"They're saying at least another week—mostly for the therapy."

"And then what?"

"And then a couple more months of recovery at home."

Angie bent over and kissed him on the forehead, then stepped away. "Can I come visit you and Janet sometime?"

"Sure. We'll have dinner together."

"Good." Her smile was quick, forced. "You take care, all right?"

"Thanks for coming."

He watched her bounce toward the doorway, and just before stepping through it, she turned and leaned against the door frame.

"You want me to bring the champagne?" Her voice was hoarse, a failed attempt at the old flipness.

"Sure. But leave the plastic glasses at home."

She blew him a kiss and disappeared.